STAY OUT OF NEW ORLEANS

STRANGE STORIES

P. CURRAN

New Orleans, LA

Crescent City Books is an imprint of Commonwealth Books, Inc.
Distributed to the trade by NBN (National Book Network) throughout
North America, Canada, and the U.K. Crescent City Books and its logo
are registered trademarks of Commonwealth Books, Inc.

Joseph S. Phillips and Susan J. Wood, Ph.D., Publishers
www.blackwidowpress.com

Author photo (back cover): Louis Maistros
Cover design & text production: Geoff Munsterman

ISBN-13: 978-0-9986431-8-2

Printed in the United States of America

Some of these stories appeared in print magazines. (The author's files were destroyed
in 2005.) Among others, from memory: "Very Old Things" appeared in John Benson's
superb *Not One of Us* sometime in 2000; "Fever" appeared in *Tribe* in January 1996;
"Higgins" was sold to Peggy Nadramia's wonderful *Grue* but I think they suspended
publication; either "Tim from Texas" or "Cadiz & Cadizn't" appeared in *Skin N' Bones*
around 1999.

THIS IS A WORK OF FICTION. Businesses and celebrities are mentioned only
for verisimilitude. The characters are not real people, and besides, they're all dead
now anyway. Specifically, the author cannot prove and does not contend that John
Dillman of Kaboom Books is the capo da tutti capi of the used-book mafia, if it
exists.

CONTENTS

INTRODUCTION

BY CHRIS ROSE

IT WAS ONE NIGHT IN the fall of 1981. I was living with my parents in London. My dad was out of town for business so it was just me and my mother in our two bedroom flat in Chelsea.

From my room, I heard a constant stream of laughter coming from behind the closed door of my parents' bedroom. No judgment here, but this was not a sound I was accustomed to, whether my dad was in town or not.

I gently knocked on the door. She could barely get out the words "come in," and when I walked in I saw her sitting up in bed clutching a book, with tears running down her cheeks. She told me about the book she was reading, which my dad had given her before he left. It was called *A Confederacy of Dunces*, a strange, incomprehensible novel about an equally strange, incomprehensible universe of New Orleans misfits, dreamers, grifters and survivors. I read it after her and I thought is was hilarious, if not a bit bloviated. Purple is the color they call that kind of prose.

And then by chance I wound up moving to New Orleans for work in 1984. So I read the book again on a lark and as a refresher. It was as long and arduous a read as I remembered, but something else struck me this time, now that I had been walking the streets of New Orleans for several months.

I remember clearly the phone call I made to my mother upon finishing the book that second time. "Mom?" I said. "Remember that novel we all read when we were living in London—the one about that Ignatius Reilly guy and all those other weird New Orleans characters?"

She said yes, what about it? I remember covering the phone mouthpiece and whispering—lest any of my neighbors hear the new guy revealing secrets of this mysterious city. "Mom," I said. "It's not fiction. They're real."

It took me thirty-five years to find another book of revelations like that about my adopted home town. But *Stay Out of New Orleans* is no extreme and comic portrait of the inhabitants of America's most unusual city. Not by a long shot. It's a whole 'nuther kettle of fish.

OK, yes, it is purported to be fiction. And yes, the avenues of self-regard on which the characters comport themselves are equally unflattering and, at times, distressing. But whereas *Confederacy* is pure satire, a lavish screed against normalcy and a pox upon the powers that be, *Stay Out of New Orleans* is as close to journalism as fiction can get.

There are no kings and queens, no saviors and savants. Just people. Real people. Wearing thrift store clothes, living on top of each other in ratty cribs, making music nobody wants to hear, just trying to get by and, if unsuccessful at that, to get over.

Call it documentalism, for lack of a better term. Stories, profiles, landscapes, caricatures, composites and personal interactions and exchanges that uncover the depths and breadth of the human condition in pre-Katrina New Orleans. From the stark but universal experiences of disappointment, delusion, stasis and malaise to the incandescent yearnings of possibility, revelation, redemption.

And sex. Naturally.

I've known Peter Orr, or P. Curran as he goes by here, for thirty years, which means I likely know Drake, Gary, Audrey, RayAnne, Enoch and Diane and most of the other "characters" in this collection of stories. Because Peter is not a fabulist, but an observer. Not a creator so much as a recorder. He's a Mark Twain of St. Claude Avenue, the Bywater Faulkner, the....oh never mind all that bullshit. The fact that I put him in the same notion as John Kennedy Toole has no doubt already earned his eternal enmity towards me.

But hell, he asked me to read the book and say something about it. He knew what he was bargaining for.

Point being, I cannot in great confidence call this a work of fiction. The portraits here are unequivocally dire, downbeat, amusing and, yes, ironic. (Another term that's gonna get me in trouble. There's nothing less ironic these days than irony.)

What Peter has written here is a bracing, sometimes toxic capsule of a time and a place that are both gone, for better or worse, but never forgotten, as these stories of lost souls and desperate lovers attest.

There's no better recommendation I could give to a book than to warn you that, when you finish, your clothes will smell like cigarette smoke, you'll flail for that last shot of Jameson's and you might even consider flossing for the first time in months.

All I wanted after finishing *Confederacy* the second time was a Lucky Dog.

STAY OUT OF
NEW ORLEANS

HIGGINS

You TRY BEING KOREAN IN FUCKING KENTUCKY. *Then* you can tell me I was better off there. I spent forever in ESL classes with two Mexican kids who hated me because my father's produce store put their family out of business. When I got to high school, one guy ever asked me on a date, and he ripped my pants trying to see if my crack went sideways.

My parents would not report me missing even if they knew how. Koreans don't like involving police in family problems. For my father, telling someone official that I ran away would mean admitting failure as a parent. Although really, he should only care if other Koreans found out, and we were the only Koreans in the state, as far as I could tell. My high school had a few Vietnamese kids.

I caught a ride to New Orleans from this guy I met at a diner near where my family lived. Along the way he took me to a bar he knew in Tupelo and taught me how to shoot pool. I already knew a little bit, but he said I was really good. When we got to New Orleans, he sent me into the Circle K on Esplanade to buy him cigarettes, and when I came out he was gone. He took my suitcase.

I had fifty-six dollars in my pocket. A room cost fifty dollars a week, and that was on top of Kagan's, where you could never sleep anyway. I don't have big tits, so I could only dance in the bars where you go home with the guys. I couldn't do that.

Staying on the street didn't scare me so much because I met more people than I had ever known in Kentucky. They hung out all day spare-changing tourists. We would sit outside the A&P or the Circle K on Royal, which closed since then. The smaller your crowd, the better your chance that some hick on vacation will play the big shot and hand you a dollar.

The first morning I hit Royal Street, this girl sitting by herself in a doorway asked me for change.

"I was going to ask *you* for change," I said.

"Honey, what's your name?" she said.

I told her. Not my real name, but the name I go by.

"Chloe, my name's Nilda," Nilda said, making room on the threshold beside her. "Why don't you sit down here with me? You feel like some Co-Cola?"

Nilda was from Alabama. Everyone from there says Coca-Cola that way. They call every brand of soda Co-Cola. Besides soda she let me take a drag on her cigarette, though she wouldn't give me any of her malt liquor. Then this crewcut white family came heading for us, and Nilda handed me her cigarette. When she stood up I realized she was pregnant.

"Could you kindly help out an expectant mother?" she asked them. The parents flinched but shook their heads as they passed. The children stared at her belly. Then Nilda started cursing the parents. "Stupid fucking hypocrite Christian scumfucks!" Nilda called them.

Nilda could get away with that attitude because she was pregnant. At the end of the day she'd have something, one way or another. Screaming at strangers won't work for anyone begging without a round belly. I learned that as soon as I met other panhandlers.

"You can't hang with a pregnant chick," this skinhead named New York Larry told me. "No one's giving you a dime when there's a baby ready to drop right next to you. Stay the fuck away from Nilda. She's a fuckup anyway."

New York Larry believed in dogs the way my father believed in produce stands. "You've got a dog, especially a puppy, that guarantees you a certain amount every day, plus it makes it a hassle for a cop to bust you because he has to call the SPCA," he said. "You just can't get attached to the dogs. I've fucking sold more dogs than I can count. Somebody just sees me hanging down the street from Kagan's with a puppy, they come right over and buy it off me. One woman gave me sixty bucks for a puppy they were going to gas at the pound."

He had this cute little black dog that day. I loved the thing as soon as I saw it. New York Larry gave me half a hot dog. I played with the puppy for about an hour. Finally I got up to leave.

"What do you have, a date?" he asked me.

"Well, I have to..." It surprised me that he didn't mind me hanging around him. Did he want me sexually?

No, he wanted me to keep playing with the dog. New York Larry had done very well while I sat there. People thought they were giving money to a destitute young couple and their pet, rather than some drunk.

New York Larry bought me two packages of those crackers with the soft cheese you spread on them. I drank some of his beer. He bought another whenever he finished one, sixteen-ounce Budweisers. By the time it got dark, I was drunk. We met some of his friends, but I don't remember which ones.

Pretty early he took me to someone's backyard across Rampart where he said we could sleep. When we got in there he fucked me on top of a dirty slab of wood, either a table top or a door. I threw up. People barbecuing on a terrace three floors up watched us and laughed.

Just before morning the next day I woke up sore, alone. I found my way out of that yard and walked the wrong way for half an hour, then got directions from a black kid at the projects. I had never seen a housing project before.

Anyway, I found New York Larry on Royal Street talking to some girl with three rings through her lip. He acted as if nodding hello to me cost money.

Fuck him, I figured. I needed to use a washroom, anyway. I found Shoney's and ordered pancakes. The waiter wanted to see my money before he took my order. Then I got up and went to the ladies'.

I thought at first that I had dust rings around my eyes, but when I looked closer in the mirror I saw that a fine layer of dirt covered my whole face except there. Because I kept blinking and rubbing them, my eyes did not hold dirt as well as the rest of me.

I didn't have another pair, so after I washed the blood out of my underpants I had to dry them in the hand dryer.

I ate in Shoney's that day, and the next, and the next. They let the freaks come in and eat at the salad bar during the afternoon as long as we all left by two. We always did. I ate there every day until I ran out of money.

At the time I thought I spent months in that routine. It must have only taken a few weeks. I started with fifty-six dollars and I didn't earn much on the sidewalk. People don't like Orientals down here. After a long time I noticed that certain tourists would talk about their friends dying in Vietnam loud enough so I could overhear it. Until I figured out that they meant it to threaten me, I just thought Americans wherever these tourists came from talked about that war all the time.

Sometimes people gave out free food on the St. Peter side of Jackson Square. You had to be there when they drove up, the stuff went fast. I saw a girl get beat up for trying to cut in line.

All the freaks hung around Jackson Square, even older freaks, the ones with saggy leather skin that smells the same as dirty jeans. Some of those men were in Vietnam, so I kept away from them, and the women would drink sometimes and want to fight someone my age for being better-looking. Drinking makes women look old fast.

When my money ran out I just concentrated on staying drunk. When I couldn't get any money I snatched people's drinks on Bourbon Street. One night a cowboy caught me grabbing his Hurricane and punched me hard in the stomach. It fucking hurt. As soon as he hit me he wished he hadn't, because all these other tourists saw him do it, so he started going, "You all right? You all right?" I couldn't talk. I put my hands up and walked away. This cop who saw it happen laughed.

I threw up all over the alley alongside the church at Jackson Square, and my vomit had blood in it. So I laid down on a bench in front of the church. I kept shivering and I didn't see anyone else. It may have been cold or I may have been dying.

I lay there staring at the sky and this man suddenly appeared and said, "You've got blood around your mouth, did you know it?"

I nodded.

"Are you all right?" he asked. I shook my head.

"You been snorting any junk?" he asked. "Huh? Why is there blood around your mouth?"

"I drank a lot," I said.

"Empty stomach?"

I nodded.

"Answer when I speak to you," he told me, firmly, without raising his voice.

"I didn't eat," I said.

"Since when?"

"I don't know," I told him. I could barely cry.

He stood me up and walked me across the square. We got as far as Pirate's Alley before I got sick again. I tried to apologize.

"That's okay," he said. "Just get it all out, like a good girl."

Normally I would have told him to fuck himself with this good girl shit. But at this point he could have called me a chink, it would've made no difference. He walked me down to Bienville and caught us a cab. The driver made a point of speaking about me as if I could not hear him, and commenting on how I smelled.

"She better not throw up in my car," he said every half-block.

When we got uptown this stranger took me up to the second floor of a house, put me in a bath, fed me toast and milk and washed my hair. He scrubbed me all over with a washcloth. My stomach burned inside, but otherwise I had not felt this good in months.

After a while that burning stopped. He dried me with a towel. Now I felt sober, and standing in front of him naked bothered me.

He could tell.

"Kind of interesting," he said, working the towel gently back and forth upon my inner thighs. "You know?"

I almost didn't answer, but I didn't want to hear it again about not answering. "What?" I said.

"We should know each other's name, don't you think?" he said. "They call me Higgins."

"I'm Chloe."

"No, you're not," he said. "What's your name in Korean?"

I hate my Korean name. I told him, anyway. He promised he would only use it when no one else could hear. I didn't want him to call me that at all, but when I saw how happy it made him to share this secret with me I didn't mind as much.

He stood before me, assessing my body while he spoke. "Well, let me tell you something not too many people know: My first name is Mitchell. If you want, you can call me Mitchell sometimes. No one else does anymore."

"Why don't they?"

He held his face still for a minute before answering. "Because they all died."

I fought against my body, which suddenly wanted to shake. All my skin became bumpy. He did not notice. His face changed, as if listening hard to something I could not hear. I stared directly into his eyes and he did not see me. Whatever he saw, it was too far away for anyone else to know about.

When his sight met mine again, he acted confused, the way someone does after waking up from a dream if they don't know yet that the dream has ended.

We stared at each other a long time.

"You feel like calling for a pizza?" he asked, finally.

Later that night, sometime between when the pizza came and when we went to sleep, I fell in love with him.

❀ ❀ ❀

Mitchell let me move in there. He did not tell me it was not his house.

That first night we made love right on the living room floor. He asked me if I was a virgin and I told him New York Larry had fucked me when I was drunk. We talked about that for a long time, and smoked a lot of pot. Mitchell made me feel a lot better about that.

So then we're making love on the floor and two men come in. Mitchell says, "Hi, Lou," and keeps fucking me. The shorter guy rolls his eyes girlishly and leads the other one inside.

The next day Mitchell introduced me to Lou, who was gay and did not like me. Mitchell set up a cot for me in a tiny half-room behind the washing machines at the rear of the house. I washed the dishes that night, then sat on my bed waiting until Mitchell came home.

Since I had nothing to do, every so often I went to the front of the house to check if Mitchell had come home. Lou had some friends over, and I interrupted them snorting coke.

"Look, just sit back there where your bed is," Lou told me. "I'll send Romeo right back there to you the minute he comes in, believe me."

"Do you want me to do anything else?" I asked.

Lou couldn't believe what he'd just heard. "What?"

"Do you want me to clean up anything?" I said. "I did the dishes."

"No," he said. "I'm not the one who wants maid service."

His friends laughed.

I sat on that bed forever. Beside it there was a tiny window that leaked cold air into the house. I turned down the lights and stared out the window for a long time. The night had no moon, and a million stars had come out instead.

Mitchell came home high. He brought me into the living room and we shared a styrofoam takeout tray of Thai food. Lou had gone to bed. After I ate, Mitchell and I smoked pot and made love.

My stomach burned again. "Eat two of these," Mitchell said, and handed me a roll of candy. I did what he told me, and my stomach felt better right away. I couldn't believe candy could do that.

We watched TV until very late. At one point Lou knocked on the wall to tell us we had the TV too loud. Finally we went to my cot and went to bed. The cot was too small but after sleeping in doorways on Jackson Square I did not complain. The room had gotten cold, so Mitchell went to the kitchen and cut a plastic bag to cover the tiny window. It helped.

The next day Mitchell took me shopping. On Decatur Street he bought me a skirt and a flannel shirt in one antique store, then two pairs of second-hand jeans in another. He spent almost thirty dollars on me, just on clothes. We bought a sandwich at the Verti Mart and ate it on a stoop across the street. An old man came by and we gave him what we didn't eat.

Then Mitchell took me to a bookstore down Royal Street. This store had a million paperbacks. I picked out six books, and Mitchell bought them for me. He said these would occupy me when he was out and I could not watch TV. I picked all books with interesting covers, three science fiction, two true murder stories and an old book about street gangs.

We brought home jambalaya. I had lived in New Orleans all this time without tasting it. I offered some to Lou, and he snorted the way a horse does when a fly goes up its nose.

I really wanted to spend the evening with Mitchell, even if we only sat around the bed reading to each other. He said he had to go discuss business for a few hours.

He didn't come back. My stomach burned again, worse than the first night. I read for hours and hours. The pages of this old book I began reading had turned dark yellow, nearly orange, and the color dimmed the tiny print to a blur unless I held it close to my face. The story took place on a planet where these space pirates hid out and ate boiled roaches. The roaches had lived through a nuclear blast. I kept expecting to find out the planet used to be Earth. But I fell asleep first.

"You have to go, sweetie," Lou said to me.

I sat up. My eyes itched, I think from the dusty army blankets on my bed. It took me a minute before I understood what Lou meant. "Where do I have to go?" I asked him.

"That's for you to decide," Lou said. "What's for me to decide is that you don't belong here. Where's Higgins?"

"He said I could stay here," I said.

"Too bad it's not his house," Lou. said. "Where the fuck is he?"

I rubbed my face. Lou angrily dropped his shoulders and put his hands on his waist. "I don't know," I said. "I'm sleeping."

"Well, when you *see* him, tell him I am *looking* for him," Lou told me slowly, with his teeth closed.

I didn't see Mitchell later that day, or the next day, or the day after that. But that first afternoon after I left Lou's I got a job at Shoney's. They needed someone to make the freaks behave and leave on time while the day manager went on vacation. He said he would train me, and paid twelve dollars for me to stay at the LeCinque Hotel on St. Charles. Then he gave me ten dollars to ride the streetcar for the week. He really wanted to go on this vacation.

I did not learn his name until the next day when I came to work. Brian. Three years earlier he had realized how much business Shoney's could do with the freaks weekdays at lunch time, using mostly day-old food at the salad bar. It made Shoney's a lot of money. The owners let Brian run Shoney's his own way. That's why he could hire me on the spot without any questions.

But no employee except Brian could handle the freaks without a crisis. He had been there every single week, Monday to Friday, for three years. This vacation meant everything to him.

"You're perfect for this," he said. "You don't have to worry about anything but watching that salad bar. Anybody steps out of line, you call Danneel. I promise, as soon as I get back, you can work whatever days you want. While I'm away, they'll train you for the floor whenever you're not watching the salad bar."

The other people working there knew me from when I used to pay to eat there, and they did not trust me. One girl called Shelly tried to talk Brian out of hiring me right in front of my face. He told Shelly to shut the fuck up. She did.

I paid attention to everything Brian did, and he told me who he didn't want in the restaurant anymore—Nilda, for one. Brian introduced me to a great big black man named Danneel, and he said I could tell anybody to leave and Danneel would make sure they did.

"Listen, is that hotel okay?" Brian asked me later, when we were alone. He must have thought talking where someone could hear would embarrass me.

"Yeah, I like it fine," I told him. "Thank you."

"Okay, I'll put you up until I get back," he said.

"What?"

"It's only thirty-eight bucks by the weekly rate," he said. "It's worth it to me. And you know, you're getting back on your feet and all."

I wanted to argue with him, but I had to let him do it. Shoney's would not give me a paycheck until next week. Brian told the other manager I could eat in the restaurant, and that I was allowed to take food home until my first paycheck. That other manager was an ugly woman. She gave me a mean look.

I don't know why I expected Mitchell to come find me at Shoney's. I could not remember seeing him around before the night he picked me up. It seemed weird to me that I loved him so much so soon. I knew nothing about him, least of all what went on in his mind. Somehow I knew he would not return to Lou's house. Besides, that was far, far up in the Garden District.

I only began to understand the geography of this city when I worked at Shoney's. Danneel explained everything to me. Unlike everybody else who worked at Shoney's, he would talk to me. But all he talked about was New Orleans.

All the street people remembered me and said hello. I had no problems. New York Larry came in and I told him to leave. He laughed, but he left.

I had one day off before Brian went away. I spent it walking. I did not want to spend any money, so I followed the streetcar up Saint Charles on foot. It took me a long time to reach Lou's house. When I rang the buzzer he stuck his head out the window.

"Hi," he said. He looked more surprised than angry.

"Hello," I said. "How are you?"

"Fine."

"Have you spoken to Higgins?" I asked him.

He nodded yes. "Everything's fine," he said. "We settled it."

"Oh," I said, and we looked at each other for an instant while he realized I didn't know what he meant. "Where did you see him?"

"Well, he came by, that's all. I don't remember which day it was."

"Oh," I said again. "If you see him or talk to him, please tell him to come see me? I am at the LeCinque Hotel on Saint Charles. Or he could see me at work, at Shoney's on Decatur Street. I'm there during the day."

Lou's face changed when I said that. He stared at me as if I were a small child who could drive a car. "You got a job?" he said. "At Shoney's?"

"Yes," I said.

"Well," he said. "Good for you."

"Thanks," I said, smiling at him. "Listen, I left some books here."

"Where, back by the washer?" Lou said. "Give me a second." He pulled his head back inside and spoke to someone else. Then I heard someone come down the stairs. The door opened, and a big guy with a beard handed me my books, a joint, and a piece of paper with Lou's number on it.

"Okay? You call me if you need to hook up," Lou said from the window. "That jay's free because I was nasty to you the other morning. I'm sorry, I wasn't mad at you. I'm glad things are working out."

I thanked him again and left. A couple of blocks later I came to a park where I could smoke the joint without anyone smelling. Then I walked all over the place. I had only been around the Quarter and by Frenchman Street, really, so I hadn't seen how pretty New Orleans is. None of the freaks I met ever came up this far.

When I got back to my hotel, I watched TV. My set only got two channels. But I had a bed to lie in and a TV to watch. I felt really good. I smoked the little bit I still had left of that joint and fell asleep.

My first day without Brian I almost overslept. The lady at the front desk called me and woke me up. When I thanked her, she told me Brian had paid her ten dollars extra to give me a wakeup call every day. He also left a number she could call to have someone contact him if I disappeared.

When I got to Shoney's, I wanted to learn how the waiting system worked. The other manager told me I didn't need to know. "Just take care of what Brian hired you to do," she said. Everybody but Danneel acted rude to me. The freaks were nice to me, too, at least.

After work I went home. I spent some time in the hotel lobby, sitting on a couch. The TV there worked way better than mine. I talked to an old man and the woman at the desk. "My brother-in-law died in Korea," the old man told me. It was all he talked about.

"Lester, she don't want to hear about your war stuff," the clerk said to him.

After a while the old man went to bed. The clerk asked me, "How long you been in town?"

"A few months," I said. "I just got a job. In the Quarter."

"Oh, is that right?" she said. "What did you do until now?"

"Well," I said, and looked directly at her for a second. "I had money with me."

"Get checks from your folks?"

I nodded.

"Where they at, back in Korea?"

"Nope," I said. "They run a fruit store in Los Angeles. That's where I grew up."

The clerk nodded. Then she wrote something on a pad and held it up to show me. "How do you pronounce this word?" she asked. The word was Sepulveda. Naturally I guessed the wrong way to say it. She nodded again and smiled. "So where you from, really?" she asked.

"Kentucky," I admitted. "I was born in Korea but I don't remember anything from there. We left when I was five." Or four, in American.

"You run away from home, right?" she said and didn't wait for me to answer. "Listen, I'm telling you something I know: Save your money and leave New Orleans. You ain't going to meet anyone you can depend on down here.

Do a lot better somewheres else. And if you're ever going to decide to go back home, decide that now."

Sorry I had started speaking to her. Now she would not shut up.

"When you meet Mister Wonderful down here, don't leave him alone with your purse. Just talking to you, I can tell what type of hawk's going to look at you and see dinner. Honey, ain't a decent man in this town, and if there is, he's gay. Let a guy buy you drinks, go to his room if you want. But falling in love in New Orleans is like getting gum on your shoe."

"I am already in love," I said.

"With somebody you met down here?" she asked.

"Yes."

"Sweetheart," the clerk said, "you are fucked."

The first day I got a paycheck from Shoney's, I cashed it at a dirty department store on Canal Street and walked to Kagan's in the rain wearing my work clothes. I met Nilda there. She was pretty drunk and got mad when I said I would not let her back into Shoney's. "It's a fuck of a thing, ain't it? I mean, I'm the oldest friend you have down here," she said.

So I put two quarters on the pool table. I got to play this guy who acted really nice to me. He said his name was Carl. We played Eightball and I had lows. Then I bent over the table to aim this shot. Everybody watching us started smiling. I peeked over my shoulder and saw Carl squinting and sticking his teeth out behind my back.

When I stood upright and looked at him, he made his face normal. It bothered him that I caught him. I dumped my stick on the table and walked out of the bar. Everybody watched me leave. Nilda called out to me, but I pretended I did not hear.

Outside, I didn't expect it to be night already. The rain had stopped and a fog had come from the river so heavily I could not see the sky. That did not bother me, because I only needed to walk down Decatur to the streetcar, and I did not wish to have strangers look at me. Every figure on the street now started as a shadow and only up close came clear enough to see.

As I passed that park where all the horse buggies line up I spotted from far off one shadow. This tall man came toward me in the fog. Outside the park there were no streetlights to make his face visible. I told myself, *He walks like...* and then I said out loud, "Mitchell!"

My voice startled him. He jumped a little, and looked so confused that I doubted he remembered me at all. Which made me feel stupid. I had thought about him every day and night, and he had not thought twice about me.

But then he called me by my Korean name, and took me in his arms. "Where have you been staying?" he asked. "I was so worried about you! Lou just threw you out, I couldn't believe that. Where did you go?"

"I live at a hotel on Saint Charles," I said. "I got a job downtown. Didn't Lou tell you?"

"Haven't seen Mister Lou," Mitchell said. "Where do you work?"

When I told him, I could tell he did not approve. "Don't work around food, honey. It's awful for your skin," he said.

"Where do you live?"

Mitchell's eyebrows did pushups, and he checked for spies in every direction while he got ready to answer me. "I was staying at this loft," he said at last. "I can't get my stuff out of there now. The guy who owns the loft has it in for me. I think somebody told him some bullshit like I talked bad about him."

We walked to the streetcar. I asked Mitchell if he wanted to stay with me for the night. He did.

At the hotel the clerk saw Mitchell and told me, "No guests."

"He is not my guest. He is my boyfriend," I said.

"Fiance," Mitchell corrected me, and a tiny thrill went through me to hear him say that.

"Look, honey, Brian did not pay for two people to stay in your room," the clerk said. With her eyes she tried to tell me that Mitchell was the kind of trouble she had warned me about.

I got her message, but I think for myself. I offered to pay her the difference to make tonight a double. She breathed very heavily out her nose and would not take any money from me.

Upstairs, Mitchell could not believe that my room had no shower or bathroom. We had to use the one down the hall. Pretty soon after we came in we began making love. Then Mitchell dressed me in my regular clothes and took me across the street to eat oysters, which I did not really want to try. It turned out I loved them. Mitchell couldn't believe I would eat them with just hot sauce.

Mitchell also couldn't believe that I had walked out of Lou's and found myself a job. "That's just phenomenal, baby," he said. "You got what it takes to hold it together down here. I thought for sure you would've just gone home."

"Where have you been?" I asked him. I did not want to nag him.

Mitchell sat there without talking. For the first time I saw that his eyes were not light blue but the same gray as the sky. Finally he said, "Been right down here, honey, where am I going?"

The beauty of him, the way his face made me hungry to lie near him, stopped me from complaining that he hadn't come looking for me. I wanted to ask him a million questions: How old was he? Where had he come from? Why had he taken me home from Jackson Square that night? Why did I feel so much love for him, such desire, when I hardly knew him?

"How old are you?" I asked.

"Twenty-nine." He didn't ask how old I was.

"Are you from Mississippi?"

He nodded. "How'd you guess?"

"People from Mississippi come in my father's store sometimes."

"What kind of store's your pop got?"

"It's a produce stand. But it's a store, not just a trailer," I told him. I kept my voice even so he could not tell how much I hated talking about my family.

"What, like a convenience store?" he asked.

"Kind of."

"Talk to your folks, at all?"

I shook my head. He dropped the topic. The waitress brought the bill and Mitchell paid it.

We walked around on St. Charles a little, although nothing much seemed open. We came to where the road made a circle around a hill with a statue on top. In the fog the place would have scared me if I was walking by myself. Mitchell started making out with me.

"Thank you for the clothes you bought me," I said. "And the books."

"I got you another book," he said. I had just reminded him of it.

"Oh, yeah?" I asked. "What book?"

He turned me around toward the hotel. "You'll see, later on. It's a surprise."

"I don't like surprises," I warned him.

Back at the hotel I said hello to the clerk, who nodded without looking at us. Mitchell and I went up to my room and immediately made love some more. When we finished he pulled my new book from the pocket of his coat, *Alice's Adventures in Wonderland & Through the Looking Glass*.

They never made me read this book in school. Mitchell could not believe I had never heard the story. I had seen something like it on a rock video. He read aloud to me. Lying there in my bed naked beside him, with him reading so gently to me, I felt happier than I could ever remember.

Soon the sound of him reading became blurry, and I thought about his growing up in Mississippi. The men I had met from Mississippi kept their feelings hidden around anyone they did not know well. They covered that up by having good manners and smiling. A man could cover anything that way.

At work everything went well enough. No one except Danneel wanted to explain to me how anything worked, and I could tell the others did not want him helping me. We handled the freak crowd. It grew bigger every day.

I did not care whether the other waiters liked me or not. Brian could handle training me when he came back. Until then I would just take it easy and do my job.

"Hey, I'm sorry about last night," that asshole Carl said to me when he came in to eat. "I just always try to get people to laugh. I wasn't goofing on you."

"I didn't care. I just had a hard day at work," I told him.

Knowing I would see Mitchell afterward made work easier, but also harder because it made me wish I was home.

Only, of course, when I got back to the hotel a little before dinnertime Mitchell was gone. I walked down to the clerk and asked her whether she had seen him. She shook her head. I went back up to my room before she could say she told me so.

I watched TV. Tonight my reception improved. After an hour I went down to buy dinner somewhere. I walked around a little before I decided I didn't feel hungry. Then I walked back to the hotel.

This time I came in to find Mitchell talking to the clerk.

"Hey, here she is," he said when he saw me. "Where'd you go?"

"I went to get something to eat."

"What's the matter, baby?" he asked as I came closer.

I did not answer, because I did not know what he meant.

"You look like you're crying," he said. I wasn't. He acted very concerned, though. He put his arm around my shoulder and held a paper sack up to show me. "Too bad you went out, I brought us Chinese food for supper."

"Good."

"But you already ate, I thought," he said.

"No, I went out. I didn't eat."

"You're not allowed to eat in your room," the clerk said.

"Okay," Mitchell said. "How about down here in the lobby, then? Want to join us?"

We all wound up eating spare ribs together. Mitchell finally got this clerk to treat him nice. She said to call her Jocelyn from now on. It made me feel good that she hung out with us two as a couple. Mitchell made me so proud. After that she even let us bring a six-pack up to my room.

Later, after he spanked me and we made love and he hugged me on his chest to keep me warm, Mitchell said, "So how's about us moving in together, huh?"

"I want that," I said.

"Working on it," he answered.

That was no lie.

By the end of the week, we had a house in a neighborhood called the Bywater. Mitchell explained it to me differently each time I asked how he got the house, just as he gave me a different story every time I asked what he did for money.

The truth is that I did not care. Having a two-story gray house to live in and a job to go to every day made me happy. Mitchell was the kind of man who always lives where someone else's mail comes.

A lady with fake red hair lived next door to us. As soon as we got there she introduced herself to Mitchell. She wanted Mitchell to have sex with her, I could tell just from watching them. I spied through a window while they talked in the driveway between our houses.

She said to him, "But you're such a good-looking young man, and I don't mean this to offend you or sound forward, but you are so very handsome and all, so why is it you wouldn't marry a white woman?"

That made Mitchell laugh. "No, I'm not offended," he said. "I don't think you can pick who you love enough to marry."

Hearing him talk about me as his wife, whether it was bullshit or not, made me part of something with him. Nothing had ever happened to me before. Even living a lie felt good with Mitchell. Too good.

One day I got to Shoney's and that girl Shelly came out to meet me. Brian was not due back for almost a week yet.

"We got a phone call from Brian," Shelly said, smiling really wide. "He says he's never coming back. He got a job as a lifeguard."

"Wow," I said. "That's great."

"You're fired," Shelly told me, and laughed.

I went and asked the other manager, that ugly woman, who acted annoyed that I would even talk to her. She told me they would mail me my last check.

"Have a nice life," Shelly called after me as I left.

I stopped and asked her, "What'd I do to you?"

She said nothing.

"Why do you have to be a bitch to me? I just want to make money so I don't live on the street," I said. "How come it makes you happy that I lose my job? Why you get jealous of somebody else working at fucking Shoney's, like this is some great job, I'm not good enough?"

She tried to talk to me but I left. When I got home I met Mitchell on his way out. I cried a little, and he brought me upstairs to lie down for a nap.

"Baby, you're going to find another job," he told me. "They'll hire you. There's tons of jobs down here. Fucking Shoney's sucks, anyway."

He stared out the window while I went over the whole story. I suppose he did not listen very closely, because all of a sudden he jerked up at something I had said.

"You gave them this address?" he said, startled. "I told you not to do that."

This was true. He had insisted that I not give my job our address or phone number. "But you said you just didn't want them calling me in to work on Saturdays," I reminded him. "Now I don't work there anymore. They just want to mail me my last check."

"I don't want any mail coming here under our names," he said. "You go down to Shoney's and pick that check up. Tell them you've had to move. I'll go with you, if you want."

I nodded, and searched around the room for something else to talk about. "Mitchell, whose house is this?" I said finally.

He smiled. "Ours, baby. We live here."

"Why does this man Tom McFaye get his mail here?"

"He used to live here, honey," Mitchell said.

"Where does he live now?"

Mitchell laughed. "How should I know?" he said. To make me feel stupid, he spoke to me the way you talk to children. "See, that happens a lot in New Orleans. People show up here and disappear and move around and everything else. It's not like Kentucky or Korea. Lots of people move through here and the post office delivers their mail forever. Certain things like the phone bill, it's easier to leave it in whatever name it's in. The rest's only junk mail, anyway."

I almost corrected him. I almost told him that I'd seen letters from the bank, and other handwritten ones, maybe from Tom McFaye's family—they should know he had moved. But I pretended Mitchell had made me understand.

With my job gone, Mitchell left me home alone during the day. Only once or twice did he disappear overnight. Two days after he told me McFaye had moved, a letter came from Montana addressed in ballpoint pen. I held it up to a lamp and studied it. The paper inside came from a spiral notebook.

To reach our mailbox I had to walk out to the street. I left the rest of the mail out there, so when he came home Mitchell would think I hadn't checked the mail at all. But I brought this letter inside and opened it.

Dear Tom,

I don't know what's your problem? Why is your new phone number un-listed? You refuse to speak or write to us, and seem to have lost the simple common decency to tell us why. Either that or you're in trouble, and to tell you the truth, I actually wish you were in trouble, rather than dick-ing around which is what you must probably be doing, sad though it makes me to say it.

If you don't want to talk even to tell me why you don't want to talk, fine, you can just leave a message on my machine while I am at work. Just to let us know that we shouldn't worry about you, we should just forget about you. That's fine.

He signed it Teddy, and he wrote his phone number under his name. Next to it he put *So you can't say you lost my number.*

After I read the letter I sat for a long time, trying to see anything it might tell me about who sent it. Then I had to consider what to do with the letter itself. If Mitchell found it he would freak.

I decided to throw away the whole letter but keep the name and the num-ber. I would bring the letter when I went for a walk later, so I could throw it where Mitchell would never dream to look. And I decided to call Teddy.

I got his machine but did not leave a message.

As far as I knew, the sink downstairs had never worked right. It had a garbage disposal, something I never had seen in real life before. Mitchell told me not to use it.

The neighbor lady told Mitchell our laundry room used to be a kitchen back when a landlord owned this house, because the downstairs was a separate apartment. Then Tom McFaye bought the house and made the downstairs into a cellar. Nobody has a real basement in New Orleans, I guess.

I never used the sink, but the washing machine used to drain into it after each cycle. It would fill to the top, and sometimes spill over and I had to mop the floor. Once it poured into the sink, the water level would gradually drop.

The day after I tried to call Teddy, I went downstairs to see how much time was left on the dryer. I already had another load in the washer, and the machine filled the sink. But magically the sink drained in a flash.

I rinsed the sink from the tap. The water disappeared immediately. Mitchell would be glad.

I did another two loads after that, and went upstairs. When I heard the washer turn off down there, I took a shower.

I came downstairs to find dirty soap suds sliding out from under the door. Drain water had flooded the washroom. And it smelled so badly I gagged a couple of times while I mopped.

When Mitchell came home I said, "We need to call a plumber."

"No, we do not," he said, extra-firmly. I thought maybe I hurt his pride by not letting him decide that. He checked out the washroom, and he acted as though he had some reason to feel responsible for causing this. Or that it alarmed him personally in some way I could not know. Making an effort to sound innocent, he said, "Boy, it sure stinks, don't it? What's that smell like to you?"

I thought about it awhile. "A raccoon died in our attic, and we didn't find him for a long time," I said. "It made the attic smell something like that." I had not recalled this story until I said that, but now I remembered the smell very clearly. Mitchell watched me closely, trying to tell what I thought. So I said, "Maybe a mouse went down the drain."

He nodded. "Probably. I'll put some acid down there."

The acid made black stuff come up the drain. And we could not use any sink in the house, or the shower, without more water rising into the washroom sink and onto the floor.

The next day Mitchell brought home a long coiled metal rope with wire brushes on one end. He forced this down the washroom drain. In fifteen minutes he had pushed through the clog.

The water went down better than ever after that, until the next day, while Mitchell was out. He had left me some pot to smoke, so I stayed in bed until the soap operas came on. Then I took a shower and got dressed. That day I wanted to go for a walk around the French Quarter to find another job. But I went downstairs to the front door and heard *drip-drop drip-drop* inside the washroom. Flooded again.

I sat down and stared at the mess. It stunk as badly as before, and the washroom had not gotten rid of the smell. Cleaning this place up would suck.

Someone rang the doorbell.

I did not want to answer. Instead I slipped up as near to the door as I could without showing myself. The lady from next door, the one who liked Mitchell, was standing out there. Beside her stood a man in a blue shirt. A mailman, I thought at first. She rang the bell again. I stood still. Parked on the street I saw a plumbing van.

"No one's answering," she told him.

They walked over to the driveway between our house and hers, where I had watched her flirting with Mitchell that time. I moved to the side window so I could spy on them.

"Well, look, I'm sure Tom won't mind," she said. "You have my permission. Tom isn't even going to see this. He never comes around anymore. Not that I miss him."

"No one's living there?" the plumber asked.

"Oh, there's a young couple living there," the neighbor lady explained. "I know they won't mind, though. Christopher won't mind."

"I'd feel better if he told me so himself," the plumber said.

"Well, he keeps odd hours. His wife's probably in the house, but she's not allowed to answer the door," the neighbor lady said. "She's not supposed to talk to anyone but her husband. She's from an ancient culture."

"Is that right?" the plumber said, walking away. "Be right back." He returned with a sledgehammer and some goggles. "Best step back, ma'am. These little chips fly."

The neighbor lady went inside. He cracked the cement pretty quickly, because it's not a real driveway, just poured on top of the dirt. He turned over a great big chunk and started digging.

The lady came back. "Real fag, the guy that owns that house," she said, though the plumber had not asked. "He's one of those obnoxious-type gays. He lived here seven years, and he didn't even come over to say good-bye.

I mean, come on, honey, I have to find out from the tenant that you're renting your house? What kind of neighbor's that?"

"Not much of one," the plumber said, because she wanted him to say something. He kept digging and hit something.

"Well, I'll tell you, it's fine with me," she said. "I'd rather have Christopher for a neighbor any day. He's charming, and his little wife never bothers a soul."

Hearing her call me his wife didn't give me any thrill. Why did he tell her his name was Christopher? I dropped the curtain and went inside to see how bad the washroom had gotten. Filthy, as a matter of fact. Hair floated along the brim of the sink, clumps of hair with gray foam caught in it. I stood in the water, and a small hole in my sneaker let my foot get wet.

I got the mop from behind the washer, and while I stood there trying to figure where I could squeeze it out, the water dropped out of the sink.

I ran back to the window to see. The plumber had removed a piece of the big pipe, and I could not tell if he had cut it or the pipe naturally came apart that way.

"Phew!" the plumber said. "Smells like you got a rat in the drain."

She put her hand over her nose and walked up behind him, eager to peek at this secret underground place.

Then the plumber said, "Oh, Jesus God, that's a *hand*."

And the neighbor lady spun around and threw up on her bushes.

They went inside to call the police. I grabbed as much clothing as I could fit into a plastic bag from the grocery store and I left. I still had sixty-three dollars from my last paycheck.

One night I saw a story on the front page of the newspaper about Thomas McFaye. I read what I could see through the rack on the front of the vending machine. It said the police wanted to find the couple who had lived in his house but the two had fled New Orleans. The wife was Chinese and couldn't speak English.

I have not seen Mitchell since then. I called home and my father said he has no daughter. I had sex with some older guy I met in Jackson Square one night and he paid me eighty dollars. I'm pretty sure the baby is Mitchell's, though. And I have some kind of infection. It really fucking itches.

MESS

WHILE RAYANNE WAITED OUTSIDE THE HOUSE she read a flyer stapled to a telephone pole. The flyer showed a murky photo of a guy leaning against a pool table; in magic marker someone had written that a bar on Esplanade Avenue would host a memorial for him in a few days. His name had been Desmond.

Then the landlady came with the keys. "I can't climb the stairs anymore," she told RayAnne.

"That's all right," RayAnne said, and held her hand out.

"Well, you can't trust anyone nowadays," the landlady went on without handing over the keys. "Rented to this couple in the back, and they had drugs and everything else going on, and fights and everything else. You ain't on drugs, are you?"

"No," RayAnne said.

"Good," the landlady said, still keeping the keys. "There's a bed up there, but you need to buy a, what do you call it? The bottom part."

"A boxspring."

"No, the part with the wheels."

"A frame," RayAnne said. "No problem."

"Do you have any furniture?"

"Everything I have's in storage," RayAnne said. "Once I get settled in, I can send for it."

The landlady unlocked the gate and handed over the keys at last.

"It's at the end of the alley," she said. "You go up them stairs."

RayAnne walked down the alley, surprised at how narrow and dank a tunnel it was. The building next door had aluminum siding, a sight she always disliked. At the end of the passage the alley turned and widened and led her up three concrete steps to a green door with two locks. The keys unlocked them both. A metal plate reinforced the doorjamb around the locks, probably because at some point a burglar had pried this door open.

The stairway ran upward a little too steeply. Someone had ripped the carpet from the steps, and RayAnne could see that whoever built these stairs had used mismatched scrap wood. This passage was narrower still than the alley; as she ascended she could rub one elbow along each wall at the same time.

Upstairs she found an attic divided to form a kitchen, a bedroom, and a bathroom. The ceiling met the walls at slightly obtuse angles. Cheap beige tiles covered the floor; as she crossed the kitchen to the bedroom RayAnne knocked a few loose with the soles of her shoes. The kitchen and the bedroom each had its own gabled dormer window overlooking the street.

The bedroom had two walk-in closets. One smelled of mothballs, the other held both a queen-size mattress sealed in plastic and a matching boxspring. A scratched dresser stood in a corner of the room where it didn't fit. The bedroom also had two side windows showing RayAnne the neighbor's front yard and part of the sidewalk.

When she returned to examine the stove, RayAnne saw that the kitchen too had its pair of side windows. The one she had noticed when she came in housed an exhaust fan. The other stood beside the sink, blocked from her view by the refrigerator when she'd first entered. Someone had recently replaced this window's sill. Clean paint made the fresh woodwork too white.

The chrome handle on the refrigerator curved outward so smoothly that at first glance she assumed it had come from the factory that way. Someone had bent the metal by pulling on the handle, maybe with a rope. A quick wisp of something foul reached her nose, though she couldn't see a trashcan anywhere.

The water heater had a closet to itself. A shelf at shoulder height in there held a few tools and a box of fuses. The bathroom had a slat window, cranked open upon the kitchen. Entering the bathroom made RayAnne think of standing in a fish tank. When she turned the cheap plastic taps the faucet spat a few times before filling the basin with grainy black water. After five seconds the water ran clear.

RayAnne went back downstairs and found the landlady sitting on the steps. The landlady seemed confused to see her.

"I'll take it," RayAnne told her. "The apartment."

The landlady nodded and said, "I need three hundred dollars for the first month, plus two hundred for a deposit."

RayAnne paid it in cash. Then they went to the landlady's house down the block, where the landlady wrote out a receipt. "Don't make me come looking for you when it's rent time," the landlady warned her.

RayAnne spent the rest of the afternoon moving in. Then she went to the Schwegmann's three blocks away for a broom, a dustpan, a mop, and the least expensive bottle of pine cleaner she could find. After a moment's thought she also picked up milk, for her cereal and coffee. Waiting in line at the checkout in New Orleans seemed different to her than she remembered it feeling back where she had come from, so she began scanning the store for details.

As she walked home she noticed that her new city lay so very flat and her new street ran so very directly east to west that the two horizons conflicted: To the east loomed night, yet day still shone in the west. This contrast made RayAnne put down her bags and dig the notebook from her pocket, and while she located her pen the dusk thickened. For half a minute or more, she could actually watch the dark seep across the sky above her. Everywhere the shadows swelled visibly, rapidly, scoring every line and sharp corner on the faces of the shotgun houses along the street. Then it was night.

She found her pen. For a brief while she wrote in her notebook, but words failed her.

Soon after rising to her first morning in the apartment, RayAnne felt something sharp poke her bare sole near the refrigerator. A nail had pressed its way from a floorboard through the tile. She didn't have a hammer, so she laid the blade of a butterknife flat upon the nail's point and pounded the knife with the heel of a shoe.

After breakfast she swept out the closet where she had found the bed. Rather than the tiles that covered the rest of the apartment, this closet had a crudely cut sheet of linoleum lying unfixed upon its floor. By lifting the linoleum RayAnne disturbed a colony of termites.

She replaced the floor covering and closed the closet door. As she crossed the kitchen to leave she smelled garbage again. The odor came from the sink.

Outside the day was balmy but clear. RayAnne walked to Schwegmann's, where she bought a can of crevice poison and then used a payphone in the parking lot to call New York. Alan answered. She thanked him for letting her reverse the charges, though she knew he would say it was no problem.

"I got an apartment," she said. "I haven't got a phone yet, but let me give you my address."

"Great," Alan said, and copied down the address she told him. "So is that in the French Quarter?"

"No, it's right next to the French Quarter. They call it the Marigny. Do you have any work for me?" she asked. "I might could have my computer set up by tomorrow."

"Okay, well, all I need at this point are letter sections," he said, "unless you want to wait for the next book."

"No, that's fine," she said.

"Then do voyeur and oral. Normal length."

RayAnne wrote that down in her notebook.

"And look, this stuff about the scenery's got to go, all right?" he said. "Stick to the point. And watch your grammar."

"How do you mean?"

"You sound peculiar sometimes," Alan explained. "This time you said 'damned' all the time. Damned this, damned that, 'it was damned hot,' whatever."

"That's how people speak, sometimes," she said, and cleared her throat. "Where I'm from."

"It's not a big thing, just watch your grammar."

For a long moment they didn't speak. Finally Alan asked, "Is everything okay with you, otherwise?"

"Yeah," she replied.

"Has he tried to find you? Or does he know where you are, or what?" Alan asked.

"Everything's fine," she said quickly. "I have to call the phone company, though, and get my phone turned on. Plus, I don't want to run your bill up."

Next she called the phone company. They gave her the address of a building where she needed to bring a deposit before they could begin service. Finally she called her moving company, who promised to deliver between six and eight that evening.

RayAnne brought her bug spray home, then took a bus and a streetcar to the phone company. After that she walked home across the French Quarter.

On Decatur Street she went inside a coffeehouse that rented computer time. As she looked around the room for the computers, it crossed her mind that a bank or something close to it had once occupied this building. A sign led her upstairs to a seat at a terminal. This computer used only programs she had never seen before, so the clerk showed her how to create a file. Having to help her annoyed him.

When the clerk returned to his desk, a bearded man sipping a cup of coffee stood beside RayAnne's chair. "What programs are you familiar with?" he asked.

"Just the ones on my computer," she said.

"Oh, has your computer crashed?"

"No," she said. "I just moved here, and they haven't delivered it yet. I just want to get some work done."

"Where'd you move from?"

"I'm real sorry," she said. "I just need to get some work done here."

"Okay, sorry," he said, and walked away.

After that, RayAnne couldn't concentrate. Other customers kept staring at her, people dressed in black with pierced eyebrows. At last she got up and paid the clerk. As she headed for the stairs she realized that the bearded man was speaking to her again.

"Excuse me?" she said.

"I said, 'Take it easy, Michelle,'" the man said, grinning.

For a moment RayAnne studied his face, waiting for him to explain. At last he did: "I just saw your name in the log. I'm Jeremy."

"You saw my name where?"

"In the log," Jeremy said, and pointed at the clerk's desk. "That book you signed when you rented the computer."

She had not signed in, but instead of telling him so, she nodded and left. Outside the coffee shop she passed a group of dirty kids with funny haircuts. One boy squatting on the ground asked her for spare change. RayAnne shook her head no.

At Barracks and Dauphine she found a second-hand bookstore. A tall man behind the counter pointed out two shelves of writing manuals, and she combed through them book by book. Near the far end she found one called *On Writing Well*. It didn't concern grammar but it caught her attention anyway. Just skimming through this book, RayAnne found herself agreeing with points the author made, things she knew but had never considered. The way he wrote seemed friendly, too.

"If you like," the tall man offered, "you can sit down there by the window and look that over. That's fine."

"Thanks," she said, and sat in a wicker chair by the front window.

In a park across the street a half-dozen people played with dogs. She read by the window for a few minutes, then she checked the price on the book and carried it to the counter.

"Good choice," the tall man said.

"Do you have any books on grammar?" she asked him.

"Grammar? No." He shook his head. "You might want to try some of the bookstores uptown, near the colleges...although they're not doing as much textbook business anymore, because the colleges stopped professors from giving out their reading lists in advance."

"That's probably going to be expensive, then," she said.

"Is it a specific textbook you need for a class, or a particular publisher?"

"No," she said. "Just any book on grammar. I need to brush up."

As he spoke the tall man wrote a title and publisher's name on a pad. "Just go to the library. This book is the best book of its kind, and I know the library on Loyola Avenue has it." He tore the sheet from the pad and handed it to her.

RayAnne crossed the Quarter on foot again. The library had a computerized card catalog. Along with the grammar text, she picked out a Henry Miller reader and a history of New Orleans street names. At the front counter she asked to fill out a card application.

"You got to have a local ID with that," a woman behind the counter warned her.

"I just moved here," RayAnne said.

"Then you got to bring your out-of-state ID and a local phone bill or a utility bill. It has to be in your name."

"All right," RayAnne said, and after a moment she asked, "Does the card have to be in my real name, with my real address?"

The woman nodded, almost incensed. "Of course it does. How would we find you if you ran off with a book?"

"No, the library could have my name and everything," RayAnne said. "I just want to keep it private."

"Well, you got to sign your real name on the card," the woman said.

"I just don't want to hear from certain people who might look for me, is all," RayAnne told the woman. "I haven't gotten a phone bill yet."

"Hey," a voice said behind RayAnne, who turned to find a pretty girl with red hair pointing at the books RayAnne had laid on the counter. "If you want, I'll take those out for you on my card."

"Sure," RayAnne said. "Thanks."

Her name was Courtney. They left the library together, and RayAnne accepted Courtney's offer of a ride. Courtney drove an old Impala.

"My stepfather had a car like this," RayAnne said as she buckled herself into the passenger seat.

"Oh, I love this car. She's my baby," Courtney said, and kissed the steering wheel.

"Does she have a name?"

"Lilith."

RayAnne smiled.

"You know who Lilith was, right?" Courtney asked. "Adam's first wife?"

"I had no idea he got married twice."

"You been married, ever?" Courtney asked.

RayAnne nodded. "Not anymore."

Courtney parked in the Lower French Quarter, near RayAnne's neighborhood. At a bakery on Ursuline they each bought a croissant and coffee. Courtney led RayAnne out a back door into a courtyard with fountains. They took a table beside a two-foot-tall brass angel peeing into a pond.

"Did you just move here?" Courtney asked.

"Yes," RayAnne said. "Is this where you're from?"

"I grew up in Los Angeles," Courtney told her. "I've lived here for seven years."

Overhead RayAnne noticed two sparrows clinging to a rail along the second story, their heads darting back and forth as they scanned the tables and floor for food. On the opposite wall she spotted three more birds, and still others peered from the roof.

"What do you call a group of sparrows?" RayAnne wondered.

"I have no idea," Courtney admitted, then guessed, "A flock."

"No, there's got to be a specific word," RayAnne said. "Like, it's a gaggle of geese and a murder of crows."

As they talked RayAnne relaxed. At last Courtney announced that she had to go to work and gave RayAnne a book of matches with her home phone number written inside it.

"But I'm usually at Checkpoint's," Courtney said. "I tend bar there. You know Checkpoint's? On Esplanade."

"I heard of it," RayAnne said. "Actually, I read about it. There's a sign by my house about it."

"A sign? What do you mean?"

"Like a poster," RayAnne said. "They're having a memorial there for somebody who passed away."

Courtney's smile dimmed. "Desmond," she said. "My friend Desmond hanged himself three weeks ago."

"I'm sorry, I didn't realize you knew the person," RayAnne said.

"Don't be sorry," Courtney said. "He was hanging two days before his neighbors noticed him."

"His neighbors actually went inside his apartment and found him, though?" RayAnne asked, because she could not help herself. "I mean, how did they know—?"

"He hanged himself outside," Courtney said. "He jumped out a window with an electrical cord around his neck. The window wasn't visible from the street, so nobody saw him there for two days. They didn't find him until crows were eating his face."

"Oh, my *God*."

Courtney grinned without a trace of humor.

"I'm so sorry I reminded you of it," RayAnne told her.

"Don't be," Courtney said again. "I have to tend bar at the memorial, anyway. You should come. Desmond was a writer, too."

"What makes you say I'm a writer?" RayAnne asked.

Courtney gave her a kiss and winked at her, but said nothing more as she left. RayAnne sat alone at the table for a while, taking notes and paging through her new books.

When she returned home her kitchen smelled bad, so RayAnne switched on the window fan and opened the other window. She peeled the linoleum from the closet floor and sprayed the termites. A few small spiders perished too. Something about the sight disturbed RayAnne, though she certainly didn't mind killing bugs. The poison stayed too wet for her to sweep up the dead termites, so she left the linoleum leaning against the wall while the closet floor dried.

Her phone worked. She called Alan again and gave him her new phone number. He congratulated her. When she hung up she realized it was almost six o'clock in New York. Whenever she called him this late in the day Alan sounded glad to have company. "That man must live at work," she said aloud.

The movers actually arrived at quarter of five, and finished in half an hour. They didn't seem to mind that RayAnne could only tip them five dollars apiece.

Suddenly she had all her belongings, which weren't many, in her new home: curtains, towels, a fair number of books. The sight of her bookshelf in this odd new environment excited her. She tried it against each of the walls, and then reasoned that it should go next to wherever she placed the table she used as a desk.

And that table, she decided, belonged in the corner now occupied by the dresser. For one thing, she wanted a window beside her workspace. Sliding the dresser out of the corner was clumsy at first, since she had to tug it until she could squeeze between the dresser and the wall and push. Several tiles came loose under the dresser's legs as she moved it to the far wall. RayAnne laid those tiles back into place.

Behind where the dresser had stood, someone had painted the lower wall another color, just a faint shade lighter than the rest of the room. The new paint all but covered something written there in magic marker; staring at it, RayAnne could detect several lines of characters, but only the last line was legible, and barely: SORRY ABOUT THE MESS.

Her desk fit this corner much better than the dresser had. She set about putting her computer together. The box that the printer came in still retained its stereo-store smell, reminding her of the day she bought it. To reach her new bedroom's only three-prong outlet she plugged her surge protector into a battered orange extension cord she found on the tool shelf in the water-heater closet.

As soon as she connected all the cables she turned the computer on, just to make sure her hard drive had survived the move. The extension cord struck her as unreliable, too, since a stretched part near the middle probably meant someone had used it to haul something. A few feet from this stretch the cord had a bend where she found embedded in the orange plastic a small sliver of wood painted the same drab white as all of her windowsills except the new one beside the sink.

Then RayAnne went in the kitchen for a glass of water, and the smell made her gasp. With one hand pinching her nose she searched around the sink. She found nothing in the cabinets, top or bottom. The drain didn't smell, either.

The window. The odor came from outside.

She thrust her head out the window. The stench rose from the alley below with such intensity that the air weaved, the way it would above a desert road. A huge wet blotch marred the concrete walkway. RayAnne pulled her head back inside and closed the window. She also shut off the fan.

In her bedroom she opened both the side windows. She had yet to unpack a lamp, and preferred natural twilight to the harsh overhead fixture. Her next job was to unload her books into her bookcase. It didn't take long. All of her reference books went at the end nearest her desk, and when she finished she grabbed her *Word Menu* and looked up sparrows in the index.

Before she could find the page, the light changed.

She studied the western horizon over her neighbor's roof. Overhead the sky was changing tide just as she'd watched it do last night. Shadows flared along what she could see of the street. Even the light pouring into her room from the west deepened somehow around her.

On the wall behind and below her desk, the writing became clear.

The ink from the marker bled through the paint. During high school RayAnne had seen a boy cause this same effect to happen by removing a certain-colored filter from a stage light.

The message on her wall now read: I HAVE HAD AN ANOMALOUS EXPERIENCE. I NO LONGER HAVE ANY CONTACT WITH THE PEOPLE WHO SHARED THIS EXPERIENCE WITH ME, A DEVELOPMENT I DISLIKE. THIS MEANS I AM DELUSIONAL. SORRY ABOUT THE MESS.

Outside, night prevailed. When RayAnne flicked on the overhead light, the message had faded back into the paint.

RayAnne awoke just before nine the next morning. Immediately she snatched her notebook from beside her bed and wrote: *I dreamed about places that are open but have been closed for so long that I can tell they are abandoned. These places were in New Orleans but I know the intersection of Gormley and 45th Avenue (where Aunt Kelda lived, with the aluminum siding) was one of the locations. I had a strong impression of nearly figuring out some important point just when I woke up.*

From the floor beside her bed she picked up the notes she had taken last night from the punctuation chapter in her grammar text, mostly about semicolons. A magazine article about self-education had taught RayAnne that drilling herself first thing the next morning helped her retain new information. That took only a few minutes, so she read a few pages of *On Writing Well* before hunger drove her from her bed.

For breakfast RayAnne made coffee and a bowl of raisin bran. She opened all three windows in her bedroom. In the closet where she had sprayed yesterday she had forgotten to clean out the dead bugs, so she swept it now; with their tiny carcasses in the dustpan, she realized what had bothered her about this floor yesterday—the pattern the termites had gnawed into the boards formed a map of that intersection back home where her aunt had lived. It interested her, but not enough to keep her from laying the linoleum back on top of it.

For a garbage pail RayAnne had slung a plastic bag from Schwegmann's over the knob of the door between the kitchen and the stairs. She dumped the dustpan into this bag. Suddenly the urge struck her to go for a walk before writing. Without a second's debate, she did.

In sunlight she found her neighborhood more beautiful every time she saw it. The streets weaved among one another so that she could wander aimlessly. Unlike the French Quarter, the Marigny had many closed businesses, all built in an older style that appealed to RayAnne though she did not know the correct architectural terms to describe them. As they stood quiet, their paint peeling, RayAnne pictured these buildings as the restaurants and shops they had once been.

She bought a cinnamon roll she couldn't really afford at a coffee shop on Frenchmen Street and ate it in a park across the street. On the other side of the park she walked down Elysian Fields to Schwegmann's and visited the store's magazine aisle. The editorial address was the same for every romance monthly she checked. Each listed a different editor, but such names were often made up, she had found. In her notebook she wrote that address, then the editor and title of three magazines.

Back at the house as she unlocked the gate she recalled the smell fouling her kitchen last night. No trace remained of the stain on the concrete that she thought she had seen from upstairs. RayAnne looked upward to make certain she stood directly below her kitchen window, and noticed for the first time that the fresh white paint on the sill made her window somehow more garish than even the neighbor's sooty aluminum siding.

Upstairs RayAnne poured herself another cup of coffee. The view from her kitchen window had changed. Until now, she had never known the neighbor directly across the alley to have his blinds open. In fact she had assumed the apartment empty. Yet here it stood, fully furnished. The part closest to her was a kitchenette. A man wearing an apron over a collared shirt and tie walked around the apartment, dusting.

This tenant did not notice RayAnne, partly because she stayed still but for raising her coffee to her mouth. He finished dusting and pulled sheets off a couch and an armchair in the living room. That led RayAnne to guess that this man stayed here only occasionally, perhaps on business. Two bags of groceries on the kitchen counter supported her theory.

Then the man did an inexplicable thing: He reached into one of the grocery bags, opened a box of butter, cut a bar in two and chucked half of it into the trash. The other half he placed in the butter dish in his refrigerator.

As RayAnne sipped her coffee, the tenant went item by item through his groceries and discarded a small amount of each. A handful of bread he threw out, two slices went into the toaster, and the rest of the loaf made it to the fridge. He opened a half-gallon of milk and poured at least one glass's worth down the drain. After a moment's reflection he took a glass from his cabinet and swirled some milk around inside it, then dumped it and left the glass in the sink. He drew two knives from the silverware drawer and rubbed butter on them, then stood them inside the glass. To fill the sink he added two coffee cups from another cabinet.

His toast came up. The tenant rubbed the two slices together over his sink and counter and then by the window, where RayAnne guessed there was a table she couldn't see just below window level. She imagined she could hear the toast scraping and the crumbs landing everywhere.

The toast itself landed in the garbage, followed by a small stack of junk mail, after which the tenant replaced the plastic bag in the trash pail and knotted the full one. Finally the man washed his hands, hung his apron on a wall hook, picked up his suit jacket from the back of a chair in the kitchen, and closed both the window and the blinds.

RayAnne remained in place, until she noticed her coffee had gone cold. Then she went inside and sat down to write.

After checking recent notebook queries in her reference books, she started with the voyeurism section:

SHE KNOWS I WATCH!

I know that most of your readers don't think peeping is much of a kick, but they should try it first before making their mind up about it. Like, there's this girl I know named Courtney and she's damned hot, but nuthin' would ever happen if I made a move on her, cause she thinks of me as just a nice, 27-year-old guy with a beard who lives near her. I helped Courtney with her computer once and we had coffee and croissants. You could never have a friendship like that if your gonna go pushing the issue.

Yesterday I caught her sunbathing nude again. It was the evening as I was coming home from work. There's a yard behind the building, and it's fenced in and she lives in the back apartment so most of the yard's hers.

I should describe the sky so you can picture it. We live near the equator, so the sun seems to move funny. At this time of the evening, the sky goes from aqua to indigo with all the other cyanic brands of blue in between. All the way east where the sun had just been, the sky reminded me of this clam shell I found on the beach when I was a kid; I painted this shell blue with waterpaints and then changed my mind and painted it red-orange, and then my stepfather used it as an ashtray and left it out in the rain, and after that the shell was the same color as this sky in the east. And in the west the background was so gray it made the few clouds still left from daytime look scared, like someone had mispelled the address they were looking for and now they were lost. Soon the night clouds would come attack these day clouds.

The light from the sky made everything look different, like the cracks in the fence got darker and the light parts of the wood seemed to glow. I looked through a slightly wide crack in the fence that I know about and there was Courtney, naked, going at it in her folding lounge chair. Her legs were spread obscenely wide apart and both her hands worked frantically at her pussy. The way her pubic thatch matches the red hair of her head always turns me on.

The familiar signs appeared soon. Her thighs began to tense, then she held her cunt totally still while her hands thrashed wildly at her clit. The tension visibly worked its way down her legs to her knees and calves and feet. Then she laid leisurely back in her chair, breathing heavily, still madly working her fingers in that nastily private place. Pleasure flooded hotly to every single part of her, toes and ears and fingertips.

I did something I hadn't done before, I looked up. All the people in our apartment building were peeking out their windows, like a host of curious sparrows checking for food people dropped in the courtyard of a restaurant.

The section had to be five thousand words long, so RayAnne wanted five letters of equal length. She filled this first one out with descriptions of Court-

ney and the narrator masturbating. The people watching from their apartments proved more awkward to work with, so she left that thread loose. When
she finished she looked it over and noticed that the headline she'd started with
didn't fit the story that had evolved. She fixed that by adding another paragraph:

> `Exhausted and damned happy, I fell asleep in my apartment.`
> `Next day I got a note in my mail from Courtney, thanking me for`
> `getting her into exhibitionism. She knows I'm her biggest fan.`

RayAnne signed the letter Jeremy. Next she wrote one from a woman who
moved in by herself for the first time after leaving her abusive husband. The
woman could only afford to tip the movers five dollars apiece, so as a bonus
she offered herself. She wound up having sex with each guy while the other one
watched.

After that came a letter from a carpenter helping to restore a very old restaurant. He was working alone on the second floor when he heard someone break
in downstairs. The intruders turned out to be a redhead and her somewhat
plainer blonde friend, both acting out the blonde's fantasy about having lesbi-
an sex in an abandoned building. Having the carpenter spy on them allowed
RayAnne to write some dialogue, which she hadn't done all morning. She also
got to use some new architectural terms.

The morning passed. She completed the voyeurism section a little after two
and made herself a peanut-butter sandwich. The computer printed her morning's work while she ate lunch with *On Writing Well* open across her lap. After
her sandwich she poured herself another cup of coffee and looked over what
she had written. She had used the word *your* in place of *you're*, but this time she
had not confused *its* and *it's* even once. RayAnne sat at the computer to correct
the few mistakes she had noticed, then she commanded the software to search
the entire document for misspelled words.

Pleased to finish so quickly, she put her jacket on and headed for the door.
The stench in her kitchen stopped her cold. It seemed impossible that so strong
an odor could travel from outside through two closed windows, yet when she
opened the repaired one and thrust her head out, the fumes made her wince.
Earlier she had mistaken this smell for trash but now instead she found it fecal,
even partly rancid. Something brown or dark red had definitely stained the
concrete directly below. Small wet puddles gleamed within the stain.

She came downstairs to find the alley immaculate. A chill from the Mississippi River blew past her. RayAnne stared upward from the alley, wondering if a pigeon or a squirrel had died on the roof near her window, maybe inside the eaves.

Outside the alley she locked the gate and spent a moment studying the flyer for Desmond's memorial. It didn't say where on Esplanade this bar Checkpoint's was.

A car pulled up and parked in front of her. The tenant she had earlier watched dust and then dirty his apartment climbed out of the driver's side. A woman got out from the passenger seat, too, while the tenant helped an older woman out from the back.

"Oh, this is a pretty neighborhood," the older woman said.

"Yeah, we love it," the man told her.

The younger woman deliberately looked RayAnne over and nodded. RayAnne said, quite loud, "Hey, how are you guys doing?"

The tenant seized upon it immediately and answered, "Great! How have you been?"

"Not bad," RayAnne said. "Just got back. See you."

The couple guided the older woman into the man's apartment.

While closing the door, the younger woman lingered a moment to share eye contact with RayAnne once more.

At Esplanade Avenue RayAnne entered a convenience store and bought herself a thick black marker for addressing parcels to Alan. When she left the store she headed toward the river. Two blocks before Esplanade ended she reached a loud bar with its side windows open. Without reading the sign she knew she had found Checkpoint's.

She pushed through a pair of swinging doors. Inside the bar the air hung like a cool shadow. Amber lamps gave the room an evening glow. A few people looked at RayAnne just long enough to see that they didn't know her. Across three tables pushed together lay food and plates.

Behind those tables RayAnne caught sight of Jeremy, from the coffeehouse. Before he could notice her she hurried to a seat at the bar. Courtney appeared in front of her, beaming.

"Hey, it's Book Girl. How you doing?" Courtney greeted her.

"Just great, thanks," RayAnne replied. "How are you?"

"All right. Can I buy you a drink?"

"Sure," RayAnne said.

"What do you like?"

"I don't really drink," RayAnne said. "Something not too harsh."

"Don't like beer?"

"Nope." RayAnne took off her jacket and draped it over the back of her chair. Courtney brought her a Bloody Mary. Some man at the far end beckoned and Courtney went to serve him.

No one else tried to speak with RayAnne. Behind her she heard Jeremy raise his voice so dramatically that she assumed it a joke. Then someone else said, "Jeremy, man, calm down."

"No," Jeremy said. "I'm fucking serious. You two got some fucking nerve even showing your faces in here."

"Look, you don't know—" someone else began.

"Why don't you go dance on his goddamn grave?" Jeremy asked.

"You have no idea what we three went through together," a woman said, at which point RayAnne turned so she could see the argument. No one noticed her, since all eyes in the place were on Jeremy and the odd-looking couple he was frothing at: a thin, pale man and woman both dressed in black, both somehow aloof though irked by Jeremy's abuse. They had walked in after RayAnne.

"I seen what *you* two have been going through for the past couple months," Jeremy said with a smirk. "And he saw it, too. And don't tell me he didn't. You want to act like it's just some weird coincidence he jumped out a fucking window. Well, so what? You two got each other now. Fuck Desmond."

With his jaws clenched, the man gestured for Jeremy to follow him away from the center of the room. To RayAnne this move implied that the man was inviting Jeremy outside for a fistfight. Yet the two walked together only as far as the corner near the cigarette machine, where the pale man waved his hands in the air as if he were pulling a curtain around himself and Jeremy.

Everyone in Checkpoint's stopped paying attention to them. RayAnne blinked at the crowd around her. So instantly did everyone ignore Jeremy and the pale man that they both might have turned invisible. The pale man spoke, but all the noise in the bar shrouded whatever words he said. The spectators all had forgotten the show mid-scene.

She focused on the pale man and concentrated. He formed his words testily, showing his teeth more than he wanted.

Suddenly his voice came clear to RayAnne. "...all there is to it. No one owes you any explanation," he said. "You weren't there, you'll never know. We went places you haven't. He made choices, by himself, then he lived up to them.

Choices. He knew what was behind the doors before he..."

RayAnne realized she had stopped hearing the other noise in the room. All the other people seemed to move slowly, but she only saw them from the corners of her eye because she could not pry her sight from the pale man's face: Cracks had appeared in his lips, and deep lines in his cheeks surrounded his eye sockets. Several gray streaks she hadn't noticed limned his hair. Jeremy resembled a sheep.

Then the pale man's woman stood directly in front of RayAnne. "How did you know Desmond?" she asked.

"Roommates," RayAnne said, "kind of."

The woman extended her hand. "I was his wife," she said. "I don't recall his mentioning you."

RayAnne shook hands but said no more. The background din had returned to fill her ears. Desmond's widow joined the wizened pale man and they left. Jeremy stayed by the cigarette machine, scowling at the floor, still wrapped inside the pale man's curtain.

For a while RayAnne sipped her drink. The jukebox played nothing she had ever heard before. At last Courtney came back to her. "Ready for another?" she asked, pointing at RayAnne's glass.

"I don't think so," RayAnne told her. "Thanks, though. I better go home. I only came out to take a break from work."

"All right, baby," Courtney said. "Thanks for coming."

RayAnne walked home down Frenchmen Street instead of Esplanade, feeling the alcohol. By the time she arrived at her house, euphoria had given way to fatigue. The alley didn't smell. Neither did her apartment.

The red light on her phone meant someone had left a message. She pressed PLAY and heard Alan's voice, softer and more somber than she'd ever heard it before: "RayAnne, this is Alan. Call me as soon as you get this. Whatever time, it doesn't matter. I'll be up."

She called him. He answered, drunk.

"What's the matter?" she asked. "You sounded upset."

"Maybe a little," he said. "I got fired this afternoon."

"Oh, no!" RayAnne said.

"Yeah, and you too," he added.

"Fired?"

"Well, we lost the contract on all the digest books," he explained. "You could probably go write for whoever they give the contract to, though they'll probably have their own free-lancers, but who knows? But anyway, I'm totally fucked. I turn forty-six next month, and I won't be able to make my rent."

"That's not true, Alan," she said. "You can find another job. You're good at what you do. I've always liked working for you."

"You're in even worse shape," he said, "because you just moved to a new city and you need the money."

"Don't worry about that," she said. "I can make the money I got last. And I've got some ideas about other places to write for."

"You should," Alan told her. "You're good."

They talked awhile. Alan assured her that she would receive all the checks for which she had already invoiced the publisher. Then RayAnne excused herself, saying she needed to go write. Alan wished her the best.

First she poured herself a cup of coffee. Out her kitchen window she could again see into the apartment next door. The younger woman read a magazine at the kitchen table, smoking, with the window open. In the living room behind her, the tenant himself sat chatting with that older woman RayAnne had seen them bring here earlier. The younger woman reminded RayAnne of a chorus girl sneaking a smoke backstage.

Alcohol still pulsed through her head, so she lay on the bed. Rather than read anything important while impaired she picked up the New Orleans book Courtney had taken out for her. In a short while she felt inspired.

At the computer RayAnne created a new document, not allowing herself to dwell upon the fact that all of her work so far today would count for nothing and be read by no one. Instead she began typing:

```
    At Esplanade Avenue the French Quarter ends. Locals call
the neighborhood that begins across Esplanade the Marigny, or
the Faubourg-Marigny, or the French Marigny. The name honors a
Frenchman who in 1813 imported a new Parisian dice game in hopes
of bilking the early Creoles; his ploy succeeded well enough
that Americans came to know this game as Craps, which derived
from the Creole nickname Johnny Crapaud, but by then debts had
forced de Marigny to sell off all his property holdings—the
French Quarter itself, for instance.
    The denizens of this neighborhood today include people from
the Quarter who can't stand the Quarter anymore, people from
other cities who moved to New Orleans yet can't pay top dollar
```

for luxury in the Quarter or Uptown in the Garden District, people who were born in the neighborhood and will only leave in a
hearse, and spiritual descendents of de Marigny himself—men of
comfort turned desperate by a brand of bad luck peculiar to this
city, where wicked habits hunt victims. Locals claim that more
former millionaires live in the Marigny than anywhere on earth.

Night falls with great stealth on the Marigny. Morning gives
much clearer warning. The residents prefer this arrangement.

Outside, as if on cue, the sky changed. Twilight filled the room, and the writing appeared on the wall behind her computer: I HAVE HAD AN ANOMALOUS EXPERIENCE. I NO LONGER HAVE ANY CONTACT WITH THE PEOPLE WHO SHARED THIS EXPERIENCE WITH ME, A DEVELOPMENT I DISLIKE. THIS MEANS I AM DELUSIONAL. SORRY ABOUT THE MESS.

RayAnne pulled the new marker from her pocket and knelt before the sign. When she touched the tip of the marker to the wall, the ink diffused, the way a felt pen would on damp paper. She changed the period between *dislike* and *this* into a semicolon. Quickly the dusk waned and the message sank back into the wall.

RayAnne sat in her chair again, satisfied. The word *this* should never appear in a sentence that does not contain whichever noun *this* modifies. By inserting a semicolon, she let *this* modify *development*. The sentence does not end until the period.

FEVER

FOUR DAYS AFTER THE RESTAURANT LAID HIM OFF, GARY GOT SICK. Any boyfriend he'd ever had always deserted him the minute he took ill, whether he came down with a bronchial infection or colitis or a persistent earache.

Eckhart, a German who had shared Gary's apartment for just shy of three weeks, left without a word the morning Gary woke up hacking and groaning.

Eckhart's departure said: *I desire you, but not enough to take care of you. Life is too short for that shit.* That made sense to Gary. He could live with that.

But understanding his lover's motive did little to make Gary's lonely sick-bed tolerable. None of his friends called on him, other than Roger, the old queen from around the corner on Dauphine. Roger dropped by, stewed, with a container of minestrone from the Nelly Deli.

"Mangi, mangi," Roger said, dropping ash from his cigarette on Gary's throw rug.

"Actually, I think I'm getting a headache from the smoke," Gary said. "Just a little headache."

"No, it wouldn't be from the smoke," Roger said. "What do you think is wrong with you?"

"I don't know, I just have a fever. Had it late yesterday, too," Gary said, wishing Roger would leave. "This morning I couldn't get out of bed. I keep ralphing."

"Why isn't Eckhart here?" Roger asked.

"He's out," Gary said.

"Out where?"

Gary sighed as Roger put out his cigarette and lit another. Roger smoked long, thin brown cigarettes that reminded Gary of his Aunt Gwen. "Oz or the Pub, probably," he answered at last.

Roger rolled his gin-stained eyes. "He's out dancing," he said, "and you're—?"

"I don't want to talk about this," Gary told him, his voice sharper than he intended.

Finally Roger took the hint and rose from Gary's rocking chair to leave. Drunkenly he closed his eyes and waved down Gary's apologies. "You are ill, my lad, wracked by fever," Roger said. "No explanation needed. Have a restful night, and feel better."

"Thanks for the soup," Gary called after him, briefly sorry that he had chased away company.

And Roger was his last visitor all week. After a few days alone Gary decided that if he died—not that he wanted to, or had any reason to suspect he might, but after all everyone did eventually and Gary couldn't count on having anyone around when it happened—if he died here in his apartment, no one would notice until his bills turned up unpaid.

Gary spent the next five days alternately kicking the covers from the bed in sweaty disgust or trembling with chills. He threw up so often during the first two days that the third one seemed positively luxurious just because his head never had to leave his pillow. Not until the fourth day did he realize he hadn't eaten all week, not a bite since Roger brought him that minestrone.

A roach the size of a turtle scooted across the sink when Gary turned on the kitchen light. In the breadbox lay three different grain loaves, each with three or four slices left. The pumpernickel had huge papules of white fuzz, the largest growths swelling around yolk-like yellow chunks; the other two sported more conventional blue mold, albeit dense with black spores.

The bread reminded Gary of his mold garden for the science fair in seventh grade, when his growths had sprouted hair so long he could comb it and he won some stupid medal. This boy Gary had a crush on threatened to make him eat his own project but never did.

In the refrigerator Gary found some apples Eckhart had bought.

The skins had shrivelled slightly and the apples themselves felt mushy, but Gary ate one and made himself enjoy it. Then he moved a package of English muffins from the freezer to the fridge, in case he got hungry later.

The next day, he awoke famished in the late afternoon. With the fever still roasting his skull from inside, he pulled on some shorts and a sweatshirt and staggered to the Nelly Deli.

As he approached Bourbon Street, a woman said, "Hi!"

Gary grunted at her and walked into the store. Nine minutes later he came back out carrying a roast beef po'boy, several cans of soup and a pint of ice cream.

Again the woman greeted him.

"When did you get back in town?" she asked.

"I'm sorry," he said. "I don't feel well. Fever."

"You look sick," she agreed. She held a drink in her hand, something dark in a go cup. A rum and coke.

Gary staggered home. Not until he reached his gate and took out his keys did he consider what the woman had said to him. Back in town? Obviously she thought she knew him.

He opened the gate and carried his groceries into his apartment. Inside, he glanced for the first time in days at the mirror over his bureau.

He did not recognize himself. A full beard of greasy blond hair covered his jaw.

Gary did not know he could grow a beard. Ordinarily he shaved every other day. At the time he got sick he had gone three days, unusual for him. Apparently life in the Quarter had stimulated his facial hair, although the last time he had tried to farm himself a goatee he had been maybe seventeen and now he was twenty-six, so he might merely have matured.

When his fever dissipated Sunday morning, Gary left the house and walked to the A&P on Royal. He hadn't washed his hair all week, so he wore a fishing cap. Outside the diner on St. Peter's Gary saw Roger chatting with James and this other great-looking boy who tended bar at Oz on Tuesdays.

None of the three recognized Gary, even when he glanced at them while passing not four feet from Roger.

Then Gary saw his own reflection in the supermarket's big windows and remembered that he no longer looked the same. The cap especially changed his appearance.

Inside the A&P he wound up waiting behind a redneck in line for the register. All at once the redneck began speaking. "Hey, goddamn," the man said, his voice more cultured than Gary would have expected.

Gary nodded at him.

"Where the fuck you been, bro?" the redneck went on, grabbing Gary's hand and squeezing it. "They been keeping you under a rock or what?"

"No, I've been sick," Gary said.

"What you got, AIDS? No, I'm fucking with you. You okay, though?"

Gary nodded, his face grinning blankly. His sight fastened itself to the coat of dirt ringing the redneck's flesh along his collar. For one mad instant he tried to imagine any human being's finding this man attractive.

"Well, goddamn, it's been months since I seen you," the redneck said. "You ain't been sick all that time."

"No, I've been, I don't know," Gary told him.

"Well, come out tonight," the redneck suggested. "Party at George's to-night, up Magazine. Just take the bus to Louisiana and follow the noise from there. He says there's going to be bands and everything, he cooks up hot dogs on the grill, it'll be a cool party. You should come, seriously."

For his very life Gary could think of no way to escape this situation. The redneck genuinely believed they knew each other. If Gary pretended to have forgotten, say, a bakery item, this vulgar cretin would wait for him to return with it.

"So where you working?" the redneck asked jovially.

"I'm not."

"You got to be shitting me, Howie! You ain't picked up one night any-where?"

Howie. How grotesque.

"Look, come down to my place, it's a done deal. I need someone to start Sunday night," the redneck said.

"Which place?" Gary asked him.

The redneck snorted. "You forgot my place?"

"No, I mean—what's the address, again?"

The redneck told him the address. It was a bar in the Bywater.

"Come to George's party uptown, man, we'll talk about it there." Then the redneck apologized for leaving and, at last, did.

Gary paid for his groceries and left. On his way home he spotted Jerome and some girl from the restaurant headed directly toward him, and he wished he could avoid them. Yet they passed without noticing him.

He spent the day lounging and reading the paper. By midafternoon he had fully recuperated. By early evening he felt restless and hungry. He needed a job. Badly. His rent would come due in a week and a half.

So he set out for the party. Gary hated Canal, especially waiting for buses there. By the time the Magazine bus arrived, three streetcars had passed. As the bus traveled uptown the world outside grew steadily darker.

After nearly missing the Louisiana stop, Gary followed a dreadful grinding sound to a crowded alley where a loud rock group played. He didn't know what kind of music to call it.

When he scanned the crowd for the fat redneck, Gary's eyes met those of a pretty redhaired girl with a pierced lip. He stared dumbly until she placed her hands on her hips in mock offense.

"You're not even going to say hello?" she asked.

"Hi," Gary said, trying to recall where he knew her from. A great many people who worked briefly with him at some restaurant or other expected him to remember them forever.

She threw her arms around him. A second later her breasts pressed against him and her tongue probed his mouth.

"Where the fuck have you been?" she murmured, her huge eyes pleading with him not to hurt her.

Gary drew a breath and exhaled. "Uhm," he said.

"Howard!" a longhair smoking a joint exclaimed, and several heads turned to greet Gary. Then, sensing he had interrupted the couple, the longhair glanced from the redhead and back to Gary and said, "I'm sorry, man, just meant to say hello." He turned away.

With an all but tangible start, Gary realized his hands had come to rest upon this girl's buttocks. Stranger still, when they broke their embrace, his cock was hard.

By the time Gary and his self-proclaimed date had woven their way through the party to the grill, a dozen strangers had shaken his hand or hugged him. Everyone told him how glad it made them to see him back in New Orleans.

"Thanks," Gary said, a dozen times, and meant it.

"Well, look who the fuck the cat dragged up here!" the fat guy Gary had met in the A&P said, patting him on the back.

The redhead kept caressing Gary's arm.

"Want something to eat, Howster?" a nerd working the grill asked.

"Sure, a hamburger," Gary said, smiling, nodding.

"Looks like Audrey needs a hot dog," the redneck snickered, his mouth full of food.

A few guys laughed in a half-hearted way. The redhead let go of Gary's arm and looked at the fat guy, her face angry and hurt. She spun on one heel and left.

Gary looked at his new boss, then at this girl storming out of the party. Instinctively he knew how she felt, an odd mixture of embarrassment for being so foolish to believe someone wanted her and resentment that this someone had led her to believe it.

As she moved through the light from the garage, the girl's ass swung from side to side beneath her skirt. In his jeans, Gary still hung semierect. He had not even jerked off in a week.

"Audrey!" he yelled, and ran after her.

He caught up with her around the block, stamping past the guitar store on the corner.

"Audrey," he said, and she turned around. Tears smeared her cheeks. Her eyes had turned pink already.

"What?" she asked him.

For just one split instant, Gary wondered what he was doing. Then his mouth opened and sentences began to flow from it, and he marveled at them.

"Audrey, where are you going? Don't leave. I haven't seen you in how long, and you're going to run off like that?"

"You haven't seen me since Thanksgiving, and you couldn't give a shit," she said.

"That's not true."

"It is so, you fucking disappeared and never called me and you've been back for days and you haven't called me," she went on. "And you let fucking Alvin make fun of me in front of everyone like I'm some slutty piece of shit."

"He's my boss now."

She paused for a moment, then started crying harder as she said, "You're working for that fat douchebag?! He can talk to me like that and you'll let him?"

"For Christ's sake, he made a goddamned joke!" Gary said. "So it was a stupid joke, all right, but don't go running away over it!"

"The last time I saw you, I had your fucking cum inside me, and you don't call me to tell me where you are all this time, and now you act like I'm some whore you—"

"*Bullshit!*" Gary snapped, and Audrey's head recoiled as if from a slap. Her eyes widened, and her weeping halted. The shock of his temper made her submissive.

That sensation drove him forward.

"Audrey, there's some things I can't explain, just like you have secrets from me. Don't act like you don't." He glared at her. She dropped her gaze to the pavement. His cock swelled anew. "You want me? You just have to accept that I've been gone and you don't know where. I haven't been with any other women, I promise you."

"I'm sure," Audrey said, rolling her eyes.

"Hey!" he barked. Again she shut up. "Don't you call me a goddamned liar."

"I didn't," she said, averting her eyes. She sniffled.

"Here," Gary said, handing her a tissue from his pocket.

Sullenly she blew her nose and said, "Since when do you carry Kleenex around?"

"There's a lot about me you don't know," he told her. "We'll probably be better off if you pretend you just met me tonight for the first time ever."

In high school he had dated girls. Nobody in Marshaltown, Iowa grew up gay; people there believed homosexuality happened when you moved to New York or San Francisco or Los Angeles. Or New Orleans.

He had had female lovers twice. One was his girlfriend, Sarah, whom he balled every weekend throughout the second half of senior year. His other tryst took place in New York before he dropped out of NYU. During his last semester there he and an acquaintance from the journalism department discovered they were both fucking the same boy, who had warned neither of them that he was bisexual.

That son of a bitch, Bernadette had said while they commiserated. *You know what the sweetest revenge would be? You know what would really burn his ass?* So they spent the night screwing at her apartment. In the morning he awoke feeling sated and powerful, and she told him he had been a satisfying and considerate lay. They did it again that afternoon and a third time that night. He spoke to Bernadette a few times before he left New York, though he had no idea what later became of her.

Thus, the notion of seducing Audrey did not disgust him, especially since he had not had an orgasm in a week. Out there in front of the guitar store, with drunk bums studying them from doorways, he patted her eyes dry with another tissue and said whatever she needed to hear.

"Hey, Audrey, I'm sorry, honey," Alvin said when they returned to the party. "I was just playing with you, baby, I didn't want to hurt your feelings."

"Got nothing to do with you, Alvin," he replied. "This was just a little something between me and Audrey, is all. It's cool now."

Audrey nodded. He put his arm around her and she could not keep a smile from her lips, though she tried.

He could tell that Audrey got off on the girlfriend role, and that she would never admit that. "You didn't even mention my pierced lip," she said, acting crushed.

"What pierced lip?" he said, and she slapped him playfully.

"You used to hate Abita beer," she taunted him.

"Well, I've grown up now."

Having never tended bar, he tried to glean clues from what Alvin told him in between swills of beer. How hard could the job be, after having had to deal with the bar in the restaurant?

"Listen, Alvin, I'll see you tomorrow night, okay?" he said, putting his arm around Audrey to lead her away.

"You kids got some catching up to do, huh?" Alvin grinned.

Audrey had a car, a decrepit Toyota parked around the corner. When they climbed in, she started the engine and gave him another French kiss while waiting for it to warm up. Her hands went to his crotch. This time he responded aggressively, and in a minute she had his fly unzipped and his erection in her hands.

"Wow," she said with a smile that turned him to granite. "Your dick got bigger."

The next morning "Howard" woke up on Audrey's futon with a hardon and put it to fine use. He'd fucked boys with almost the same exact blunt haircut as Audrey's, yet he had to admit that this look worked better on her.

Around noon they walked to La Peniche on Dauphine for breakfast. While they ate she asked about a variety of names he did not know. At every chance he steered the conversation toward TV shows, Anne Rice books, anything. Every so often he would glance up from his scrambled eggs and catch her staring at him curiously.

She insisted on paying the check.

Outside, Audrey squinted at the clear blue sky overhead, deciding how to express what she meant to say. Finally she asked, "Can I ask you something?"

Howard could not refuse.

"Did you have an accident?"

This question startled him. He could not guess where it had come from or where it might lead. "What?" he said, feebly.

"An accident," she repeated. "Did something happen to you? Have you had amnesia?"

That made more sense to him, and he relaxed. "You're pretty much on the money," he nodded. "How did you know?"

Audrey shrugged. "You're so different," she said. "Like, you eat eggs now. And you don't trim your beard the same way."

"Wow, you noticed, huh?"

She rolled her eyes. "Christ, Howard, I used to trim it for you," she said. "Have you forgotten everything?"

"Well," Howard said, amazed at how easily his arm slipped around her waist, "why don't we go back to your place and you can remind me?"

As they walked, she said, "You still haven't told me where you're staying."

"Nope, I haven't," he agreed.

They walked on. She chuckled and said, "You're a lot more mysterious now, and a lot less mean."

"That's not so bad, is it?"

"I'm still in love with you," she answered.

That sentence hung in Howard's head, echoing as they reached the house where she lived. The words would not go away. *I'm still in love with you.*

He liked the way she shaped his beard, since so far he had not examined it closely himself. He also liked the way she pressed her tits onto his shoulder, his back and finally his face.

This time he took her on her kitchen counter. As soon as he entered her she clung to him and donned the expression of an awed child. It drove Howard utterly insane. He pawed her flesh.

"Easy, easy," she pleaded when he grasped her thighs.

He pulled her off the counter and slid her all the way onto him. Her face quivered, ready to cry. She wrapped her legs around his back. Still pounding, he walked slowly into the bedroom and did her in front of her full-length mirror. They came together.

For a while afterward they lay quietly on her futon.

"I like you better these days," she said at last, and got up. "Want something to drink?"

He nodded and grunted.

She brought him a glass of cranberry juice. He sipped it while she examined her ass and thighs in the mirror.

"Hope you didn't bruise me," she said. "They'll get pissed at work."

"Where do you work?" he asked innocently.

Her cheerful demeanor dropped to the floor.

"Same place," she said, worried.

"Where's that?" Howard asked.

A beat elapsed. She shifted her gaze to the wall when she spoke.

"The Pink Flower," she said in a low voice.

He had never heard of it.

"You forgot about that, too?" Her voice did not hide fear well.

During the past twenty-four hours he had developed a technique of remaining silent until conversation told him whatever he needed to know for his role. This ploy did not work when dialogue faltered.

They remained in the same position, avoiding one another's eyes.

Finally he ventured, "What do you do?"

"I dance," she whispered.

"Naked, you mean?"

"Topless. In a G-string."

He exhaled through his nose, struggled to conjure something neutral to say. An odd sensation struck him, an anger he had never felt: In his mind he could see Audrey naked but for a thong—gold lamé, *Christ!*—bending over to show her ass to a dark club full of leering men. He wanted to punch the shit out of them all.

"Why do you do *that*?" he asked, unable to hide his disgust.

Her eyes went off like a land mine.

"You been gone how many fucking months without a fucking note or a fucking phone call, you come in here and fuck me and won't tell me where you're staying, and you have the fucking nerve to say *that*?!" she snarled, smashing a cassette cover on the floor for emphasis. "I don't give a fuck if you forgot, you got some fucking nerve!"

He glared back at her for several taut seconds, trapped because he knew she was right. Sort of.

"I'm sorry," he said.

"You're *sorry*," she sneered. "You're sorry I'm a fucking whore."

He leaped up and embraced her from behind, hugging her, holding her arms at her side. "You're not a whore," he said.

Tears flowed down her cheeks. He licked them away, tasted her salt on his lips. "You're not a whore," he told her again. "I'm sorry I said that. It came out wrong."

Her breathing returned to normal. Still she did not speak. In that moment he wanted more than anything to make her smile.

"Don't stay mad at me, Audrey," he beseeched her.

A tear that had escaped his mouth fell from the tip of her nose.

"It just hit me bad. I'm jealous," Howard said, listening to his words as though someone else had said them. "I don't like the idea of other men looking at you nude, because I'm in love with you."

She turned and regarded him, her eyes enormous and fragile, and pressed her warm beautiful body against his.

Shit, why had he said that? Worse yet, did he mean it? His dick seemed to think so.

That night, after dropping by his apartment to change his clothes, Howard began work at Alvin's bar. His memory of the restaurant led him to expect tricky drink orders, but everyone just drank shots and bottled beer.

Nothing about the job demanded much concentration, so his mind kept returning to Audrey, her alabaster skin fully exposed except for a tiny strip of fabric covering her crotch and waist, strangers drinking and laughing and tipping her, her nipples contracted tight into bullets as she swayed to crappy rock music—Guns 'N Roses, probably, though he did not know what they sounded like.

Alvin's bar was called the Night Side. Around ten-thirty a band arrived and began to set up their amplifiers and drums in one corner of the room.

"Hey, man, you're new," one longhair said. Howard nodded.

"I'm Davey," he said, extending his hand.

"Howard," he said, all at once realizing he had never called himself that before.

"Pleased to meet you, Howard," Davey said. "Where's Alvin at?"

"He left an hour ago. He'll be back by midnight."

The band played generic rock music. Spectators began filling the bar up as the noise grew louder. These people were locals, which meant they weren't obnoxious tourists, and in fact they tipped reliably.

His thoughts returned to his new lover, and he let himself fantasize. He imagined ordering her to quit her job, having her move in with him.

Then he thought about her seeing his mail addressed to someone else's name. And he saw her wondering why so many of his neighbors snickered when she walked past with him.

At twenty after eleven, as Howard wiped a few shotglasses, Audrey entered the bar. Everyone—male and female—watched her saunter past the band and lean across the bar to kiss Howard hello. He felt...proud.

"How's work?" she inquired.

"Not so bad. How was your work?"

She sighed. "I don't know, some asshole kept trying to touch me," she said.

Howard put his rag down. "What do you mean, 'touch' you?" he asked, helpless to bottle his anger.

She watched him calmly. "He was drunk, that's all."

"Yeah, and he tried to touch you?"

"Well, he—he..." Her mouth formed a barely perceptible grin. "He tipped me twenty bucks, and he wanted to touch me. Vinnie threw him out."

"Who's Vinnie?"

Now her grin spread into a full-blown smile, increasing the heat at the base of Howard's skull. "He's a bouncer. He's gay."

At the other end of the bar someone called for a Heinekin. Howard held up his index finger, meaning he would take care of it in one minute. "Could this guy follow you home or—?"

"Oh, Christ, he was some drunk tourist," she said, laughing. "Give that guy his beer before he gets pissed."

Howard served the guy at the other end. By the time he returned to Audrey he realized how stupid he must have sounded.

She leaned across the bar again, this time to whisper in his ear. "You never got jealous over me before, Howard," she said.

"Yeah, well," he said, "I'm not the same person I used to be."

Weeks slipped past. Only the bills piling up in Gary's name at Gary's apartment recalled his previous life, and each night Howard learned a tiny bit more about the old days he had never lived.

With the passage of time Audrey too revealed much more of herself, and Howard came to adore her. In her bedroom, as well as her living room and on a few occasions her kitchen, he devoured her, his lust so fierce that it seemed to Audrey a new appetite, just awakened. She answered his every craving eagerly. In any case, he had certainly learned a few new tricks.

She did not know about Gary's apartment and never ventured into that neck of the Quarter. When Howard stopped by to check the mail, Gary's neighbors never recognized him.

One Wednesday at least a month after he had begun sleeping at Audrey's, he arrived to find Gary's answering machine blinking. That surprised him, not just because no one left Gary messages but because he believed the phone company had cut off his service.

"Hello, Gary?" the man on the tape said. "This is Dave at Commander's. I can put you on the floor tomorrow night, if you're into working here again. Call me by tomorrow."

Gary called the restaurant immediately, with a silent prayer that the message was not days old already.

"Commander's?"

"Dave?"

"Speaking."

"Dave, this is—" He swallowed. "This is Gary. You called me?"

"Yeah, thanks for calling back," Dave said, and in his mind Gary could see Dave's face, older and leathery, all its lines sinking comfortably into a smile. "How have you been, Gary? People told me you'd left New Orleans."

"No way."

"Glad to hear it," Dave said. "So, you want to come back to work for us? Can I schedule you?"

"Oh, yeah," Gary told him. Then he thanked him and hung up. His waiter's uniform, pressed, awaited him in his closet. His hair had grown slightly, but he could get a trim on Bourbon. The beard had to go.

The thick bristles jammed his razor so badly he threw it out and took a new one from the package. Halfway through the job he paused and stared at his own cheeks emerging through the foam, and he thought of Audrey. How in Christ's name could...?

With his old face back, albeit slightly rougher and pimpled, Gary walked to the payphone on Royal and called Audrey. Her machine answered. He had expected her to be home now.

"Audrey? This is—" He stumbled on his tongue. "Howard. When you get in, will you—"

She picked up. "Yeah, hello?"

"It's me," he said.

"Uh-huh," she replied.

"What's the matter?"

She did not answer quickly. "Just talked to Billy," she said finally.

"Billy?" he prodded her. "Do I know Billy?"

"Yes, you know Billy—you went to fucking New York with him," she reminded him. She sounded really hurt.

"What did he have to say?"

"That you died, shooting bad dope."

Gary dropped his lower jaw.

"What kind of shit have you pulled, Howard? Did you scam an insurance company? Billy says he went to your wake and it was definitely you."

He stammered for a moment, then he said, "I can't explain it, if I didn't say it, can I? I don't look dead to you, do I?"

She said nothing for fully half a minute, then, "I have to go to work, Howard."

She hung up. He stood holding the payphone to his ear for a long, long time.

Audrey had warned him that boyfriends were not allowed to visit at the Pink Flower. He didn't care. He wanted her out of there, anyway.

He arrived and brushed past the barker at the front door. Inside the club he peered through the weak light. The girl dancing was not Audrey. Finally he saw her, sitting alone at a table next to the door, her eyes fixed on some place no one else could see, some awful place where she had lived a while ago and would soon return.

Before he caught her attention, he wanted to decide what he would tell her. But then she looked up and saw this cleanshaven stranger studying her.

Audrey cleared her throat and spoke, slurring. She was high, and not on pot. "You feel like buying me a drink, Mister?" she muttered.

Gary left without a word. He walked slowly to Dauphine Street till he rounded his corner and came face to face with Roger, the old queen from around the block.

"When did you get back in town?" Roger asked him warmly.

TIM FROM TEXAS

SHIT, THIS YEARS BEEN SO BAD I HAVE TO LIE ON MY TAXES and say I earned more money than I did. Made twentythree hundred on my W2. Thats it. Tell that to the goddamned IRS, good as saying Here I am, audit me. Those sonsabitchesll cut me in half, I go claiming twentythree hundred bucks. Seasons so damned slow, is the thing. Been here seven years, aint ever seen the Quarter this empty. I mean, all right, where I work we get the cheaper end, so we actually do the kind of business that keeps us alive in August when a waiter at a better restaurant might not necessarily make it through if he aint squirreled money away since like Jazz Fest. But this years been insane. The goddamned Baptist convention didnt even show this year, how you like that? Not that they ever tip more than two bucks even if they spend three hundred, but they kept the place busy at least. I actually got high at work the other day, is how fuckin empty the place is.

[Tim takes a drag on his cigarette, shaking his head in disgust. Nobody in Giovanni's ever actually listens to what someone else says, not after three in the morning. Right now the naval clock above the poker machine says quarter to five. Around the pool table, three off-duty waiters stand nodding at Tim while a fourth shoots. A new CD begins on the jukebox.]

Fucking Roy. Oh, the greatest voice ever. Ever. No one else touches him. Should be on a stamp. Roy should be on the fucking hundred dollar bill. Practically claim him as a saint back home. I remember the first time I ever saw Roy live. You know Roy should have been bigger than Elvis, right? If it was all about talent. Nothings ever just about talent or who deserves what they get, Im telling you.

[Three drunk girls saunter in from the street, talking loud, furious that the Blacksmith Shop on Bourbon closed before the sun came up. Quickly this trio combines with the four pool players to become a merry band of seven, laughing and flirting around the pool table and ignoring grim Tim, his eyes ringed by black circles that deepen as he grumbles to himself.]

Nobody gets what they deserve. No shit. Im telling you.

❁ ❁ ❁

I lost seven pints of blood on the floor of a titty bar outside Houston. They couldnt believe I lived. Was a miracle.

[Tim shifts from foot to foot on the corner of Bourbon and Toulouse, hawking roses nobody wants. And even if they did, few customers would venture to speak to Tim, whose constant grimace has lately cemented itself onto his features.]

Twentysix years old, and I talked to God. Fuck, who is this shithead? Keep him away from the—dont let him get sick here! Nuh-uh, cause I aint moving this goddamned cart through the crowd at this hour, get that guy out of here. Im serious. No, honey, I got to work here.

[The drunk squats on the sidewalk against a wall and runs one hand through his hair. His woman tends to him and ignores Tim entirely.]

Hey, Im not shittin you, all right? If he gets sick, Im dumpin this bucket of water over your head.

[The girl turns on Tim, cursing and slapping him. Meanwhile, her drunk boyfriend gets up unnoticed and leaves. When she spots him, he has nearly reached St. Louis Street. She tears after him, swearing.]

Bitch. So God says to me, He says, Tim, you got a date with greatness. And He sends me back to life. So Im back among the living, and I get the urge to move to New Orleans. I dont know, I mightve come back from the other side with the idea. You know how you dream something, and you forget it when you wake up but later that day something reminds you of it? So I had Divine inspiration to come here.

[Tim wipes his nose on his sleeve. No one's buying roses.]

When I came here, I made enough money waiting tables that I could do coke at least twice a week. At that point, you didnt even have to report your earnings. They just paid us cash.

❀ ❀ ❀

Mostly I was just trying to have a good time.

[Leaning against the Lucky Dog wagon, Tim gets too deep in his own story to notice that the hot dog vendor doesn't care what Tim has to say. The vendor just wants to drain his cart and go home. He wants his night to end.]

I mean, I spent years just hanging in one bar or another. Always knew how to have a good time, believe it. Used to be different down here, though, used to be you didnt have to worry about starving. Look at the runaways now. They aint like they were five years ago. Man, they didnt used to all end up whoring.

[Were the vendor to pay Tim the slightest attention, he would note with some alarm the pall that suddenly bends Tim's features. Tim staggers back from the cart, leans against the lamppost.]

I met this runaway outside Kaldis on Decatur Street. This was, I dont know, it had to be a year ago now. I come walking by round dinner time on my way to work, theres all these punks that hang out there. Kagans is right on the next block, by where I work, and theyre always all over the place so you get used to them. Anyways Im walking by and this girl goes: Spare any change so I dont have to sell my ass tonight? Just like that. So I stop. Shes dirty—I mean, theyre all dirty, but theres a certain point they cross after they been on the street awhile. And shes past it. Shes this dirty Oriental girl. I go: Whats your name? Chloe, she says. I go: You really dont want to be out here? Cause I work on the next block, you know, I aint some tourist you can jerk around. You really dont want to be here? And she goes: I asked you for some fucking change, not your life story. So I gave her two bucks. Couldnt believe I even did it, after. She said thank you like it pissed her off I didnt hand her ten.

So after that I start seeing her around. When Id go to work, whatever. Theyre always around the Quarter. Used to hang round that Circle K on Royal Street, its a furniture store now. Whenever Id see all of them somewhere, Id check and see if she was in the crowd. First thing I noticed was shes really fucking dirty. Maybe the dirt just showed up better on her skin cause she was Oriental. And the other thing was shes pregnant. And I found myself really boiling about that. I started thinking to myself: Which one of these dickweeds with the blue hair and the metal shit sticking out of his face knocked her up?

[The vendor has already departed for the night. Tim didn't notice. Still doesn't.]

Began to think maybe I lost my mind. Some nights I couldnt sleep, Im all by myself thinking about her. Id keep hearing Roy Orbison songs and Id picture living with this little Oriental and her baby. The way I imagined it we lived on a beach, and she was clean and so was the kid. Corpus Christi, say.

❀ ❀ ❀

One night I went drinking here and I walk back toward Canal along Royal Street.

[Tim sits alone at a table in the Blacksmith Shop, a Bourbon Street bar, formerly a stable and headquarters for the pirate LaFitte. It's not very crowded tonight.]

Shes sitting in this doorway down the block from the A&P, her heads lollin. I can see she wants to sleep but shes afraid. Every time she snaps awake again she looks both ways down the street real quick. Finally I come right up to her and she goes, real halfhearted: Spare some change at all? I say: Why you out here?

She tells me: I just asked if you have any change. I say: I heard you fine, and I see you around the Quarter so its not like I dont know what your life is like. Why are you out here? She says: Where am I goin to fuckin go? She had this way of sayin shit like that, made me feel like I was the one who put her on the street.

[Shaking his head, Tim takes a pull from his Dixie beer and lights a cigarette. Lately he rations his smokes.]

Anyways it didnt take a real long argument. Something was scarin her in the Quarter, I never found out what. But that made her give in pretty easy. I took her to my place. She could sleep on my couch, I told her. She just rolled her eyes.

I made her take a shower. At that point I was living in the Third Ward in this brick house, it was pretty nice, actually. Mustve been the only white man for miles, but that dont bother me. So I make her take a shower, I make her go in there. I go out to the kitchen to get a beer, and I come back and the waters not on. Im like: You done already? Cause she didnt look like under three minutes worth of dirty. She was filthy. So I go: You done? And she hasnt started the shower yet. Shes waiting for me to come in and watch her. I didnt say a thing about it, she just assumed that was the deal.

I tell her: No way, I didnt say nothing about you having to do anything. I said you could sleep on my couch. She didnt want me to see that it relieved her to hear this, so she goes: Okay, whatever you want. Which makes it like Im the fool. Shes saying: Sooner or later youre going to want something, and whenever or whatever it is, youre just one more trick.

Of course, having her at my house at all was a big risk. These street kidsll rob you in a breath.

[Tim has a window seat at Clover Grill, a small diner on Bourbon and Dumaine. It's real late. He's drunk and eating a grilled-cheese sandwich with a cup of water.]

I didnt tell no one she was there. For the first few days she left when I left and hung out in the Quarter all day and then met me when I got off at the restaurant in the evening. Then we took the bus back together. I figure shes hangin out with her friends, but turns out shes goin in this bookstore on Dauphine and reading all day. She buys a paperback for like seventyfive cents and sits in this wicker chair there readin it, and then leaves when he closes at seven. Im getting out of work at eight. I didnt realize until a couple of days into it, Im like: How are these spaceship books showing up in my house? She goes: What else can I do, get drunk? You dont want me hanging out with my friends.

Now, Im not even gettin laid at this point. I dont need to hear what a crimp I put in her social life by giving her a place to sleep. So I say so.

[Behind him, a table of five starts singing along with "Tainted Love" on the jukebox. Tim does not react.]

I go: Why go to the same bookstore every day? She says the guy there is nice to her. Okay, but why every day? She goes: Well, if I hang out with kids by the A&P youll get pissed and I wont have anyplace to sleep. So I say: Then why go out? She goes: I cant just stay home all day, you go to work. I say: So why cant you stay home when Im out? Watch TV. She looks at me like Im crazy and goes: You want to let me stay at your house all day while youre gone.

I mean, it was ridiculous. She had a point there. But I just knew she wouldnt rob me and split. Somehow. I knew it.

❀ ❀ ❀

Besides, at this point Im thinkin she needs to take better care of herself. I dont want to pry and ask how long she been pregnant.

[Tim sits beneath the dartboard in Giovanni's, watching two off-duty busboys from an upscale restaurant shoot pool. They regard Tim as part of the furniture.]

Wasnt like I was trying to fuck her. Well, obviously I felt an attraction for her, but I wasnt doing this to get in her pants. Wouldntve even been necessary, she made that plain enough herself. I couldve just said: Take a shower and get in here and fuck me, and then get lost tomorrow.

This one night I come home from work pissed off cause some redneck stiffed me. And shes like: Whats the matter? And I start telling her, shes lookin at me like she cares. And then we go to bed. It just happens like that. I didnt even want to let myself enjoy it cause it was just how Id always pictured it. Not everything exactly, but the way she was acting.

[From the bar several men wearing clean, pressed shirts that clearly mark them as tourists eye the dartboard and Tim. They want to play darts but don't want to give Tim a reason to start unloading on them.]

But see, these were the happiest days of my life. I didnt even know it. Probably most people dont know when that happiest little piece of time happens until it ends. With me it happened exactly that way. One night I realized I had everything I wanted, or I would soon anyway. It just all sank in on me one Friday when I got paid. My check covered the rent and the electric, plus some drunk Shriner tipped me a ten-spot, so we could order Dominos that night. Says to myself: Tim, this is as good as its apt to get. Then by the time I get home, Im thinkin about this baby. I mean, she aint been takin care of herself, let alone this kid inside her.

So I bring the topic up.

❀ ❀ ❀

Big mistake.

[Tim's back on Bourbon and Toulouse. He puts more enthusiasm into stamping out his cigarette than into hawking these roses.]

She freaks out. Im fuckin controlling her and all this shit. It was never the same after that. The next mornin I went to work figuring when I come home itll all be over with, but uhuh. She just never let it go. Every night I come home and we cant just relax, be ourselves.

[A couple stagger up to him, and the woman makes a show of snatching at the rose in Tim's hand. He doesn't notice.]

Even lyin in bed at night, its like tension.

❀ ❀ ❀

Get the fuck down here.

[Tim mutters as he waits for his dealer to come downstairs and let him into the courtyard so he can buy some crack. The door opens. The crack dealer wears—no exaggeration—a professional clown costume, with some of his makeup rubbed away. The dealer's clientele get used to the sight of him, so Tim does not flinch as he hands the Crack Clown fifty-five dollars. The Crack Clown gives Tim twelve vials of rock. Tim darts back onto the street and leaves briskly.]

So I come home from work a couple nights later and shes gone, along with my CD player.

I seen her since then, but shes always with these gypsy street shitheads. Never says a word to me, wants to act like she never met me.

[Tim lies on his mattress, trying to smoke his rocks slowly enough that they'll last, which they won't. None of his belongings made it out of the Third Ward to his new one-room off lower Magazine. Roaches patrol the walls. Beside him he has a glass of tap water.]

One night I seen a guy pick her up outside the A&P, for money. Swear to God.

"THEY DON'T DO THIS IN TOPEKA"
—OR—
FELICITY, THE TENTH MUSE

JAMES LET THE REST OF THE BAND SET UP while he watched the street from the doorway. Eventually the girl out front found a sponsor she liked, and yanked her sweater up to her neck. She had big pink nipples. A strand of beads like oversized pearls dropped to her from the balcony above.

"There's a song in that," James said, walking back to the bandstand. Bourbon Street was packed. No one had come inside the bar yet except employees. The crowd wouldn't venture up the two steps from the sidewalk until the music started, yet once any customers came inside they tended to ignore the band. James had to respect anyone drunk enough to successfully ignore a banjo.

While he was tuning, two people came in. A couple.

The German woman behind the bar said, "No," in a tone that implied she'd told them already.

"Uh-uh, I got money," the man slurred. James looked at him. This man wasn't a tourist. He wore a ragged blue football jersey on which white block letters spelled words that James couldn't read from this angle.

"Just sell us beers and we'll go," the girl offered.

"Where is your ID?" the bartender asked the girl.

James had seen the girl before, on the street. She looked different right now because she'd bathed and she wasn't drunk yet.

"What do you mean?" the girl asked.

"I need to see your ID," the German woman said. "To check that you are old enough for alcohol to be served."

"Vhere are your papers, Fraulein?" the man asked his date.

Very quickly the bartender replied, "I do not have to hear this from you." She walked down the bar and called out, "*Richard!*"

The couple left. At the front door the girl turned and said, "Hey, sauerkraut!" and flashed her tits at the bartender. By the time Richard arrived from the dining area, the couple had reached the sidewalk.

James read the name printed on the back of the drunk man's jersey: VAN EYENS. He tried to recall why it rang a bell. Maybe he had seen it while skimming the sports section years ago. James went back to tuning.

James met her at Molly's on Decatur Street one night in the summer. Two guys he'd known in high school had arrived in town and arranged to meet him there, then never showed. While waiting, James started talking to a college kid standing next to him at the bar.

Then that girl came in and asked the college kid to buy her a beer. The kid refused, so James bought her one instead.

"Thanks," she said to James. "I'm Nilda."

The college kid had begun talking to someone else, so James asked Nilda, "Where's your boyfriend tonight?"

"I'm in the market for one just now," she said.

"Oh, you guys broke up?"

Her smile faded. "Who are you talking about?"

"The guy you were with last time I saw you," James said. "Must have been— well, it was Fat Tuesday."

"Fat Tuesday?" Nilda gasped, and rolled her eyes. "You think I remember back that far?"

"I was playing at Tricou House," he explained. "The bartender wouldn't serve you. That German woman."

"Oh," Nilda said. "Oh! That was fucked up. I was with Christian that day."

"Who?"

"Christian Van Eyens," she answered.

"That's him. I remember seeing a Dutch name on his shirt," James said. "Why do I know that name? Was he a real football player?"

"No, he's a painter," Nilda replied. "I don't know, maybe he used to play football in school. He paints now."

"What does he paint?"

"Comic books," she said, finishing her beer. "The covers. He did covers for these magazines that used to come out in the nineteen-seventies, like *Creepy*. He has that up on his wall."

"I remember that magazine, when I was little. That's pretty good exposure, I guess, for a painter," James said.

"Actually, he hasn't had anything published since he moved here," Nilda said. "Someone keeps paying him, and he keeps working on this same comic. But he gets so fucked up, I can't tell what it is. I don't think even Christian knows."

When she came closer to say good-bye James caught a whiff of the girl's hircinous odor, which made him glad to see her go.

"Thanks for the beer," she said.

"Wish your friend good luck with the comic books," he said.

"Maybe I'll see you play sometime," Nilda said. "What do you play?"

"Banjo," James said, as the girl left without waiting to hear his answer.

One night weeks later, rounding the corner onto Frenchmen Street after smoking half a joint during a set break from the Dragon's Den, James nearly collided with Van Eyens. The painter sprang back against the building.

Once a rush of panic burned itself off, James found he could not help staring into these drunk, tormented eyes. He realized he had seen this man around the Quarter for years. During Mardi Gras Van Eyens had looked different because he'd shaved and worn a clean shirt. Normally he paced around Decatur ranting, his hair and beard matted into knots, his clothes so filthy that they always matched whatever else James had seen him wear.

"Mister Van Eyens?" he said.

Van Eyens cocked his head in surprise, and said nothing.

"You're Van Eyens, the painter, am I right?"

Suddenly the man lunged at James, who dodged backwards against a parked car. A second later Van Eyens had dashed around the corner and up the street where James had just smoked his half-joint.

James stayed leaning on the car for just a moment. After that he left, avoiding the chance to peek around the corner and see where the mad souse had fled.

The crowd left Dragon's Den en masse during James's ensuing set. Within fifteen minutes Bret at the bar signaled him to finish. James gladly complied, and used the bar phone to call Carla. She didn't answer, so he didn't leave a message; late calls annoyed her sometimes, in particular when she could guess that he hadn't called earlier because some girl at his gig had flirted with him but then left before he finished.

Everyone else in the band sat at a table to eat while James packed his banjo and amp. He had Angela the waitress bring his food in a styrofoam box and carried his gear down the stairs by himself.

Later that night James woke from a dream so vivid that he could not recall stirring from it, could not tell when the dream stopped and wakefulness began. The dream lacked any narrative or logic. Instead it sparked an intense gloom that outlasted sleep itself. For as he lay in the dark, blinking at the hammered tin ceiling above his futon, James continued to feel exactly as he had while dreaming.

He held very still so sleep might resume. This dream meant something, though. In the dark his room reminded him of the house where he'd lived with his mother twenty years ago. It surprised him to find sadness so appealing and secure.

All at once James knew where the dream had come from:

A man his mother dated right after James's parents divorced, the guy who worked for the phone company, used to bring James comic books. James only liked scary comics. Somewhere or other the man came across a poster-sized replica of a cover of *Creepy*, and this poster adorned James's wall for however long it took his mother to determine that the picture kept the boy awake at night.

This entire recollection came to James with a clarity that unnerved him. Yet he could not recall the cover image itself, beyond its cool nocturnal color scheme (surf pounded moonlit rocks across the bottom of the painting, he could say almost for certain) and the name VAN EYENS in tiny block letters near the lower right-hand corner.

James had noticed before that the Crack Clown lived on Dumaine, within sight from any window seat in the restaurant where Carla usually took James before they went to her place for the night. On a few occasions when Carla's conversation had bored him, James instead watched customers come ring the Crack Clown's doorbell.

The Crack Clown lived up a flight of outdoor stairs; from the restaurant James could see him creep out onto the balcony to check the block, sometimes still wearing parts of his clown costume. Then he would bound down the stairs and bring his customer inside the courtyard, after which the customer would leave, exuding a culprit's forced nonchalance.

One night in August, the Crack Clown didn't come out even once throughout their meal. Over the summer Carla had adopted a sarcastic tone whenever she took James out, as well as a habit of proffering career advice.

"What do you keep looking at?" she asked, turning in her chair to see Dumaine Street empty behind her.

"The Crack Clown lives there," James said, "or he used to."

She waited to hear the rest. He shrugged. They ate some more.

"Two people got fired at Tower, did I tell you?" she said.

"Yeah?" James said. "Sorry to hear that."

Carla paused, glaring at him, and put down her fork.

"What's the matter?" he asked her.

"You make it sound like I'm—*what* are you *looking* at?" She spun in her seat again.

"Him. That's what's-his-face, the painter. He's a well-known painter," James said. "I never saw him cop crack before."

"And this is more interesting than me or what I'm saying."

"Jesus Christ, something catches my eye out the window and you take it like I'm staring at another woman," James said. "What is the big deal?"

Irate, Carla began to explain exactly what the big deal was, while James paid attention to Van Eyens, who didn't ring the bell after all. Instead he pulled out a key to the door.

"You don't even listen when I complain," she complained.

"That explains why he can sell crack like that," James said.

"What?"

"The Crack Clown has a bunch of weirdos for neighbors. That's why they don't stop him from dealing out of their courtyard."

Normally Carla would let him abruptly lead her onto a new topic this way. Not tonight. She ate in silence.

Over her shoulder James saw Van Eyens climb the staircase to the Crack Clown's door.

When his eyes met hers again, Carla let her lower jaw drop, just faintly, to show anger. "I guess the Crack Clown doesn't live there anymore," James said.

"Do you want to go check?" she asked, gesturing toward the building. Upstairs, the Crack Clown opened his door to admit Van Eyens, then crossed the balcony to scan the street, from force of habit.

Carla paid for dinner and went home without James. It had happened before. After her cab disappeared down Dauphine, James hung out awhile, watching the Crack Clown's building. He thought of ringing the bell, but had never noticed which button on the panel customers rang. He didn't know the Crack Clown's name, either.

Whatever Van Eyens had gone upstairs to do, it took longer than half an hour. James left. He crossed the Quarter to the Dragon's Den, where he drank sake and failed miserably at talking to strangers.

One afternoon in September James rode his bike uptown. On Oak Street he chained it to someone's fence and walked into a comics store, although he couldn't afford to buy anything and didn't really want to.

He found the *Creepy* section in the used bin, but none of the covers were signed Van Eyens.

"Can I help you with anything?" asked a man James had taken for a customer rather than a clerk.

"I doubt it," James said. "I'm looking for any magazines with covers by Christian Van Eyens."

The clerk pursed his lips and shook his head slowly. "You won't find that in a store," he said. "Anyone who collects Van Eyens owns a whole set, and that's the only way to buy them. They don't even list Van Eyens in the *Comics Buyer's Guide*."

To illustrate, the clerk slid a mid-1970s issue of *Creepy* from its plastic bag and opened it to a two-page spread featuring tiny reproductions of covers from back issues. A white diagonal banner with the words SOLD OUT! blocked each Van Eyens cover the clerk pointed out, save the most recent one. "Some of these even sold out on the newsstand," the clerk marveled.

James held the ad very close and squinted. The clerk handed him a photographer's lupe. The one cover he could see clearly was not the one from his dream. "Which ones did you say were by Van Eyens?" he asked.

The clerk pointed them out again. James found the right one; the white caps on the waves sent a chill between his shoulder blades. Yet the print banner hid most of the image.

"It's kind of odd that you're interested in Van Eyens but you haven't actually seen his stuff," the clerk commented.

"I had it on my walls as a kid," James said. "And I know him."

"Really?" the clerk said.

"He lives in the Quarter."

The clerk shook his head. "Christian Van Eyens wound up in a nuthouse in, like, Massachussetts. You can't even write to him."

Immediately James could tell that nothing short of dragging the crazed artist in here, birth certificate in hand, would change this clerk's mind. The opinion of anyone who took comics so seriously didn't matter enough for James to argue.

"Is there any way I could just see some of his work?" James asked. "Do you know a person with a collection who would let me just look at it?"

"My friend near Hattiesburg owns a Van Eyens set," the clerk said. "He's a pisser, too. He grows pot."

The clerk gave James this friend's number. James thanked the clerk and left. When he got home, James chucked the number into the drawer of his nightstand and forgot about it.

In October, Carla stopped calling James. After two weeks, he called her and left a message on her machine, then another the next day. The third time he called, three days later, her recording stopped and the line clicked on.

"Hello?" Carla said.

"Hey, it's me," James said.

It seemed to him that she paused deliberately, to make him think she didn't recognize him. "James," she said finally. "How are you?"

"Fine, I guess," he said. "Haven't heard from you."

"Yeah, you haven't," Carla agreed.

"Is everything okay?" he asked. "Are you mad at me?"

"No," she said. "Everything is really good. I just don't think we should see each other anymore."

"Why not?"

Carla sighed with the effort of replying, then gave up and said, "I don't have to tell you why. I just don't want to see you. It's nothing personal."

"That's how you tell me? By not calling me," James said. "I'm supposed to guess."

"You have to be kidding," she told him. "Honest to God. It took you *weeks* to call me."

He hung up, pleased she'd at least given away that she'd counted the days he hadn't called.

So James went down the Quarter to get drunk. He lost several racks of pool at Giovanni's and only managed to drink one beer. Finally a Cuban waiter cleared the table from a break, and James left.

The Blacksmith Shop had changed hands the previous New Year's, and James had only gone in once since then; the new owner had replaced the old crew with workaday Bourbon Street bartenders. Tonight James thought he might have a beer there anyway, out of nostalgia. Yet at the corner of Bourbon and St. Philip he changed his mind and kept walking away from the river.

Just as James reached Dauphine, a man smoking a cigarette entered the intersection. The red-and-white sight of his face made James stare. It was the Crack Clown, wearing a blue satin costume and only the crudest remnants of his greasepaint. Without slowing his pace at all he nodded at James and muttered, "All right."

"Hey, man," James called to him.

The Crack Clown pivoted around. "Yeah?"

"Hey, uh," James began, trying to recall Van Eyens's name. "You know that artist, don't you?"

"I don't know any artists," the Crack Clown said vehemently.

"No, that painter that, uhm..."

"I hate art *and* artists," the Crack Clown assured him. His eyes looked high, but he meant what he said.

"I've seen him go inside your house," James insisted. "His name is, like, Von something. He's Dutch."

"You mean Christian," the Crack Clown told him. "Christian Van Eyens."

"Yes! That's it," James said.

"He's just my roommate," the Crack Clown said. "I don't really know him." He continued on his way down Dauphine. As he did, a breeze riffled his baggy satin pantaloons.

James's bass player went back to Mississippi for Christmas and never returned. The search for a replacement kept James occupied until the middle of January, by which time every club in the city had finalized its Mardi Gras schedule.

The Dragon's Den told him not to call even for March bookings until after Fat Tuesday.

At first bitterness over having to work at the bookstore on Barracks Street just to cover his rent led James to decide he would blow off the entire month of February. Yet, as beads and lights spread along balconies across the Quarter, it occurred to him that he had never lived through Mardi Gras as a mere spectator.

The weather was great. He drank and got high with strangers at parades uptown, and hopped bars in the Quarter or the Marigny almost every night. The final weekend coincided with the beginning of Spring Break, so a million college kids on X filled the Quarter; watching them stare at the bands, dumbfounded—not applauding or tipping, sipping only water or fruit juice—made James glad he hadn't booked any of these shows for himself. A college girl from Minnesota gave him a hand job in front of her friends at a booth in the Hog's Breath that Saturday.

Late in the afternoon on Fat Tuesday James actually worked his way through the crowd on Bourbon Street. Girls flashed their tits. Drunks came to blows over plastic beads. Two cops arrested a fifty-year-old woman and the Iowa frat boy she was fellating.

James let the crowd move him. The streetlamps came on, a spectral pall upon the writhing mob. James walked a side street toward Dauphine and finally knelt to lean against a building for a few minutes.

A gay man came out the front door and said, "You're not getting sick out here, are you?"

James shook his head.

"What's the matter?" the man asked.

Slowly James said, "I think someone gave me a dose of acid without telling me."

The gay man came over and said, "Look at the streetlight." James did, and the man said, "Yeah, boo, your pupils are having a hard time contracting."

"Fuck," James said. "I don't even know what it is or how much."

"You've done acid before?"

James nodded.

"So this seems like acid to you, now," the man said.

"I guess, kind of," James said. "I'm not sure if I'm high or just not feeling good."

"Drinking don't make your pupils do that. There's liquid acid all over the Quarter this year," the man said, and fished a joint from his pocket. "Here. If this dose you're on gets out of control, just smoke this and mellow."

James took the jay. "Thanks," he said.

"I'm serious," the man said, reentering his house. "It'll take the edge off, if your trip gets heavy. Happy Mardi Gras."

James meandered down the street, away from Bourbon, and turned onto Dauphine. From a balcony thirty or so men shouted, "Show us your dick!"

A woman in an antique dress sauntered off the next side street. She walked ahead of James.

"Nilda," he called.

And it was. The clean state of her, even at a glimpse, had given James doubt, but it was she.

"Hi," she said, peering at him as if they'd never met before. Her skin glowed; she'd gotten an actual haircut and used makeup.

"Happy Mardi Gras," he said.

"Happy Mardi Gras," she said back, still baffled.

"Want to smoke a joint?" he asked.

"Sure!" she said, beaming. "Light it up."

"Well, where are you going?" he asked her. "Are you on your way to see Christian?"

"Yes," she said. "I'm sorry, where do I know you from?"

"Around town," he said. "Just, you know, here and there. We've had a few beers together. You don't remember me?"

She shook her head.

"Well, my name's Kevin," James told her, not sure himself why he had chosen to lie. "Can I come with you to meet Christian? I'd really like to smoke this joint with him, too."

Nilda shrugged. "Sure. But he's got pot."

"Is that right?"

"Where do you think I got all this shit?" Nilda said, gesturing at her dress, her hair, her rouge. "He got his check."

James offered her his arm, and they strolled Dauphine. A pensioner waving a string of beads from a hotel balcony called down, "Show me your tits!"

"What, for beads?" Nilda hollered, letting go of James. "Get bent. You want to see my tits, show me five bucks."

The old man pulled a five out of his pocket and showed it to her.

"Show me your tits," he said again, his polite tone inappropriate, grotesque.

"Throw it down here first," Nilda demanded, cupping her hands. "You could just put it back in your pocket after I take my tits out."

He dropped it. The bill fluttered too much to fall straight, but she caught it.

"Show me your tits," the old man said again.

"Eat my ass, you old crust," Nilda shouted back, and ran. James ran with her. They turned at the restaurant. Nilda giggled as she rang the Crack Clown's bell. James didn't think of it in time to watch which button she pressed.

She had the nervousness of a chased high-school vandal. James thought this mood odd in a street person, especially since that old man on the hotel balcony certainly couldn't pursue her.

Up on the terrace, the Crack Clown smiled and waved when he saw them. "Here, baby," he said to Nilda, and chucked the key into the street.

"Christ," she said to James, "he looks *fucked* up, even for him."

James retrieved the key, then held the door open for Nilda. As she entered she gave him a shy glance that became her more than she knew.

"Things are going better for you, though, these days?" James asked as they crossed the courtyard.

"Right now, they're fine," she said. "Then his check runs out."

The stairs shook with each step as James and Nilda climbed. At the top the Crack Clown greeted them. Whatever costume he had put on this morning, its tattered fragments did not suggest anything clownlike. A great deal of silver body paint dripped down his naked torso as he spread his arms.

"Hey, Happy Mardi Gras, y'all!" he said.

Nilda and James said in unison, "Happy Mardi Gras!"

The Crack Clown hugged Nilda hello. When he turned to shake James's hand, Nilda spun around to make a bewildered face at the back of the Crack Clown's head.

"Come on in," the Crack Clown said, holding his door open.

"Thanks, man," James said. He had visited drug dealers' apartments before; the mess did not impress him, but this building's ruined opulence did. Flensed of stains, the wood floors and the staircase would be among the finest James had seen. A heap of garbage filled one corner of the room so completely that he had to look twice to spot the kitchenette buried beneath it.

"Listen, baby, I want to buy a rock," Nilda said to the Crack Clown, pulling out her five dollars.

"No, darling," he said. "That's not necessary. It's Carnival."

While the Crack Clown fetched her a glass pipe and loaded it with crack, Nilda silently signaled her astonishment to James.

"Where is Christian?" James asked.

The Crack Clown said, "He's working."

A spark passed between Nilda and the Crack Clown, and she said to James, "You can just go on up and see him."

"Yeah, you can go on up," the Crack Clown said. "You haven't been to his space before, have you?"

James shook his head.

"Go up the stairs," the Crack Clown said. "Upstairs, walk to the bed and turn right. There's a ladder."

The stairway ran up a narrow passage to the third floor. As James climbed the steps he overheard the Crack Clown say to Nilda, "I've always thought so."

The walls bore an ancient coat of grease, even up here away from the kitchenette. When he got upstairs James saw that the third floor had a balcony, too; from street level he had always assumed it was an awning that protected the lower balcony from rain.

The bedroom had its own fireplace. James didn't see any ladder, though. He entered all the way and peered into every corner.

Something heavy thumped the ceiling, though not directly overhead. Partly obscured by the chimney, a set of four cleats ran up the wall to an open trap door.

James climbed the ladder. At the top he thrust his head into darkness and wondered how to greet Van Eyens.

As his pupils adjusted he could make out a brick wall and plank floor. Light refracted into the attic from around a turn. James hoisted himself onto the aged planks and walked.

"Hello?" he called. Words died quickly in the thin air. "Christian?" Around the turn he found a whole new room, lit by the outside through its missing far wall, which faced the Tremé. The view, and the hum from the packed streets below, arrested him as he entered, until he noticed a series of three easels, each loaded with a canvas, and on the floor behind the easels, a collapsed person.

James came to him. "Hello? You all right?" he said, and knelt beside Van Eyens, whose beard was not yet unkempt enough to mat. The painter did not have the mad, unwashed quality James knew him for, but would, soon. James pushed him a few times. "Christian," he said. "You okay, man?"

In the manner of a soldier's swordpoint surrender, Van Eyens opened his eyes. "Who might you be?" he asked.

"Nilda said I could come up," James said. "She thought you'd want to smoke a joint."

"She thought right," Van Eyens said. "You got one?"

"Sure," James said, and pulled out his jay. "But is your head all right? I heard you fall from downstairs."

"I just fell asleep, is all." Van Eyens shrugged and struck a match for James. They smoked the joint.

The canvases contained geometric shapes that appeared abstract at first, but James could tell these were comic panels in some early stage of design.

On the bare wall behind the easels, Van Eyens had mounted three posters, two of them covers from *Creepy* and the other from *Eerie*. In the middle of the trio hung the one from James's childhood bedroom, except that Van Eyens had flung bright red paint onto it. James could not bring himself to examine the defaced poster up close.

"I got some pot, over there. Roll another one," Van Eyens said, rubbing his eyes.

James noticed layer upon layer of paint drops on Van Eyens's hands. "Yeah, I heard you got your check," James said.

"Fuck my check," Van Eyens spat, climbing to his feet. "Their checks are never here in a crisis." From behind one of the easels he fetched a bottle of beer and took a long pull. When he'd swallowed, he said, "I don't need their fucking checks, anyway. I'm probably the best pickpocket you ever met. I work Bourbon Street, in full public view. I have the best fucking disguise."

He handed the beer to James, who held it but didn't drink any. Van Eyens picked a palette up from the same place he'd gotten the beer.

"If you don't need the checks," James asked, "why do you sell those people your work?"

Without taking his eyes off the canvas Van Eyens said, "Because they want it. Are you rolling another bone or are you writing a book?"

"I'm going down to use the bathroom first," James said.

"Just piss out there," Van Eyens told him, nodding toward the missing wall. "The only true northern exposure in the Quarter."

"No, I'll just go downstairs," James said. "I'll be right back."

"Suit yourself," the painter said, mumbling the last syllable because he'd already begun to forget James's presence.

James returned the way he had come, conscious this time of the huge dust wads on the attic floor as he lowered himself through the trap door.

Downstairs he found Nilda naked, masturbating on the couch in front of the Crack Clown, who sat in an armchair. They both glanced at James. The Crack Clown didn't show any sign of embarrassment. Nilda did, though she didn't stop.

"You want to get high?" the Crack Clown asked James, holding out a glass pipe.

"I guess," James said.

"Why don't you fool around with Nilda?" the Crack Clown suggested. "This rock's on me."

"Fool around?" James said.

"He wants to watch," Nilda explained. "Come on, it's Mardi Gras."

James closed his eyes and scratched his scalp.

"What's the matter?" Nilda asked.

"Aren't you," he asked her, "involved with Christian?"

"'Involved with'?" she asked, and rolled onto her side with her legs closed. "You're asking if I'm 'involved with' Christian."

James nodded.

She glared at him a minute, then said, "How do you know us if you don't know Christian and I are married?"

The Crack Clown watched, his legs crossed, as though observing some friends' conversation at a casual party.

James stalked out the front door and down the steps to the courtyard. For a moment he wondered if he would need the key to leave, and he looked upward to see the Crack Clown's bleary paint-stained face studying him from the window. But the door opened and let James back into the streets, where he dissolved into the crowd.

James sold his banjo and moved back to Chicago.

THE LOST GIRLS

A LITTLE AFTER MIDNIGHT the owner sticks his head inside the kitchen door and says, "You can close it down, man."

"All right," Abel says. He has already run the dishwasher, so he needs only to wipe down the prep surfaces. Twenty minutes later he's seated at the bar inside, with two shots and a Sam Adams in front of him. When the band upstairs finishes, some of the patrons will come down to this bar instead of leaving, maybe. For now, Abel and Dilcia the bartender have the room to themselves.

He drinks and pretends to listen as Dilcia tells him about Richmond, Virginia. Once he's sure he has drunk a little too much, Abel rises from his stool.

"You taking off?" Dilcia asks.

Abel nods. "I have a date."

"Anybody I know?"

He shakes his head and leaves.

Outside he gets in his 1986 Datsun and drives Basin Street up past Claiborne. On the other side he takes a right onto North Prieur, and drives more slowly.

Several motels operate on North Prieur between Orleans Avenue and Esplanade, one of which appears to Abel to serve middle-class black people cheating on their spouses. Closer to Esplanade another building stands vacant at a desolate five-way intersection; its huge unlit sign says House Of Joy. But the outright whore dens are down here, by the projects at Orleans.

On a side street he glimpses a girl with waist-length hair. He brakes the car, right in the intersection. She's white, strutting alongside a man Abel takes for a pimp. They walk into the Rainbow Inn, and as Abel drives away he wonders if the motel's name means to attract black men who want white prostitutes. He decides that's not likely.

⊛ ⊛ ⊛

The Crack Clown hands his customer two twenty bags and says, "All right, you know about my hours now, right?"

The customer shakes his head.

"I thought I told you," the Crack Clown says. "Whatever. Next two weeks, I'm only over here between midnight and three. No exceptions. All right? I got to cut off anybody who pisses off my neighbors. So don't."

The Crack Clown unlocks the door and lets his customer leave the court-yard. Then he climbs the stairs back up to his apartment. Before going inside he trots down to the end of his terrace and checks the street. No one's down there.

As he enters his living room the girl on his sofa says something incoherent, probably not to him. He has seen intense reactions before like the one this kid is having, usually in girls under twenty who began their first psychiatric pre-scription at fourteen or younger.

Another flight of stairs leads up to the Crack Clown's bedroom and the loft where his roommate stays. He stands at the foot of the steps, trying to decide whether to go up or not. Apart from the sofa, there's no seat in this room that isn't full of clutter. For some reason he doesn't want to sit close to the girl.

But he doesn't want to go lie down, either, so he walks to the sofa, picks up the girl's naked legs, sits, and places her calves across his lap. She does not react. He takes the pipe from her hand and loads a rock into it.

As he smokes it, she says in a dead voice, "I hear someone up in your room."

"Maybe you hear Christian," the Crack Clown says. "Up in the attic."

The girl shrugs, her head bobbing just faintly. "Doesn't bother me, if it doesn't bother you," she mutters.

At one intersection in the Tremé where Abel likes to go spy on hookers, he has learned the names of two girls. Both Shila and Dynette are black and full-figured. Shila lives above a laundromat with her old man, a grouchy drunk Abel sometimes sees wearing phone-company workshirts. She and Dynette work the corner together.

About a quarter after one he sees a man drop a girl off from a truck. It isn't Dynette or Shila, because this girl's thin. White, also, with auburn hair. When the truck pulls away she clears her throat and spits—emphatically, although she has no idea anyone can see her. Whatever has gotten in her mouth tastes really bad.

The girl stumbles a little, pulls her skirt straight, passes under a streetlamp. For a flash Abel can see her face.

He sits bolt upright.

Now the girl slips inside the shadows. Frantically Abel starts his car and pulls over to the spot where he saw her. She's gone. He leaps out of the car and looks in every direction.

After a moment, he begins to feel foolish, so he climbs back in and drives home.

The Crack Clown finally cuts the kid off around dawn. "You got to get dressed," he tells her. "I'll walk you down and let you out."

"I," the girl says.

"Let's go."

"I don't," she says, "have anywhere to go."

"I'm sorry, you can't stay here."

"Can I just sleep here?" she says. "For a little while? I can't go walking around like this. I'm wiped out."

"I'm sorry about that," he tells her. "I didn't say I could put you up. I would, but I can't. Not today."

The girl's face becomes weary to the point of pain.

The Crack Clown says, "Not today, you can't stay here. I'm not going to be here and I can't leave you here alone. Sorry. I have to go to the airport, to pick up my daughter."

"I sucked your *dick*," the girl sobs.

"I'm sorry, but you can't stay here," he says again. "I see my daughter once a year, and I didn't see her at all last year so now it's like two years. We're house-sitting someone's apartment for the next two weeks. I'm not going to be here."

The kid cries. It takes a few minutes before she can dress herself, and at that point she becomes sullen. The Crack Clown neither notices nor cares.

Downstairs, when he opens the door for her, she sneers, "Thanks."

Preoccupied, the Crack Clown sincerely replies, "You're welcome, baby," and shuts the door to the courtyard. Whatever else she sees fit to add from outside on the sidewalk, he misses it.

❀ ❀ ❀

Abel dreams about a neighborhood a lot like North Prieur yet at the same time recognizable as another place, one where he lived awhile after his parents died. On this street he sees Shila and a social worker he met briefly in Vermont; both wear tight spandex biker shorts.

"That new girl's called Polymnia," Shila tells Abel.

"You know her?" the social worker asks as she shakes her ass at a passing produce truck.

"Yeah," Shila says, and nods toward Abel. "He knows her."

Abel tries to speak.

"Now, your name's Eric, am I right?" the social worker asks Abel.

"You know her, definitely," Shila assures him. She pulls up her shirt to expose her breasts at a car driving past them. The car slows but keeps rolling. "Yeah," Shila says as she pulls her shirt back down. "You know her."

"Why are you here?" the social worker asks him. "I'm not saying you can't be here, but why? And since we're asking why, you of course don't have to answer."

Abel says, "My name is not Eric. It never was."

"Well, we can make it Eric if you want," the social worker assures him. "Let me just check and make sure no one else is using that name. I can tell you for sure by, like, Tuesday."

Abel wakes from this dream and sees it is one o'clock in the afternoon. He needs to do the shopping for work today, since the kitchen's out of too many things for him to put it off.

By the time Abel has showered, dressed, and climbed into his car, his dream has vanished forever.

This is the first time in more than a year that Jimmie Fiegal steps directly into the midday sun dressed in anything other than his clown costume. Immediately he feels drenched, as though he didn't towel himself after the bath he just finished, his first here in his new home.

"Hello," a woman outside his gate says.

"Hi, there," Jimmie says. The skin around his eye sockets feels oily, as if he hasn't cleaned all his makeup off properly.

"Did you just move in?" the woman asks.

"Sure did," Jimmie tells her, and introduces himself.

The woman's name is Donna. Up close she appears about Jimmie's age, slightly eager for company. She dresses deftly, well enough to almost conceal the thickness of her legs. He explains that his daughter's coming to visit, and Donna's eyes light up.

The sun pounds on Jimmie. He touches a hand to his breast pocket, as though searching for something he suddenly realizes he left in his apartment. "Oh, you have to excuse me," he begs Donna. "I forgot something, and I better get it before my cab gets here."

"Right, well, nice meeting you," she says.

"Tell you what, let's get together one evening," Jimmie says, "while my daughter's here."

She smiles and nods as she crosses the street.

Jimmie darts back into the house, through the back hallway, to his apartment. Inside, he goes to his bedroom closet and pulls one of three shoeboxes off the top shelf. Quickly he opens the box, loads a chunk into a glass stem, and smokes it. Then he puts everything back inside the box and places the box on the shelf alongside its two brothers.

The thought washes across him very abruptly that he has broken his vow not to smoke any product whatsoever in this apartment, at least not until his daughter has returned to Canada ten days from now.

Jimmie hears a horn honking out front. His cab's here.

One of the waitresses—a Scandinavian named Kreckle or Krekka or something close to that—has discovered that the owner is married, so she has stopped sleeping with him and will quit the instant she finds another job, which should take her all of three minutes.

After shopping, Abel arrives in the kitchen to find the owner drunk, nearly crying. "Hey," he greets Abel.

Abel puts the paper sacks of groceries on the service counter. "How you doing, man?"

"I'm fucked." The owner holds up a half-finished bottle of red wine. "You want?"

"No, thanks," Abel says, but then, with a shrug, he decides, "Yeah, all right. If it's dry."

The owner pours him a glass. Abel puts all the groceries away before he picks up his wine. It's dry, all right.

"Listen, you got mail," the owner says. "I had to sign for it."

"Wait, *I* got mail here? Or the kitchen got mail?"

"No, *you* got mail," the owner says. "It's inside on the bar. Probably some tax bullshit, or whatever."

Abel carries his wine into the front bar. The sepulchral air of this nightclub when it's empty always soothes him. He sits on one stool and throws his feet atop another, then he picks up the certified letter lying on the bar beside him.

The envelope has a printed address, but it can't be a government document because it has stamps on it rather than a meter mark. In fact, when he holds it close to his eyes Abel can tell that someone printed this envelope on a home printer, and not even a laser model.

Below Abel's name and the restaurant's address run the words: PERSONAL & CONFIDENTIAL—PLEASE FORWARD OR RETURN. Abel reads these words and says aloud, "Why write that if you're going to send the thing certified?"

Inside the envelope Abel finds a single sheet of paper containing several single-spaced paragraphs beneath an obviously homemade letterhead. A handwritten postcard addressed to a woman whose name Abel does not recognize hangs from the letter by a small paper clip. The letter reads:

Dear Abel Fitzpatrick:

Please excuse this intrusion. I am an author of books about real-life crimes. An agency that helps me track people I need to interview turned up your name in a search for Abel Milani, because you are paying taxes using his Social Security number. If they've made some mistake, please say so on the enclosed postcard, and I thank you for your time. I have attempted to reach you at your last workplace, but since I sent the letter certified, I know for certain that no one opened it or knows its contents.

But if the agency's right and you are Abel Milani, I want to ask if you would consent to an interview with me, at your convenience. I'm sure you realize by now why I want to speak with you. I'm completing a book about Gerald McVries, and it includes remembrances of every known McVries victim except your sister. According to the account

of the one policeman I've spoken to who knew anything about her, you
were Paula's only close companion during the time that she pursued
the lifestyle that resulted in her tragically meeting McVries. None of
the girls working around the bridge now have been there long enough
to remember her.

Abel, even if you choose not to help me (in which case I totally understand) please know that I am on Paula's side. I do not intend to make
money by glorifying McVries, and he will not receive a penny from
the book. I know it's not something you enjoy talking and thinking
about, and I know it's caused you enough pain already.

The woman goes on for yet another paragraph, hinting that participating in
her research could open the door to a career in the media, but Abel has read
enough. He reaches beside the cash register for a pen, which he uses to write
on the postcard: *Fuck yourself, ghoul.*

He does not sign it.

When Abel opens the kitchen door, the owner's head sways a little. "What's
up?" the owner asks. He has begun slurring.

"Where is there a mailbox near here? I have to mail this right away," Abel
says. "There's one on Dauphine, isn't there?"

"I don't know," the owner says miserably. "I always just drive by the one on
Rampart."

Abel sets off to mail the postcard before work.

Jimmie Fiegal's stomach has tied itself into knots. He stands watching through
the big windows as planes taxi to and from the runway. A prickly layer of his
own sweat has dried inside his clothes.

Last summer he actually came and waited at the boarding gate. Genevieve
did not arrive on her flight, so he phoned Toronto collect. That's when his
ex-wife told him her father had forbidden the girl to come. It had to do with
Jimmie's legal troubles, of course, though his former father-in-law particularly
objected to the fact that, the previous year, Genevieve had spent her vacation
with Jimmie in a set of motel rooms on the North Shore.

The new apartment solves that problem. She'll go home telling them about
the nice way Jimmie lives and how everything is brand-new. She'll tell them

about Jimmie's nice friend across the street, pretty much the same age as Jimmie and a little bit fat. Jimmie lives in a big, pretty house with an automatic gate across the driveway, and Genevieve has her own bedroom there.

A plane rolls to a stop right outside. Jimmie watches, his mind suddenly blank except for the gnawing feeling that he really, really needs a hit.

DUST

Two days after Snack Pak's miscarriage, they let her out of Charity early in the morning, and she went walking in the Tremé. She passed a house where a black dog nursed a litter of puppies on the side porch.

New York Larry had taught Snack Pak to always keep an eye peeled for puppies, and the gate to this yard didn't have a padlock, so she started to memorize the address.

Then she remembered that New York Larry had money now. Even though at the time the car hit him New York Larry had had a blood-alcohol level that astounded the paramedics, he somehow had won a settlement. Nilda said he had a lawyer uncle back home, and eventually gossip around the Quarter claimed that New York Larry had deliberately staggered into the car's path. In any case, New York Larry wouldn't need a dog for the foreseeable future.

"You like them puppies?" a woman asked from inside the house.

"Sure," Snack Pak said, only because this woman had caught her casing the yard. "They're really cute."

"You want one?" The woman opened the screen door and came onto the porch. "They're free."

"Free?" Snack Pak said. "Definitely."

At first she wanted to pick the first puppy that came to her. The litter was only four weeks old, though, and so they kept back.

"Are they too young?" she asked.

"Maybe a little," the woman said. "I'm just afraid I won't get rid of them at all. That's why I'd be happy if you took one now."

Snack Pak picked the skinniest puppy and left the Tremé carrying it against her breast. In the Quarter she went past Verti Mart and fished a cardboard box from the store's trash. An older juggler she knew by sight at Jackson Square let her use his pen to fashion the bottom of the box into a sign: PLEASE HELP SO THIS PUPPY AND ME CAN EAT.

She sat with her back against the iron fence of De Gaulle Park. Nearby a lady painted a picture of the cafe across Decatur Street. The puppy didn't behave the way New York Larry's dogs always did. Passersby barely glanced at Snack Pak, and she wondered if they even blinked at her sign long enough to see the word "puppy."

Then she thought of what New York Larry would say: Be patient. Not every tourist loves animals, but the ones who do will never let you down.

Tourist traffic increased as the morning grew later. After an hour, Drake came by and said, "Where'd you get the puppy?"

"Hi," Snack Pak said.

"Where'd you get the puppy?" he repeated, adjusting the strap on his knapsack so he could touch the dog.

"The Tremé," Snack Pak said. "I just got out of the hospital."

"Where in the Tremé?"

"Near Claiborne, but not the projects," she said. "Where they have regular houses, near the highway exit."

"Cool," Drake said, absently. The puppy did not react much to his prodding. Drake frowned, assessing the dog the way a carpenter studies tools he might buy. "What's her name?"

"I think I'm going to name it Ogre," Snack Pak said. "How can you tell it's a girl?"

Drake showed her how to sex a dog. Then he berated her cardboard sign. "Don't mention yourself," he said, as though he'd gone over sign etiquette for her before. "People know you're begging for beer money then. The whole point of the dog is that people who have dogs themselves see you and think how it would feel if they had to beg to feed *their* dog. With that sign, you're telling people this dog won't get any of what they give you. And that puppy's too young to eat anything you're going to buy it. Anyone who'd pay money to feed a dog knows you're not going to spend it on puppy formula."

"Drake, could you do me a favor?" Snack Pak said.

"What?" he replied, already leaving.

"Could you get me another piece of cardboard so I can make a new sign?" Snack Pak said. "Please? I walked all fucking morning."

Drake laughed as he walked away. "Yeah, if I see any boxes, I'll hold on to them for you."

❋ ❋ ❋

Drake had ripped off someone's clothes from Checkpoint's one afternoon a week and a half ago, and this was his first visit back since.

Seven people sat at the bar. The bartender didn't look twice at Drake, who marched directly to the laundry room and found it empty. None of the washers or dryers was in use.

Normally he would load someone's laundry—preferably from the dryer, but most times from the washer, which entailed having to rinse and dry the clothes at another laundromat before selling them to second-hand stores—into his backpack and leave. If anyone by the bar ever asked him why he should leave so quickly, he would claim to have forgotten his laundry money. No one ever stopped him, though. He didn't hit this place often enough for anyone to recognize him.

Checkpoint's always offered feast or famine. For a target Drake favored anyone who had just moved to New Orleans. Even people from bigger cities didn't guard against laundry theft. The novelty of a bar-laundromat's staying open round the clock on the edge of the Quarter disarmed new arrivals, to the degree that a street kid could easily carry their clothes away right in front of them as they drank.

But the bartenders at Checkpoint's would catch on quick, these days, especially if they saw a street kid carting out a wet load. Such a tyro could only hit Checkpoint's blatantly once or twice, maybe not even.

So far as he knew, Drake had the larger schedule to himself. Other thieves worked Checkpoint's laundry room hit or miss. They took their chances when the bar got crowded, which primed bartenders to pay close attention to laundry-room loiterers throughout peak hours. Early in the day, on the other hand, everyone showed more trust. Somehow his knapsack always helped Drake look the same leaving as he'd looked on arrival.

Yet Drake's system couldn't guarantee him a mark every time he came here. None of the seven patrons this morning had brought dirty clothes. As he stared at the empty machines Drake cursed and rolled his eyes. He would come back later, and a third and fourth time if necessary. One good opportunity at Checkpoint's was easily worth a whole morning to him.

Drake's eyes came to rest upon a shelf of paperbacks. Taped to the wall beside them, a sheet of paper read: BOOK EXCHANGE—DONATE TWO, TAKE ONE, OR $1 EACH FOR CHARITY—SEE BARTENDER.

Very rapidly Drake stuffed thirty or so books from the shelf into his back-pack.

No one at the bar or behind it paid any attention as Drake left. Second-hand bookstores wouldn't open for another hour or two yet, but that didn't bother Drake. The store he had in mind was on Magazine Street, and he wanted to take his time traveling there. He bought a pint beer at the grocer on Barracks and set out uptown on Decatur.

A block and a half from De Gaulle Park, he realized he would run into that girl with the puppy again. Even at this distance she stood out; that alone would keep her from making any money, because pedestrians would have al-ready spotted her before she asked them. A good beggar stays invisible until speaking up. Girls who learn to beg while pregnant don't believe they have to work to earn money.

To avoid her, Drake cut right and took Chartres Street to Jackson Square. He didn't see anyone he knew, which didn't surprise him, considering the hour.

He finished his beer long before he reached the bus stop on Canal. This month he had unlimited free access to all public transport, in the form of a pass filched from a drunk's wallet at Dragon's Den. On one line the pass said "Jim Harris" in red felt pen, with the same name signed on the line below it and the word MALE circled above.

The tourists gave Drake a wide berth. He cut easily to the front of the crowd to board, and no one sat next to him on the two-seat plastic bench. As the bus traveled up Magazine Street, he realized he needed a shower before going inside any bookstores.

His best bet for a shower was Lou's, a bit further uptown than he'd wanted to go. At this time of day almost no one Drake knew would even have woken up, but Lou would have smoked a quarter-ounce of pot already. A few times Drake had gotten pot from Lou, and paid for it with sex.

The last time Drake had visited, Lou had asked him to call first in the fu-ture. Months had passed since then, however. Just by ignoring a request, Drake could make it seem to have never happened.

The bus dropped him a little before Napoleon, and he walked to Lou's white and gray house and rang the bell. He got no answer. After several minutes Drake very nearly left without trying the bell again, yet by habit he pressed the button one more time.

A window on the second floor slid open, and Lou's head popped out. He'd cut his hair short and bleached it.

"Hey, where y'at?" Lou greeted him.

"How are you?" Drake said.

"All right. Wait a sec," Lou replied, and disappeared from the window. Drake could hear him gallop down the stairs.

Lou opened the door for him and said, "Good to see you." Then he winced at Drake's odor and said, "God, you must be *sleeping* in those clothes."

"I was just in the neighborhood," Drake said politely as he entered. "I was hoping you could let me use your shower. We got trouble with the plumbing where I'm staying."

With Drake already climbing the stairs, Lou could scarcely refuse. Inside Lou's apartment Drake proceeded directly to the laundry room, where he stripped and put everything but his boots into the washer.

"Well, you don't waste time, do you?" Lou asked, eyeing Drake's naked form from the hallway.

Drake grinned and waved his penis.

Midway through Drake's shower, Lou came in to watch. Drake had forgotten Lou's main kink, having street guys wash in front of him.

In the bathroom mirror Drake learned that his hair had grown longer than he'd realized. After he shaved with one of Lou's disposable razors and toweled off, he went nude to the laundry room and moved his clothes into the dryer. The thought crossed his mind that he ought to find a friend with a dryer where he could bring stolen laundry. It would save him a buck every time he nailed a wet load. Lou would let him, but Drake didn't want to travel this far uptown whenever he stole.

While his clothes dried, Drake let Lou blow him. Then he got dressed. Lou gave him a joint and said, "I'm glad you came by. Call me first, next time, though."

"Sure," Drake said, and left, pissed off that Lou had only given him a joint.

Outside, the day had become gray, though Drake did not think it would rain. He walked to Magazine Street and then headed downtown. To reach the bookstore he had in mind, he needed to cross Louisiana Avenue.

Magazine changed block by block, from beautifully decrepit homes to Art Deco storefronts to former gas stations remodeled into sandwich shops. Ivy sprouted in tufts everywhere. The street's narrow bends lent themselves to near-misses between cars, since everyone drove a little too fast.

The leaves and exhaust and food weaved their scents into Magazine Street's signature smell, one that triggered Drake's earliest memories of New Orleans.

When Drake first came here, he'd moved in with a girl on lower Magazine for several weeks, and really liked it until she asked him to help pay rent.

After a few blocks he noticed ahead of him merchandise on the street in front of an antique store, mostly furniture. As he got closer he spotted beside the door a table holding a few clock radios and smaller items. He put on a show of checking price tags on chairs before glancing in to check whether anyone was watching him from inside the shop.

Next to the register a whitehaired man cradled his chin in his hand, staring at Drake intently through the window. Drake didn't even bother casing whatever lay on the table. All the people who owned these antique stores knew each other and each other's stock, anyway. Drake had neither the patience nor the home to store swag nine months or a year before selling it.

The antique store appeared to fill two storefronts, because the two attached shops shared the same olive paint and had identical steel grilles covering their windows. Yet Drake read the peeling gold letters on the second window: LUMIÈRE BOOKS. Closer to the bottom of the pane more gold print gave the store hours and some other information; this writing was a decal, and the years had rendered most of it illegible.

But part of it clearly said: BUY—SELL—TRADE.

Drake turned the knob on the door both ways. The knob didn't connect with anything, so he shoved the door. It opened.

The shop had a fifteen-foot ceiling. Twelve-foot bookcases cut the floorspace into a tight maze of aisles. From the door Drake could see only the very top of the rear wall, and he lost sight of even that much once he stepped into the small clearing that allowed the door to swing inward. The door closed to reveal a desk.

"Hello," the girl seated at the desk said, setting down a computer catalogue. She had good tits but wore a drab blouse and jeans, and her glasses made her face flat. "Can I help you?"

"Hope so," Drake said, taking off his knapsack. "I have some books to sell."

"Paperback or hardcover?" she asked.

"Paperbacks," Drake said. He dumped all thirty books from his knapsack onto the desk.

The girl picked through them without talking. In seconds she shook her head and said, "I'm sorry, we don't carry romances."

For the first time, Drake looked at the covers of his books. Every one featured a painting of a man and woman in torrid embrace, frilly clothes atwirl in the ocean wind. Every single one.

"Oh, you don't? I didn't know that," he said.

"We hardly carry any fiction at all, anymore," the girl said, glancing over her shoulder at the fiction aisle. "Just the classics."

"Oh," Drake said. He despised feeling stupid, particularly in front of a girl. "I just have all these romances. Because I used to write them."

"Really?" the girl said.

"Yeah," Drake said. "I used to write romances under a fake name. Now I'm writing..." He paused, swallowed. "The 'real' book I always wanted to write. So I thought I'd sell these. I used to use them for research."

She adjusted her glasses and looked at him differently. "That's interesting," she said. "What name did you write under?"

"Felicity Clio," Drake said. "Had to use a woman's name."

"Wow, how cool," the girl said, smiling. She held her hand out and said, "I'm Danielle."

"Hi, Danielle," Drake said. "I'm Jim Harris."

They chatted awhile. Drake could tell she liked him now. While they talked she organized his books into piles, and handed them to him so he could load them back into his knapsack.

"Wait," she said, and held up a gray book with an orange title, by an author named Ludwig Wittgenstein. "This we sell." She opened the front cover and found something written on the first page. "Did you buy this at another bookstore? Down in the Quarter, a while ago?"

"Maybe," Drake said, squinting at the ceiling as though leafing through detailed mental records. "Yeah, I think so. Why? Is there a problem?"

"No, not at all," she said. "It's just, that man you bought it from? Roger? He passed away."

"Sorry to hear that," Drake said. "He was a nice guy, I thought."

She nodded. "It was very sad. He suffered a great deal, and it changed his personality at the end. I knew him since I was little."

"I'm really sorry to hear he died," Drake said.

"But do you remember his buy-back policy?" she asked.

Drake shook his head.

"All the used-book sellers started honoring Roger's buy-backs when he had to close his store," the girl said. "The buy-back price on this book is three dollars."

"Cool," he said. "I sure hope it helped."

"It doesn't even really matter if it did. Honoring his buy-backs is how we honor Roger." A solemn tinge entered her voice. She opened the desk's top drawer and from a cash tray withdrew three dollars, which she handed Drake. Then she tore out the front page from the Wittgenstein book, placed it carefully under the cash tray, and closed the drawer. "What's your new book about, Jim?" she asked.

"It's about a lot of things," he said, shrugging. "I can't talk too much about it until I finish it, but it's heavy. One thing it's about that my other books never had is sex."

She grinned, barely, and a spark flashed in her eyes.

"You go to school?" he asked her.

"Actually, I start back next fall," she said. "I dropped out after freshman year at USM."

"What do you want to do?"

"Write," the girl said, suddenly bashful.

No one else entered the store. She told him the place belonged to her uncle, and often whole afternoons went by without customers. Their business chiefly revolved around the beginning of semesters.

It took Drake another twenty minutes or so to get her to lock the front door and hang the sign that said she'd closed for lunch. "I'm not supposed to do this," she said, her lips quivering and wet.

Drake and Danielle snuck to the back of the store and copulated on the floor. Removing her glasses made the girl mysterious and beguiling. If anything, Drake had underestimated how fine a body she hid inside those bland clothes.

Afterward they talked some more, and she reopened the store. Still no customers came. Drake took her phone number on the back of the store's business card, and invited her to dinner at Commander's Palace on Friday, to celebrate selling his newest book, the last of his romances. Her face glowed as she accepted.

"You've got dust in your hair," Drake said, pointing at a location on his scalp.

She reached up and plucked the ball from the same site on her own head. "This place is so dusty," she said. "That's the thing I really hate about working here. It aggravates my allergies."

"Dust comes from people," Drake said. "People's skin flakes off and floats away, and that's what makes dust."

Danielle nodded slowly, with intense admiration. He could tell she'd never met a celebrity before, much less fucked one.

"Let me ask you this," he said. "How can I tell which of the books in my library at home came from that store in the Quarter?"

For a second she didn't grasp what he meant, then she said, "You mean from Roger? Look." From inside the cash drawer she pulled the front page from the Wittgenstein book Drake had just sold her, and held it up to show him. "See the two prices? The top one's in ink, and that's what Roger charged. The bottom one is the buy-back price, and that's in pencil. Usually it's half the top price."

Drake said, "And you just know it came from that store. There's nothing else on the book that says so."

"No one else did that, with the two prices," Danielle said. "And his handwriting is very distinctive. He connects the zeros and crosses his sevens."

They kissed a little bit. Drake told her to expect his call Thursday and left.

Further down Magazine, he stopped at a check-cashing place and wrote in the upper prices on three of his romances—two for five bucks each, and one for six—with a pen attached to the counter by a thin metal rope encased in dirty plastic. Then he asked the woman behind the bulletproof glass for a pencil, with which he added the buy-back prices.

When Drake reached the bookstores below Louisiana Avenue, the girl at the first one he entered paid him eight dollars without a moment's hesitation. She tore the front page from all three books and laid the removed sheets inside a drawer beneath the counter.

"Why'd you rip them like that?" Drake asked casually.

"I have to do that with certain books," she said. "My boss has to see those pages, I don't know why."

By nightfall Snack Pak's puppy developed trouble breathing. Pretty soon it died. Snack Pak laid its carcass inside one of the garbage cans in Jackson Square, shortly after the garbagemen had emptied them.

She had already given up on using the animal as a prop. No one wanted to hand her a dime today. Some friends of hers passing by had given her two Valium and part of a beer, but she didn't collect enough change to buy a hot dog.

That night Snack Pak hung out on Decatur near Kagan's. Nobody she knew showed the slightest concern that she'd come out of the hospital that morning and hadn't eaten. When she asked Nilda for a cigarette, Nilda said, "Buy your own." Nilda hadn't acted friendly since Snack Pak began showing, probably because Nilda had had a baby last year whom she now regretted giving up for adoption.

Much later, Snack Pak went with two other girls to an abandoned house near Esplanade, not far into the Tremé. They slept on the floor there. Snack Pak balled her sweatshirt into a pillow.

The next morning she felt terrible but couldn't sleep late, for the sun shone too bright through the curtainless windows. The other girls woke up too, and they went to Circle K. One of them bought Snack Pak a cupcake for breakfast.

Around eleven o'clock Snack Pak got to Jackson Square. The dead puppy had lain in the sun all morning, thus beginning to rot. The tourist hordes avoided the vicinity of the garbage can where Snack Pak had dumped its little corpse. Flies hovered above the can's mouth. She pretended not to know anything about it.

Half an hour after Snack Pak arrived at the square, the stench gagged several well-dressed people leaving a formal event inside Saint Louis Cathedral.

A garbage truck did not arrive to empty the can until after dark. By that time, several crusties whom Snack Pak knew well enough to talk to had tried to spike the puppy's severed head onto a shard of broomstick and, failing, had flung it by one ear into the ornate garden at the rear of the church.

By stealing the Yellow Pages from a laundromat next to Pie In The Sky, Drake obtained a complete list of all used-book emporia in Orleans Parish. Mentally he placed each address on a map; the stores fell into easy geographic zones. Oddly, the Yellow Pages did not list Lumière Books.

He tore the page out, and left the phone book on the sidewalk. That evening at Dragon's Den, when Drake saw a drunk stagger from the bar down the stairs, he slipped someone's empty Bass Ale bottle into his pocket and followed. The drunk barely made it into the men's room before vomiting. Drake came up behind him and knocked him unconscious with the bottle.

The guy's hip pocket contained five hundred and twenty-eight dollars, which Drake spent on a bag of heroin so big it lasted him several days—he couldn't say exactly how long because he booted the stuff inside the Algren, a twenty-four-hour porn theater on Canal Street. This binge could have lasted longer had the theater's employees not insisted on an occasional taste.

When he finally ran out of dope Drake exited the Algren and spent a day begging around Jackson Square and the A&P on Royal.

Late the next morning he rode the streetcar up Saint Charles Avenue, above the Garden District. He had only a handful of fellow passengers. The car smelled of seed oil, he guessed, or whatever the transit workers used to polish the wood seats.

Drake had trouble locating one particular store uptown called J. Robicheaux Books. The building resembled a regular home, for ivy had overgrown the sign above the front door. In the driveway stood a red Volkswagen van. He went inside and waited in line for the register. First the clerk had to help a guy wearing new clothes that didn't fit, carrying an armful of science texts to sell.

As soon as the student laid these books on the counter, the clerk put his palms forward and said, "All right, just a minute. All right?" The clerk went to a doorway behind him and summoned someone he called Jude, a man with a pepper-colored beard, obviously the store's owner.

"No," Jude groaned to the clerk, wagging his head as he pointed to the yellow stickers that adorned the texts' spines. If Jude thought his clerk possessed more intelligence than did most dogs, he hid this belief well. "How many times you need to hear this? When it has that yellow thing, we don't take it anymore."

The customer began, "But I always—"

"Not anymore," Jude said, with a hair more courtesy than he showed his clerk. "The bursar used to give us access to the reading lists as soon as the teachers made them, so we knew how to stock up before the semester started. Now the school tells the teachers they don't want any competition for the campus bookstore. Bullshit! I don't go for that."

The college kid said, "But what about me? I'm out the money."

Jude shrugged. "You can take those to the book exchange on campus, or to some of the other used-book places, maybe downtown, though they probably don't handle school books," he said. "I know none of the others up here will take them now."

The clerk looked past the college kid, at Drake, and said, "Can I help you?"

"Just felt like browsing," Drake said, newly intent upon shunning attention. "Is that all right?"

"Sure, yeah," the clerk said, and waved his hand.

Drake pretended to search the aisles. He could feel Jude's eyes upon him, so he plucked a gray-brown hardcover from the shelf and flipped through it;

the words *First Edition-$35* caught his eye on the title page. This store did not offer the privacy of the one where Drake had balled the chick with the glasses, and he needed a moment to compose himself.

Finally Drake returned to the door and said, "Bye, now," to both the clerk and Jude, who still hadn't shuffled back to the other room since rejecting the Physics texts.

"Bye," the clerk said.

"Okay, bye-bye," Jude said. His manner grated on Drake, who while leaving the shop realized that Jude reminded him of a certain guidance counselor who'd busted Drake's balls in high school.

Outside, he ambled along the sidewalk as though in mild shock. He had expected to palm off all the paperbacks in his knapsack in maybe two or three stops. Yet watching how this clerk directed even the simplest decision to the store owner's authority, Drake had suddenly grasped that he'd struck upon the greatest single scam of his career to date, and its fragility awed him.

Research that afternoon at three other stores confirmed for Drake that luck had guided his first sale, however many days ago that had been. At all three stores he now found that they employed the owner and one or more part-time clerks who allowed the owner to ignore the cash register or even leave the premises. Drake must have hit that store down Magazine during its owner's lunch hour, or his day off.

In all likelihood, these clerks were students themselves. Anything unusual—anything other than a customer's choosing books from the shelves and paying the marked prices—required the owner's say. Of course, experienced clerks ought to accept Roger's books for the penciled buy-back price, but if Drake happened to get a newly hired trainee, or someone who had forgotten how this policy worked, the boss would get involved.

Once any store owner laid eyes upon an obvious forgery, none of the stores would pay another nickel for Roger's books.

In fact, the romances Drake had sold to the store on Magazine Street could have already sunk him, if the owner there checked over the incoming paperbacks at any point before they hit the shelves. Any store that would honor this dead man's debts would alert all the other stores immediately. Probably they all belonged to some merchant guild.

At the second store he visited, Drake swiped a pencil from beside the cash register. On an envelope from the wastebasket he began a list, describing what kind of books each store carried. He came up with his own code to describe their stocks. For J. Robicheaux Books, he had to go by memory, though he hadn't paid much sincere attention to the shelves while there. He wrote: *Old hardcover, "First Edition-$35."*

By the time Drake worked his way to the Quarter, the day had grown late. On the sidewalk outside a bookstore on Chartres Street that he'd passed countless times on his way to and from Jackson Square, Drake noticed that they kept a medium-sized cardboard carton full of books. On one of the box's flaps someone had written in magic marker, FREE! *Give a book a home.*

Drake entered the store and politely completed one lap of the aisles, noting the stock. Then he grinned a farewell to the man at the register, an older fellow wearing a visor. "See you again, now," the man said as Drake left.

Outside Drake stooped to examine the free books. What lay inside the carton must have come from the store's stock, some damaged, others unbought. Drake opened his knapsack. For some reason, he had neglected to toss his romance novels in the trash after he realized that attempting to sell them could destroy his scam, so he swapped them now for the books in the box.

Drake visited every store on his list, except the last one, which lay at the back end of the Quarter, away from the river, without another store of any kind nearby. He got there just as night fell. Through the windows he saw a man standing alone behind the counter, and knew him instantly to be the owner. From the sidewalk the shop itself appeared small, and Drake decided not to venture inside.

Across the street, Dog Park had just closed. Drake had slept there many a night, especially during the spring or fall. The woman who ran the place during the day had already locked the gates shut, which meant the homeless now considered the park open. Drake jumped the fence.

In one corner of Dog Park stood a rain shelter that covered an area as large as a small house. As Drake drew closer to it, he saw three crusties squatting Indian-style against one of the shelter's painted brick pillars.

He knew two of them, Terence and Oogie, and the third by sight. They invited him to sit with them and passed him their purloined bottle of cheap Scotch.

After a while the man closed the bookstore across the street. First he mounted tall shutters over the windows, then he bolted the door and drove away.

"Do you know if that guy owns the store?" Drake asked Terence.

Terence nodded. "He's the only one I ever seen work there."

"I tried to rip off books out of there, but he never takes his eyes off you," Oogie said. Darkness made the blood clotted around Oogie's freshly pierced eyebrow a pinguid black.

Drake stayed and drank their Scotch with them. Oogie and the third guy discussed shoplifting from used-book stores, theorizing that one could steal books and then sell them in another part of town. Drake waited until a break in their conversation and then said, "It ain't like laundry. The clothes stores don't all know each other, the bookstores do. You try to sell them each other's shit and they'll call the cops. That happened to someone I know who's in Angola now. For, like, a two-dollar paperback book."

"No shit?" Terence asked.

"Oh, yeah," Drake said. "It's not worth fucking with those bookstores. Trust me, stick to cars and laundry. Bookstores'll put you in jail."

When they finished the Scotch, Drake left. He walked to the A&P, where he met a girl he liked. They shared a cigarette while she panhandled. After a while Drake bought three forties, and escorted her to an abandoned house in the Bywater where she squatted. They drank and screwed.

When they awoke the next morning she told him her neighbors down the block would let them use their shower. The neighbors turned out to be hippies, who actually owned their house. The husband repaired motorcycles in the yard.

Drake fucked her again in their shower. Afterward his clothes felt and smelled dirty to him, which didn't bother Drake except in a professional sense: The less dingy he seemed, the more easily he could gain a stranger's trust. For the same reason, he shaved with the hippie husband's electric razor.

When Drake and the girl came out of the bathroom, the hippies invited them to stay for tea and a joint. They accepted. Before leaving, Drake stole a blue ballpoint pen from a jar beside the hippies' phone.

The girl brought him back to her squat, where another couple sat smoking at the table in the kitchen. Drake hadn't heard them enter during the night. The girl Drake had fucked last night said, "This is Kara and Satch."

"Jim," Drake introduced himself.

"Hey," Satch grunted. Kara didn't glance up from her cigarette.

Drake went into the room where he'd slept, and dumped the books from his knapsack. Not all of the titles seemed appropriate for what he'd written on his list, but he managed to divide them into seven groups.

A small, tidy pile of paperbacks sat beside the girl's mattress, all self-help or occult or the shelf between those two. These fit easily into Drake's knapsack.

First he did the ink prices. Inside one sturdy hardcover Drake wrote, "First edition—$40." Then he went through the books again with his pencil, adding in the buy-back prices.

While he wrote, she came in and asked, "What are you doing?" Drake said, "Taking care of some business for later today. I'll come inside in a second." And he did, wearing a Butthole Surfers T-shirt he'd found folded and clean among some underwear in a paper sack.

"That's my shirt," his hostess said.

"Yeah, mine's dirty. I'll do laundry later today, if you want," Drake said, and before she could reply to that asked the entire room, "You feel like eating?"

Everyone was hungry. On a strip he tore from a paper bag, Drake wrote what each of his three companions wanted for breakfast. Since Drake was treating, Satch let him take Kara's bike, an old-fashioned three-speed with a basket.

As Drake wheeled the bike out the front door, the girl who'd brought him here asked, "Why do you have your knapsack on?"

He answered as though her question had implied no suspicion whatsoever. "I have to drop off these books now so I know I've got enough to pay for breakfast. They pay on delivery."

"Oh," she said.

"Listen, is there a laundromat near here?" he asked her. "I need to go wash clothes after we eat."

"Yeah, it's like two blocks that way," she said, pointing with her thumb. As Drake intended, discussing laundry reminded her that he'd left his shirt inside, on her bed, and mollified her into believing he meant to return.

"I'll be back quick as I can," he promised, and pedaled away. Drake hadn't thought of how much easier a bicycle made this project. First he went to the Quarter and used the last of his money to buy a croissant and coffee at Kaldi's. Then, his belly full, the sun warm on his neck and scalp, he set off up Magazine Street.

Whenever he came near stores on his list, Drake rode on the sidewalk, slowly, so he could peer inside the windows. In the first two shops he passed, he saw the proprietors manning their own tills. At the third one, the owner stood in the doorway with his arms folded.

At the fourth a clerk sat beside the register reading a magazine. Drake parked his bike, checked his notes, and entered. "Hi," he said, unfastening the straps from his knapsack. "I have some books to sell."

"I'm sorry," the clerk said. "You'll have to come back tomorrow. My boss doesn't work today, and only he can buy or trade."

"Look at these, though," Drake said, and laid one of his seven groups onto the counter. "Open the covers."

The clerk did, and promptly handed over thirty-eight bucks. Drake left before seeing whether the clerk would tear the first page from the hardcovers the way the others had from the softbound books. An effortless victory sometimes made Drake giddy, and further research wasn't worth the risk of getting sloppy, especially since—after today or possibly tomorrow, depending on when somebody first discovered the fraud—this scam would never work again, anyway.

On Royal Street in the middle of the afternoon Snack Pak met a very drunk man in his sixties named Norm, who invited her for a drink at the Napoleon House. When they reached the bar, the bartender of course refused to serve Snack Pak, because she hadn't bathed but once since leaving Charity.

The ordeal of having his date expelled from a venerable landmark left Norm flustered. Snack Pak sat on the curb in front of the Pharmacy Museum and bawled. Awkwardly Norm hugged her, patted her on the shoulders.

Presently their dialogue moved to the topic of sexual favors. They reached an agreement, and Snack Pak insisted that Norm show her his forty dollars—a twenty, a ten and two fives—right then and there. This way, she definitely knew he had the money and, more important, which pocket Norm used to carry his wallet.

They went to his hotel just outside the Quarter. As they crossed the lobby Snack Pak peeked at the concierge, and saw him speaking on his red phone, his manner too agitated for him to notice her. They didn't encounter any other staff on the way up to Norm's room.

Inside the room she gave Norm his blow job. He'd spent the whole day drinking, so his concentration didn't match his ambition. All his body hair was gray. It took him at least twenty-five minutes to climax. Afterward she killed the lights and curled up beside him.

As soon as Norm fell asleep, Snack Pak wriggled free and fished his wallet from the pocket of his plaid blazer. Swiftly yet with as little noise as possible she crossed the dark room and fled, closing the door behind her. Outside in the bright hall she felt vulnerable, and stashed the wallet into her jeans pocket.

If Norm suddenly woke up and put his pants on, he would dash out to the elevators to catch her. So she trotted off in the other direction, and followed two different right turns in the hallway. Up ahead, where the hall ended, she sighted a red-on-white exit sign and charged toward it.

Just as her hand pushed the door open Snack Pak worried that she might trip an alarm by using the fire stairs. None sounded, though. Down she ran, all six flights to ground level, where she pushed through a door into the lobby.

Several middle-aged guests stood expectantly at the check-in counter, their luggage beside them where the doorman had placed it. The concierge barely found a spare second to watch Snack Pak's swift exit.

The charge of victory sailed her a block and a half back into the Quarter before she opened the wallet and counted her take.

Eleven dollars, all singles.

She opened every flap and pocket and even looked between the photos Norm had placed in his see-through plastic gallery. All this work yielded her an additional quarter, which Norm presumably kept stored behind his photos for emergency phone calls.

For a while Snack Pak tried hard to recall where Norm had put his forty dollars after showing it to her. Futility began to sour her stomach, so she bought two Valiums for a dollar from Terence at Kagan's, and then bought a forty from Verti Mart.

Later, as the sky darkened, she lay on a bench along the Riverwalk and studied Norm's photos closely. He had at least one daughter older than Snack Pak, and he and his wife beamed in the girl's wedding portrait. On the brink of passing out, Snack Pak wondered whether Norm's wife was still alive.

Drake collected more than three hundred dollars throughout the day.

On his bicycle he rode from one bookstore to another, watching for signs of any owner's departure. He hit two places near each other on Prytania both at around one o'clock; sometime after three he nailed the shop on lower Magazine where he'd sold the romance novels, and even got the same wide-eyed clerk; and at four-thirty, one proprietor farther up Magazine actually left his clerk to close for the day.

With that, Drake had sold five of his seven bundles of books. Had a situation arisen where he found himself dealing with an owner, Drake would have handed over the self-help books he'd obtained that morning, and maybe even garnered an extra few bucks.

Certainty that his plan could work only this once kept Drake from heading downtown immediately and investing his earnings in dope. Staving off this temptation led him to avoid visiting the bookstores down the Quarter, for the short trip to his connection in the Marigny would prove irresistible.

Businesses in the French Quarter were the most difficult to swindle, anyway. Instead Drake stayed uptown, both to keep clean longer and to avoid that girl he'd balled last night, or her squatmates. They'd look for him downtown.

All day he monitored J. Robicheaux Books without once coming any closer than the corner. For one thing, it inhabited a residential block, so Drake wouldn't blend in if someone inside the store happened to see him pass twice. More than that, he disliked the place because that man Jude worked there. As a rule Drake never let personal issues interfere with work, but Jude irritated him. Throughout the day, each time Drake passed he checked down the block from the corner, spotted the red VW van in the store's driveway, and continued on his way.

At a little before six, Drake swung by and saw that the van had disappeared.

He cut a sharp loop and glided toward the store without pedaling. This close to night, the shadows grew longer, and might shroud from his brief passing glance anything parked in the driveway.

No mistake, the van had pulled away somewhere. Drake still had two bundles of books to sell, so he dismounted and leaned his bike against the building, in the driveway.

Inside, a girl greeted him from behind the register, slightly more assertive than the clod Drake had observed here the first time.

"I can't purchase books," she warned him as he produced a handful from his knapsack.

"These you can," Drake said. "These came from Roger's store."

"I don't know anything about that. You have to talk to my boss."

"Yeah, you're talking about Jude, right?" Drake said.

The girl relaxed slightly. "Yes. You know him?"

"I buy and sell books here all the time," Drake said. "You must be new. I'm Jim."

"It's my third week," she admitted with a grin. "My name's Dorothy. I only work two days."

"Okay, well, can you call Jude?" Drake asked. "Call and ask him about Roger's books. Roger had a store in the Quarter, and he passed away last year. All the used-book stores honor his buy-back prices, which are these pencil numbers, see?" He held open the covers of two different books.

"I don't know all that, though," the girl said.

"So call Jude at home and ask him," Drake suggested.

She shook her head. "He's not home. He went by the other store. He should be back, if you want to wait."

Drake ran a hand through his hair, dramatically weighing his desire to stay against a packed imaginary schedule. "I really can't," he said. "Listen, if you can't take care of this, that's okay. Tell Jude that Jim Harris said hello."

"I will," she said, and held up one of the books. "Maybe you want to leave these here for him."

Drake shook his head. "Uh-uh," he said.

The door slammed open.

Drake and Dorothy spun to see Jude storm in and demand to know, "Whose bike is out in the driveway?"

"Oh," Drake said. "Oh, that's mine. I'll move it."

"You can't park in my driveway," Jude said, as though disgusted he should have to explain.

"I'm sorry," Drake said, moving toward the door.

"Do you know about this Roger thing?" Dorothy asked Jude.

"What Roger thing?"

"There was a bookstore run by a guy called Roger, in the Quarter," she said. "He passed away."

"Yeah, I knew him—Roger Aickman," Jude said. "What about him?"

Drake quelled his instinct to flee. He stepped far enough away that Jude couldn't stop him from leaving, and watched.

"Well," the clerk said, confused. "Do we buy his books automatically? Or, or what?"

Jude sighed. "That was last year," he said. His voice displayed more patience than it had for the other employee, possibly because she was a girl, possibly at the mention of a deceased friend.

Then Jude's eyes fell on the book open before her, a mint-condition hardcover. He picked it up and gave a quick, involuntary laugh as he read what Drake had written on the first page.

"'First edition'?!" Jude exclaimed, and checked the spine. "Someone's smoking dope. This is a *Reader's Digest* book."

A beat elapsed during which Drake eagerly believed Jude might not uncover the scheme. Then Jude began to talk, and each sentence he uttered sounded less bemused and more accusatory.

"First off, Roger wouldn't write his prices on the fly leaf," Jude said, glancing across all the books Drake had laid upon the counter. "And I know he didn't carry *Reader's Digest* abridged novels, or Social Science stuff." He opened one book to the first page and held it close to his eyes. "And Roger never smudged the ink like this. He made a big deal about letting it dry because he used a fountain pen, and these are—"

Jude touched the page and examined his finger. Suddenly his amazement shifted to fury.

"This is *ballpoint*," he snarled at Drake. "You fucking wrote this yourself, just now!"

Drake barreled out the door and jumped onto his bike. The red van stood parked beside the curb. As Drake pedaled clumsily out of the driveway into the street, Jude burst out the front door, shouting, "Who told you about that? Where did you hear that, huh?"

Jude's hands snatched the air behind Drake's neck, and then the gears caught and the bike took off. At the corner Drake turned the wrong way up a one-way street so Jude couldn't pursue him in the red truck.

The one-way street took Drake to Saint Charles Avenue, where he headed downtown. After a few blocks the traffic annoyed him, particularly because he needed to keep an eye out for that Volkswagen van, so instead he crossed the trolley tracks and found a parallel sidestreet on the opposite side.

He passed ornate homes. A few had lawns as big as Dog Park, and twice he passed a landscaper's truck to discover that an entire team of gardeners was grooming several houses at once, trimming and pruning and edging and mowing in shifts. It interested him, especially the second crew he saw, because it led him to consider the resale values of landscaping materials. Sod, for instance.

Garden supply places must buy their sod from somebody. Suppose he dressed as a gardener—they all wore blue workshirts—and removed freshly laid sod from customers' lawns. If he said that a government inspector had found some kind of dangerous mite and his boss had to recall the sod, no one would stop him. It would require a car, at least, though. A station wagon would work better.

These thoughts engaged Drake long past the point of leaving the neighbor-hood that employed gardeners. As he crossed Napoleon and then Louisiana Avenues, houses bared their age in less flattering ways. The first step in a gar-dening scam, he concluded, was research, which would have to wait until after his victory celebration.

Night seized more of the sky above him each second, and he had no friends in any neighborhood between here and the Warehouse District, so Drake put gardening on hold and stayed alert. Rarely did he carry this much money, or travel anywhere so dangerous. He kept the bike in third gear and ignored stop signs.

Shortly after he passed beneath the elevated highway, Drake's rear tire went flat. Briefly he rode on the rim, then he climbed off and cursed. This bike would sell down at the French Market, or at the flea market on Frenchmen Street. He took his knapsack from the basket.

With his right hand guiding the handlebars and his left holding the seat, Drake walked the bike nearly to Poydras Street. Then he said, "Fuck this," and dropped it onto the sidewalk. A block away he caught a bus to Canal, and then another on Rampart Street that looped and brought him to Rampart and Esplanade.

He got off and entered the Marigny, checking each block carefully from the corner first, lest he run into Satch. At last Drake reached a small red house and rang the doorbell. No one responded. He rang again, and a third time.

His connection—Drake couldn't tell whether his name was Lennie or Rene, and the guy answered to either—sometimes conducted house calls in the Quarter, usually in the early evening. If he ever came home and found any customers waiting, he cut them off, supposedly.

Drake bought a forty-ounce and cigarettes at Circle K, and then crossed Esplanade toward Dog Park. As he came closer, he saw why Barracks Street didn't look right: The bookstore hadn't closed.

Cautiously Drake peered inside as he passed on his way to the park. The lone man sat calmly behind his counter, while two or three customers scanned the shelves. Drake didn't recall ever seeing the store open this late, though the hour might not be as late as he supposed. He still had the last handful of books in his knapsack, plus the self-help books.

"Nope," he chuckled to himself as he jumped the fence. Trying one last roll could cost him, even if this guy had no other employees on hand to help him hold Drake for the police.

Drake drank his forty in the dark, sitting under the rain shelter in such a way that crusties passing on the street would not necessarily notice someone sitting here. Drake didn't buy cigarettes often, and didn't like to share when he did.

He sipped his beer slowly. His pupils adjusted well enough that he could discern bundles along the park's rear wall, not very far from where he sat. Drunks slept inside those bundles.

A noise drew Drake's attention back the way he had come. Across the street he saw the man hanging the shutters over the bookstore's windows for the night.

Overhead the stars seemed somehow more visible to Drake from here, although the absence of streetlamps in the park could only reduce the glare minimally. His head against the bricks, Drake smoked and stared upward.

When he had less than a quarter of the beer left, Drake heard the gate to the park grind open. He stayed still. In all the times he had slept here, never once had anyone unlocked the gate before morning.

With his ears pricked, he thought he heard a few careful footsteps, though not clearly enough to gauge which direction they headed.

Then a bright light blinded him. "Hey, what's up with this?" Drake said.

The man who held the light stood about five feet from Drake and said, "Stay where you are. Keep your hands where I can see them."

Drake complied. By shielding his eyes with his hands, he could make out enough of this intruder to suspect it was the bookstore owner from across the street.

"Am I not allowed in here now, sir?" Drake asked earnestly.

"No, you aren't," the man said politely. His posture was unmistakable. "But don't worry about that. Just sit still."

Nearby Drake heard a male voice he knew yet couldn't place. Then suddenly a girl emerged from the darkness of the shelter into the beam of light, just long enough to meet Drake's gaze.

Her features possessed a sore puffiness he didn't recall, but Drake knew her from Lumière Books. The tits girl.

When she retreated into the shelter behind him, he heard her say, "Yes, I'm positive." Then she left with someone.

"What the fuck do you want?" Drake asked.

"I want you to get up now," the man brandishing the light told him.

Drake rose to his feet. Before he could break into a run, someone behind him pulled a sack down over his head. He struggled and received a sharp blow in the stomach from a weapon harder than a fist. Then they pulled the bottom of the sack tight, and someone poked him more gently with the cudgel.

"I hate violence. Let's do this the right way, okay?" the man who had held the light pleaded. "Just walk where we bring you. Stay quiet."

They led him out of the park and to the left. Drake realized they intended to take him into the store, but he didn't know how he could stop them.

When they arrived there, the owner said, "Careful, now. Step up." Drake did, and then one of his captors slammed him to the floor.

As he fell, Drake felt the tension in the cloth give. He hit the floor and almost instantly wriggled his way free of the sack. A single light shone, though not as harsh as the one he'd faced in the park.

Drake stood up, and heard that other voice again, the one he couldn't place, saying something that ended with the word *scumbag*. A fist connected with Drake's mouth, and he sprawled on the floor again, toppling a small bookcase beside the counter.

"No, not here," the tall man who owned this store said sharply. "You want to bust him up, you should have caught him up at your place, Jude. I don't need his blood on my stock."

"This little bastard took—!"

"He stole money," the tall man reminded Jude, and then said to Drake, "All right, now, I was saying how we can do this the right way. But we can do it the wrong way instead, if you want. The right way for you to leave New Orleans is on a bus tonight, we'll buy you a ticket out of the money you're about to give us back. The wrong way for you to leave town is in my trunk."

This man spoke so reasonably, with such evident distaste for affect, that Drake couldn't doubt for an instant his sincerity. The punch in the mouth had dazed Drake, and he pulled himself upright enough to count at least half a dozen men in the shop, all avoiding the light, all watching him.

"Your first step toward the bus station is telling us what we want to know," the man said. "Even if you don't think it's the answer we most want to hear, we won't hurt you for being honest with us. And don't try to lie, because I can tell. If I wasn't good at reading people, I wouldn't have known it was you staring at me through my window earlier. You wouldn't be here."

Drake nodded and rose to his feet. They had locked the front door; with all the windows shuttered, no one outside could see what happened in the store.

"Who else did you tell what you learned about Roger?" the man asked.

Drake cleared his throat. "Just my partner."

"Who's your partner?" the man asked.

Jude said, "Bullshit, he doesn't have a partner. Nobody saw anyone else pulling this shit but him."

"You asked who knows," Drake pointed out, tasting blood. "Not who was involved. You want straight answers, I'm trying to give them to you."

Books lay on the floor where he and the bookcase had landed a moment ago. Drake glanced toward the back of the store, saw that it ran further into the building that it appeared to from outside. Most of the bookcases reached just shy of the ceiling.

The man asked, "Did you tell this partner of yours specifically how it works? About the ink, and the pencil?"

Drake continued studying his environment under the ruse of straining his memory. He could see no back door. "No, I don't think so," he said. "It's hard to remember... I'm sure I didn't. I had no reason to."

All at once Drake thrust both his hands forward and sent a bookcase onto the lamp. The bulb met the floor with a pop, and the room went pitch dark. Amidst the swearing Drake heard another bookcase follow. He hoped they stood close enough together to fall like dominoes.

He turned and shoved the bookcase behind him toward the windows. It smashed into one and broke through the middle of the wooden shutter. Light poured in from the streetlamp outside.

Drake kicked more of the glass out of the window, and pushed the bottom fragment of the shutter until it snapped from its mount. Breaking it didn't take much. The wood felt brittle. One corner of it remained fixed to the metal, and the shutter dropped sideways to the concrete.

Immediately Drake threw himself through the gap he had opened. The small glass teeth still protruding from the bottom of the frame gouged his hip as he slid over the wall onto the sidewalk.

Seconds later Drake had bolted up Barracks Street toward the river. A raw sting in his hip slowed him. He checked behind him to ensure that he'd escaped unpursued. He touched his pelvis, and his fingers glistened with blood.

"Shit," he said. A tourist couple watched him curiously. He continued up Barracks to Decatur, where he entered a grocery store.

"Can I help you?" the woman asked.

"I need a ten pack," Drake said, and paid her for a package of crude hypodermic needles.

He took these outside and headed into the Marigny. The pain in his hip forced him to walk sideways, almost limping. Outside Checkpoint's he met Terence, who said, "Man, Lennie got busted, you hear?"

"No, fuck," Drake said. "I went by there before."

"Stay away from there," Terence said. The skin of his face appeared slightly shrunken, which meant he had a buzz. "They nailed him in the Quarter. Probably they're going to watch his house, now. Go talk to the Crack Clown."

"I don't want any fucking crack," Drake complained.

"No, he's got twenties of junk," Terence said. "I split one with, what's her face? Nilda. It's nice."

Drake turned back the way he had come, and turned off Decatur at Dumaine. His hip ached. He had to cross Bourbon in front of the Clover Grill and the gay club across the street. Finally he crossed Dauphine and rang the Crack Clown's bell twice.

For a flash Drake thought he might have to go search for him around Jackson Square, but then the Crack Clown appeared overhead on his terrace, weaving from wall to rail. "Oh, it's you," he mumbled, and came downstairs to admit Drake into the courtyard. They waited there a moment.

"What can I do for you?" the Crack Clown asked.

"I hear you got junk," Drake said.

"Yep," he confirmed. "Do I ever. Been running it for days, you can't even tell."

Actually, this news did not surprise Drake at all. The Crack Clown had a very distorted idea of how clandestine he kept his own drug use. But from the state of his makeup and the shriveled quality of his face, this appeared to be good dope, strong enough to dehydrate people.

"What can you do for three hundred bucks?" Drake asked.

The Crack Clown insisted on seeing the money first, then brought Drake up to the apartment and weighed him out a huge bag.

Drake departed immediately down Dauphine Street until he reached the Algren Theater on Canal. Oddly, he didn't know the ticket taker on duty, so he just paid the admission and went upstairs.

Originally three times its current width, the theater now contained two showing rooms: a claustrophobic, rat-haunted lower one, formerly the mezzanine, and an airy one upstairs with a high domed ceiling, formerly the balcony.

Both these theaters now used video projectors that hung above the middle of the room.

A giant blow job took place on the screen behind him as Drake made his way up the stairs that divided the former balcony. The carpet stuck to the soles of his boots. A few customers stared at him nervously as he passed.

At the top of the stairs, Drake poured a small amount of junk from his bag into the plastic wrap from his cigarettes. Then he crept up into what had once been the projection booth.

"Hey?" he called. "Hey, man?"

Inside he found a bearded fellow he knew by the name John, who sat up on his mattress wearily and said, "No more, man. Ricky came in and found Nilda up here with a trick. No more. You got to go sit in the theater. Sorry."

Drake handed him the cellophane parcel and said, "Come on, man, I can't deal with it down there. Someone'll rip my shit off."

John slipped the bag into his pocket and thought about it. "Well," he said, pointing directly overhead, "if you want, you can use the attic."

Drake had heard employees here discuss the attic, but had never considered how it might be reached. Even after nodding here in the booth for days on end, he hadn't noticed the open trap door in the corner of the ceiling, nor the black metal ladder mounted upon the wall below it.

"Climb the ladder," John said, and handed Drake an empty plastic bottle. "It may shake a little, but you won't fall."

From a filthy sink behind John, Drake poured a few fingers' worth of tap water into his plastic bottle. Then, as smoothly as he could with his hip killing him, he ascended the ladder. It moved, and when he reached the top he saw that someone had fastened it with wire, rather than bolts.

"Use the flashlight," John told him, pointing at one on the edge of the trap door.

Drake hoisted himself up, switched the flashlight on, and found himself surrounded by air ducts.

"John, I can't lay down up here," Drake said.

"Squeeze between the ducts," John said.

"Are there rats up here?"

John said, "No, they stay downstairs where they have something to eat. Just go through where you see the little gap between the ducts. You see?"

Drake found the gap John meant, and pushed through.

When he came out the other side, the expanse of the attic awed him. It ran the length of the building, and seemed to grow bigger the farther it got from where he stood. Playing the light among the rafters, he realized that the floor actually dropped a few feet every four yards or so because of the dome ceiling in the theater underneath it. But this attic was the width of the original theater, including the two sections that had become stores on either side.

Drake stepped carefully down the planks. They felt far more solid beneath his feet than he expected. His flashlight revealed various trash dumped here from the building below: old portable TVs, boxes, a mattress with a huge stain on it.

Soon he reached the back of the building. An air conditioner the size of a garage hummed above him, suspended from the roof, and he saw that the smooth floor beneath it was white due to a thick layer of dust that covered the attic. He trained the light behind him. It revealed the trail of bootprints he had made coming here. Drake wondered whether this dust came from the cinder-block walls around him, or if the massive AC unit's filters collected sloughed skin cells from the entire city.

Beside him he noticed a room, just larger than a closet. Over its doorway workmen ages ago had used a stencil to paint the words CURTAIN DRIVE MOTOR. Drake looked inside. The motor itself sat in one corner and resembled an over-sized sewing machine. Most of the tiny room contained rows of theater seat-backs missing their foldout cushions.

"Fuck this," Drake said out loud. He retraced his path until he reached the stained mattress, which he dragged one-handed to the tiny room. The gash in his side stung.

After standing the flashlight upright on the floor so that it shone upon the ceiling, Drake sat on the mattress and pulled a bent metal spoon from his pocket, the only paraphernalia he carried. In this spoon he diluted some junk with water. He must have used his last cotton ball without realizing it, so instead he tore apart a cigarette and stripped the paper off the filter.

With his belt tightened around his left arm, Drake heated the liquid over the flame of his lighter, and soaked it up with the cigarette filter. Then he stuck a needle into the filter and drew all of the fluid into the syringe.

He pierced the needle into a vein bulging from his left forearm, drew some blood inside the syringe, and then plunged all of it into his vein.

As Drake loosened the belt so the drug could spread through his body, he expected to throw up. Instead, he collapsed backward onto the mattress and his face turned blue. Gradually his body began cooling. The flashlight stood undisturbed, unseen, and over the next hour the bulb slowly dimmed to darkness as it spent the batteries. Shortly after that, the rats came.

Feverish after starving for days, Snack Pak stepped in front of a car on Rampart, hoping to sue or at least spend some free time in the hospital. The car hurled her against a parked truck, shattering her neck. She died before she hit the ground, and the driver accelerated into the Tremé. No one witnessed this collision.

By a coincidence, Orleans Parish prisoners in New Orleans East buried Snack Pak the same day they buried Oogie, who'd impregnated Snack Pak earlier that year. Oogie had managed to get himself shot dead while stealing dirty laundry from a parked car in the Bywater.

Though Snack Pak and Oogie had died days apart, the prisoners laid the two in a tinkers' field on the same Friday, because it had rained for most of that week. The work crew waited for a sunny day to bury them, out of the belief that even an indigent deserves that much.

VERY OLD THINGS

NINE-THIRTY TUESDAY MORNING LAUREN SITS AT THE BACK table of a coffeehouse near her apartment, alone but for a pimply clerk mopping the tiles near the entrance. Cool wind flows in through the French doors beside Lauren's chair. Since arriving home from work last night at midnight, she has nearly finished a true-crime book that Richie gave her the Christmas before he died. Only when insomnia keeps her awake overnight does she ever read enough to satisfy herself.

Outside on Magazine Street, brakes shriek, then die abruptly. Two drivers Lauren can't see have avoided a crash.

The kid near the front drops his mop and runs toward Lauren. She expects him to snatch the phone from beside the register. Instead he charges past the counter, past Lauren, out the back.

A blue sedan smashes through the glass front doors. They shatter and spray the room. Something stings Lauren's cheek; a chunk of glass, but it hasn't cut her. The car demolishes the pastry case, then jams to a halt against the wall.

The scene falls silent, save for stunned cries somewhere outside. The clerk who fled returns and jabbers, "Jesus, are you all right?"

Lauren nods. Without realizing it, she has risen from her seat. Never has she seen so much blood in real life. The car's windshield has burst in upon the driver, whose head lolls dripping onto the steering wheel.

Up close, she sees where his scalp has separated from his skull. Air has turned his forehead into a huge purple bubble.

She tastes blood. The glass nicked her cheek, after all.

"Are you all right?" a man in a blue shirt asks her. He has come in through the French doors beside Lauren's table.

She can barely speak. "Oh," she says. "Yes."

The man in blue reaches in through the driver's window and kills the engine. "He blew the light," the man says, as if she had asked. "There's another car out there. No one's hurt but they're shook up as shit."

Suddenly the driver sits upright inside the sedan and announces in a loud voice, "I need to know what time it is."

The other man checks his watch and says, "It's twenty-five to ten. Can you move?"

"I have to be at the library for Veterans Day, otherwise the crew starts mulching without me," the driver says, waving his bloodsoaked hands. A shiny pink strip between the two lips of his head wound seems to show his skull; Lauren's eyes lock upon it as he speaks.

The other man glances at Lauren, hoping she might decipher the driver's gibberish. "Listen," he tells the driver, in the same tone he would use to placate someone ornery and old, "I don't think you should worry about your library appointment. Just relax, and wait until the ambulance gets here. It'll be here."

The driver shakes his head emphatically. "But...no," he says. "It's, it's just not—"

"Relax," the man says again.

The driver lays his head back against the neck rest, forlorn, eyes aimed at the dashboard. Lauren feels her heart swell as the driver's head ceases all movement. His eyes go glassy.

"You okay?" the man asks the driver again.

The driver makes no reply.

"He's in a coma," the man tells Lauren.

"He's dead," Lauren corrects him.

An ambulance attendant advises Lauren to have a doctor stitch her cheek, but her cut is barely a blemish once she sponges the blood away. Instead she has the attendant apply a butterfly. While the police take Lauren's name and phone number, she can't stop feeling that they've caught her breaking some law she doesn't know about.

Afterward Lauren walks home down Magazine Street. Two men drinking beer on the porch of an abandoned house pause as she passes, which makes her suspect that her cheek has resumed bleeding, yet her finger finds the wound dry.

These men have not merely hushed, they actually glare at her. She smirks. They turn away. Half a block later she spins around and catches them watching her again. This time they keep staring.

As she arrives at her apartment, Lauren sees her reflection in her downstairs neighbor's window. A huge spot of blood has already turned brownish on the bottom of her blue denim jacket. The stuff has gotten on her jeans, too, and her thermal shirt.

Earlier, while talking to the ambulance attendant, she'd noticed red flecks on her shirt that had dripped from her cut. Now the sight of these large stains stops her cold: She leans closer to the window, checking her wounded cheek. It doesn't appear to have reopened.

Her eyes widen. "This," she tells herself, "isn't *my* blood."

Upstairs in her apartment Lauren starts to yank her clothes off before she has even closed the door. She dumps everything from her pockets onto her kitchen table, then chucks her jacket, jeans, and shirt into her hamper. Without thinking about it she takes a shower.

When she towels off she cannot believe it's a quarter past eleven. Her bed feels alien. Sleep still won't come. There's no way the restaurant will let her take tonight off, either.

Her television does not work. "Wait," she says out loud, "where's my book?" The things she brought inside with her—her keys, wallet, change, and sunglasses—lie on the kitchen counter. No book. "Oh, goddamn it!" she swears, realizing where she left it. "I'm not going back there."

But twenty minutes later, she does. The commotion at the coffeehouse has ended. Lauren has to duck under yellow police tape to peek through the French doors at the table where she sat before the crash. Her book's not there.

"I'm, like, twenty-five pages from the end," she tells the clerk, who's nailing plywood over the hole where the front doors were. "I'll go nuts if I don't finish it. I just started it last night, and I haven't slept."

"Wow," he says, nodding.

"You didn't see anyone leave with a paperback book?" she asks him. "I mean, you haven't had any customers since then."

He shakes his head.

"Damn it," she says, to herself.

"Sounds like you had some night," he tells her, and taps the plywood. "Soon as I finish this, you feel like smoking a joint? I got the rest of the day off, obviously."

She laughs. "Sorry," she says. "Thanks, anyway."

"I wasn't, you know, suggesting anything," he assures her.

"Yeah, I know," she says, picturing him as he fled past her in terror. "See you." She leaves.

Her physical signals of tiredness—the small aches in the backs of her knees, the way her eyelashes cling when she blinks—go away as Lauren walks home again. When she reaches her apartment, she drags her bicycle down the steps and rides to the Quarter.

Everything's quiet, especially away from the River. She rides Burgundy all the way to Barracks Street, the last block before the Quarter stops and the Marigny begins, and she turns up Barracks to Dauphine. At that corner stands the best used-book store downtown. Lauren gets off her bike and starts dialing her combination lock before she realizes that the immense forest-green shutters have not come off the windows today.

A sheet of looseleaf taped to the locked door reads: CLOSED FOR REPAIRS. WE'LL BE OPEN TOMORROW. SORRY. Around the corner she sees a man reattaching one of the shutters near the rear of the store.

For a few minutes Lauren watches dogs play in the park across the street from the store. The dogs chase one another across a volleyball field while their owners squat upon the low concrete wall of a onetime wading pool, now filled with earth to serve as a flowerbed.

Oddly, Lauren feels rested, as though she just woke up. She hasn't got enough money to buy her book new on Decatur, and hasn't liked the bookstores up Magazine Street since Richie died. She has no library card. The only other bookstore she knows to have a good secondhand crime section is on City Park Avenue, and she's never traveled there from this far downtown.

A man leaving the park with his retriever passes Lauren, and she asks him, "Excuse me, do you know how I can get to City Park from here? Do I just go up Esplanade?"

The man nods.

"How far?" she asks.

"To the end." He keeps walking, face forward.

Esplanade runs parallel to Barracks, a block away. Lauren gets on Esplanade and takes it into the Tremé. Potholes pock the blacktop. Once she crosses under the highway at Claiborne, the houses become elegant, though on the brink of ruin.

At North Miro, Esplanade forks; to the right it becomes Bayou Road. A statue, three wrought-iron benches, and some shrubbery fill the triangle.

Someone has taped a large sheet of oaktag to the statue's base, and written on it in magic marker: ESTATE SALE, VERY OLD THINGS with an address and an arrow pointing up Bayou Road.

Lauren follows the arrow off Esplanade. She once took this turn before, maybe two years ago, when she and Richie came up here to a reggae club. But in Richie's car she didn't notice that Bayou Road has no asphalt. The worn, flat cobblestones rattle her bike as she rolls over them.

On the block past the reggae club she finds the sale. The house isn't the area's most stately. She chains her bicycle to a porch railing and enters the yard. At a folding card table beneath a lattice pavillion overgrown with brown-gray vines sits an old lady in a black hat, who gives no sign of noticing Lauren. A sad woman in her forties walks past Lauren to leave, empty-handed. One other customer, a college-age guy, digs through a box of paperbacks leaning against the garage.

First Lauren scans a table full of trinkets: tie pins, tie chains, fountain pens, an "I like Ike" button, rings, a carved letter opener. She hesitates to touch anything, for the baubles give her a strong impression of the couple who collected them, no doubt throughout decades together.

Then she sees the mirror, a great mahogany hawk as tall as Lauren herself. It rests on the bottom points of its wings, propped against a birdbath. The polished wood digs into the sod. The pane is rectangular, four feet wide by two feet high with an inch-thick beveled edge. Lauren wants to buy this thing.

The house catches her eye. She turns and takes it in. When the guy by the paperbacks gives up and passes in front of her on his way out, Lauren barely blinks. This house has gables, gorgeous wooden shingles bleached by the sun to the hue of wheat, a recessed upper porch. It seemed so ordinary from the street.

"What's happened to your face, dear?" a girl asks, and Lauren glances around for the source of this voice.

It's the lady. She's not old. "Your cheek," she says.

"I got cut," Lauren answers.

The woman nods sympathetically; Lauren guesses her age at thirty-four. The hat made her look old at first. Or the shadows. Something.

"Actually, I guess I was in an accident this morning," Lauren goes on, "though I didn't get hurt. I was sitting in a coffee shop and a car drove through the front doors and windows."

"Oh, my," says the woman, evaluating Lauren from foot to crown. "That sounds awful. But you weren't hurt?"

Lauren shakes her head. "No," she says. "The driver died, though."

The woman waves at an empty chair beside her. "Have a seat, why don't you?" she says. "Would you like some tea?"

"Sure," Lauren says, and sits there beneath the vine-covered roof. "My name's Lauren, by the way."

"I'm Giselle, how do you do?" the woman says, and shakes Lauren's hand. "Now, you mean hot tea, don't you?"

"Hmm? Oh, yes," Lauren says.

"You're not from the South," Giselle says, smiling. "When you say 'tea,' you mean hot tea. What we call tea, you call ice tea."

"Ice tea'd be fine," Lauren says, smiling back. "Beggars can't be choosers."

"Nonsense," Giselle says, and then calls over her shoulder, into the house, "Whitley?... Whitley?"

"Yes, angel?" comes a man's answer.

"Whit, would you put some tea on to boil? I have a guest," Giselle asks him, and then to Lauren, "What kind do you like?"

"Oh, anything's fine," Lauren says.

"How about Earl Grey? I bet you like Earl Grey."

"Yes, I do," Lauren says. When Giselle leans back to tell Whitley what kind of tea to brew, Lauren can't pry her eyes out of the woman's cleavage.

Giselle lights a cigarette and offers Lauren one. Lauren takes it, though she hasn't smoked since Mardi Gras.

"I love your house," Lauren says.

"Thank you," Giselle says.

"I didn't when I first saw it," Lauren says. "From the street it doesn't look impressive at all."

"No, you're right. Often it doesn't."

"Whose estate is this you're selling?" Lauren asks.

"My aunt's," Giselle replies. "She passed away."

"I'm sorry to hear that," Lauren says, and points over her shoulder. "How much do you want for that mirror?"

"I'm sorry, that's not for sale," Giselle says. "I couldn't sell that."

"It's beautiful," Lauren agrees. "Why did you put it out here, if you don't want to sell it?"

"Well, it's so pretty to look at. Isn't it?"

A trim man about forty comes out from the kitchen with a pot of tea and a cup on a tray. His clothes complement Giselle's, though Lauren can't say exactly how. His beard has been trimmed impeccably. "Hello, I am Whitley," he says to Lauren.

"I'm Lauren," she says. "Thanks for the tea."

"Not at all." He bows his head a little. From his vest pocket hangs a silver watch chain. "Can I get you anything else? Cream?"

"No, thanks," Lauren says. "I drink it black."

"Then I'll have to go back inside," he says with polite regret. "I have a few things I'm working on."

"That's too bad, on such a sunny day."

Whitley says, "Oh, is it?" without checking outside the sun-blind. "Pleasure meeting you," he adds, and goes back inside the house.

"Where are you from, dear, may I ask?" Giselle asks. "You're not from New York."

"No, Chicago, sort of," Lauren says. "How do you know I'm not from New York?"

Giselle rolls her eyes. "You've spoken to me for a whole minute without mentioning anything about Manhattan. That *never* happens with a New Yorker. You can't be from New York in secret."

"That's true," Lauren snickers. "I've noticed that at work."

"So you live here now."

Lauren nods. "Uptown. Right off Magazine Street."

"By yourself?"

Fetid air from some long-sealed cellar creeps across Lauren's shoulders. Giselle blinks, twice.

"No," Lauren lies. "I have a roommate. I thought he would really like that mirror, in fact."

"Oh," Giselle says. "I *am* sorry, dear. I honestly couldn't sell it."

"That's okay." Lauren drags on her cigarette and exhales toward the yard. "So your aunt lived here?"

Giselle's brow knits as though she doesn't understand the question. "Well, at one time, yes," she says. "Whit and I live here now. We've lived here awhile. This *was* my aunt's house, though, once."

Lauren can't think of anything to say. She sips her tea, keeps both hands upon the cup to keep from fidgeting. At last she points over her head at the wooden lattice. "Are all those vines dead?" she asks.

"No," Giselle says. "That's just so they can keep growing upward. Some of them die so the others can use them as food. Vetch, you call that." She tips ashes into a bronze ashtray on the table, and adds, "I think most life needs some sort of vetch to grow on."

The two women share a long stare.

Lauren arrives at work on time, freshly showered and smelling of Giselle's imported Italian soap. In the first half-hour she serves three tables, two of which only order drinks. Everyone else sits out on the balcony tonight, within Angela's station, or stays in the front at the bar.

Bret needs a break, so he puts Lauren behind the bar and leaves. The customers ignore her except to order drinks. Soon she finds herself entranced by a couple in the corner—by the man, more specifically. A serpentine quality in his movement fascinates her. The girl he talks to doesn't matter, could in fact turn into someone else without Lauren's noticing or caring.

A longhaired man leans across the bar and says, "Negra Modelo, please." His nose comes to an impossibly sharp point. The stubby shape of his small white-block teeth, his large eyes, the paintlike texture of his skin all give him an evil puppet look.

Lauren serves him his beer and holds out her hand. The girl beside the puppet hands her a five, a girl with no definite face, who might not even be a girl for all Lauren notices.

Gradually the rest of the front room divides along these lines. In each conversation, one participant glows to Lauren, and the others seem indistinct. The ones who stand out grow in power as she watches. The others nod and laugh, oblivious. All the voices in the room weave into a hum.

As the man in the corner speaks, his mouth becomes physically longer, yet only slightly less narrow. A faint panting becomes audible to Lauren over the fugue of chatter.

The door opens. A guy carrying a bass drum comes up the stairs, followed by a guy with a guitar and a gutterpunk girl carting a microphone stand. They set up in the middle area, where they have lots of room because only one table has anyone sitting at it. The drummer goes back downstairs for more drums, and the people at the table pick up their beers and follow him out. As they pass, Lauren sees a feral leer on one girl's face as she regards the dull, handsome man leaving with her.

From beneath the bar Lauren picks up the phone and dials it. While it rings a balding guy with dreadlocks asks for a Red Stripe and she serves it to him. He never tips.

"Hello?" Giselle says.

"Hi, it's Lauren."

"Oh, hello, dear," Giselle says. "How are you?"

"I'm not sure," Lauren says. "I wanted to tell you, what we did? That's not something I just...do all the time."

Giselle listens.

"I'm not sure why I called you," Lauren says.

"Are you upset at what happened?"

"No, not at all," Lauren says. "It's not, uhm. I'm at work, is the problem."

"They can hear you?"

"Kind of."

"So you're saying today wasn't the first time you've been with a woman," Giselle guesses.

"Right."

"But today seems important, almost as if it *were* the first time," Giselle goes on. "You feel different now."

"Yeah," Lauren says. "You pretty much hit that on the head."

"Dear, the reason you feel different," Giselle tells her, "is that you *are* different now. You've become more in touch with your real self."

"How do you mean?"

Giselle falls silent for a few seconds, working on an answer, and then gives up. Instead she says, "What time do you have to work until?"

"I get off at twelve-thirty tonight, unless we get slammed later."

"Call when you know you're almost ready to leave," Giselle says. "I'll send Whit to get you. You work at Dragon's Den, didn't you tell me?"

"Yeah, he dropped me here earlier," Lauren says. "That's part of it, I think: This place is looking weird tonight."

"It's been weird every night," Giselle tells her. "You're just seeing it that way now."

They hang up. Angela comes in from the balcony with a bar order.

Immediately Lauren sees herself seducing Angela—sees Angela's features contorted, eyes vacant, body surrendered—sees herself snapping Angela's neck.

Unbidden, this fantasy overtakes Lauren so powerfully that Angela must repeat her drink order. Twice.

Bret takes an extraordinarily long break. When he comes back, it's eleven. "I'm sorry," he says.

"That's okay," Lauren assures him. "It's real slow tonight."

"Yeah, you can go, if you want," he says.

"I need the hours."

"I'll punch you out when we close," Bret promises. "Don't worry about it, go home. It ain't going to pick up."

Lauren puts on her jacket. Behind the bar Angela bends over, searching for another pad of guest tickets; Lauren casts a hungry gaze along the girl's flanks.

Outside on Esplanade, Lauren sees a cab dropping a punk tourist couple at Checkpoint Charlie's. She runs across Frenchmen, past the firehouse. One of the punks holds the door open for her. Lauren climbs in and asks the cab driver, "How you doing?"

"Been better," the driver says. He pulls out. "Where we going?"

"Up Esplanade," Lauren tells him.

As he flicks on the meter, he mutters, "Son of a bitch gave me twenty-five cents."

Lauren says, "What?"

"That guy who held the door for you," he says. "Him and his boyfriend run a fourteen-seventy-five fare, they hand me fifteen bucks even. Fucking Germans."

"They don't tip," Lauren explains as the cab crosses Rampart and potholes begin to rock the chassis. "In Germany they figure everything into the bill, so Germans just assume people do it everywhere else."

The driver nods.

"I know it puts you in a funny position," Lauren says. "They stiff me at the restaurant sometimes, and I know it's because they don't know, but I can't tell them. It wouldn't be cool for me to say anything."

They stop for a light at Claiborne. Beneath the elevated highway men lie asleep at the bottom of the concrete pillars. One lifts his head to meet Lauren's gaze with mad, yellowed eyes. Lauren thinks of a herd, how just a few of the animals will stand guard to let the others rest.

"I'd tell them," the driver says. "I go to this guy, 'You want change?' He goes, 'Keep it.' I'm like, fuck you. So I should've told them."

"Yeah, I would, too, because they should know," Lauren agrees, still eyeing the street drunks. "They're going to piss someone off, they won't know why."

The driver yawns. The light turns green and they cross Claiborne. Out her window Lauren can see one vagrant under the highway who continues watching her cab as it speeds off.

"Up ahead," Lauren directs the driver. "Where Esplanade forks? You go right."

Stifling a second yawn, the driver repeats to himself, "Forks... ?"

"It's past where that, like, closed-down bar is," she says.

"Oh, you mean Bayou Road," he realizes.

"Uh-huh, that's it," she says. "Go up Bayou Road."

"Where you going to, Gentilly? Up by the race track?"

"No, just Bayou Road," Lauren says.

"Huh. That's rough, over there," the driver announces, then adds, "Well, not so much over there as down toward the highway."

As they pass the traffic light before Bayou, the cab veers into the right lane. Outside her window Lauren spies the tiny park with the statue where she saw the sign this morning.

"How do you mean, it's rough?" she asks.

"People get killed there," he says. "Back the other way, though, the other side of Galvez, closer to Claiborne. Cops found a body down there last week."

"Really?" Lauren turns in her seat, peers out the rear windshield. "I thought this road just started at Esplanade."

"No, no," he tells her, "it goes back to Claiborne. None of it's paved, it's all these little bricks. Bayou Road is the oldest street in New Orleans. They used to unload ships from the bayou along it. I think it becomes Barracks Street the other side of Claiborne. Or Governor Nicholls, that's what it is."

They pass another block, and then the cab stops at a red light beside a corner cigar shop with a rack full of racing forms in its display window.

"You know what cross street you're looking for?" the driver asks.

Lauren says, "Nope."

"'Cause this is the end of Bayou Road," he tells her. "This is Broad. Across Broad this street becomes Gentilly, like I said."

"No, my friends live on Bayou, I'm sure of it," Lauren says. "I'm sorry, we have to throw a U-turn. I must have missed the house because we were talking."

"Sorry," the driver says, turning back.

"No, that's okay," she says. They return the way they have come, and Lauren pays careful attention to each house they pass. Giselle and Whitley's doesn't appear.

They reach Esplanade. "Are you sure it's on this side?" the driver asks her.

"Yes, I'm sure," she says. "I was there this afternoon. Can you throw another U-turn?"

"No problem." He spins back.

This time she stares hard at each building, straining to remember how far she traveled from Esplanade on her bicycle. The cab passes the reggae club, then houses and more houses, then they reach the cigar store at Broad again.

"You're sure you've been to this place," the cabbie wonders.

"Would you let me just go use that payphone?" Lauren asks. "I'll call my friend and get the address. It must just look different at night, I guess."

The phone booth is in front of a closed seafood store. Lauren dials Giselle's number. Whitley answers. "Hello?"

"Hi, Whit, it's Lauren," she says. "What's your address?"

"Why?"

"I'm trying to take a cab to your house," she says.

"No, I'll come get you," Whitley says. "Where are you?"

Lauren reads the street signs. "Bayou and Broad."

"What are you doing there?"

"I got out of work early, so I took a cab," she says.

"That's not so safe, over there," Whitley advises her. "Have the cab driver stay with you till I get there, if you would? I'll be five minutes, at the longest."

"All right," she says.

Whitley arrives on schedule, driving his Riviera convertible and wearing paint-stained trousers.

To get Lauren's attention he has to rap several times with his fist on the window of the cab. Finally she takes her eyes off the driver, who has fallen asleep.

"Unlock the door," Whitley instructs her, loud yet calm.

For a brief instant, Lauren turns her eyes back upon the driver and ignores Whitley. He pounds the window again, harder. With a clumsy jerk of her arm she unlocks the door.

Whitley climbs in and squeezes the cab driver's wrist for a few seconds. Dazed, Lauren rubs her forehead. Whitley lets go of the driver's forearm and turns off the ignition key. Then he helps Lauren out of the cab, locks the door and slams it. The driver does not stir.

The sharper air outside the car wakes Lauren, yet her head weaves as Whitley leads her to his Riviera. "What happened?" she asks. "Did we have an accident?"

"Of sorts," Whitley replies. "He'll be all right."

"I'm not sure what just happened," Lauren says.

"I can tell you aren't." He holds open the passenger door for her, then climbs in behind the wheel.

"I hope you didn't have to stop painting to come get me," Lauren says as they pull around and head back the way Whitley came.

"I certainly don't mind," he says. "How was work?"

"Not too bad, I guess. Weird, though," she says. "I'm glad I got off early."

"Weird in what way?" Whitley asks.

"I just see things differently," she tells him. "The people at the bar look like crocodiles."

"All of them or some of them?"

"Some of them," Lauren says. "Most of them seem, I don't know. Unimportant. Or at least to me. But some people look almost scary. They have this way they treat other people, the background people."

"It's called feeding," Whitley informs her. "Your perception's improving at a very, very rapid rate."

All at once the house overwhelms Lauren. Nothing else in sight compares with it. It stands taller, more elegant, less marred by age than its younger neighbors, which assume a drab sameness in the night.

In plain sight, Lauren's bicycle leans against the porch railing where she chained it upon arriving at the sale this afternoon. She forgot her bike here because Whitley dropped her off in the Quarter this evening.

"How could I not have seen this?" she wonders out loud as Whitley pulls the Riviera into the carport.

"We didn't know you were coming yet," Whitley points out.

They climb out of the car and enter the house. Inside, Giselle greets them in the drawing room, wearing an antique silk robe.

"Whit's been painting me," she explains. "How are you, dear? You look peaked."

Lauren kisses her. "I'm all right," she says. "I was telling Whit, work was really strange. People looked weird."

"Like animals," Giselle guesses.

She pauses. "Yeah."

"And some other ones look like they're hardly there," Giselle says. "They just block out the scenery behind them."

Lauren doesn't respond.

"And usually there's only one of the animal people in each group, even if there are seven or eight of the boring people," Giselle finishes.

Whitley asks his wife, "Should I change?"

"No, I don't think so," Giselle says. "Lauren, do you want to pose with me?"

"Pose?" Lauren says, still wondering what Giselle knows about her.

"Yes, pose. Take your clothes off and pose," Giselle says, shedding her robe. "It's not like letting someone take your photograph. If the world sees a nude painting of you, for all they know Whit drew someone else's body and stuck your face on it."

Lauren shrugs. "I'm not too bashful lately."

"Then take your clothes off, dear."

Nude, she joins Giselle on a plush velvet loveseat. For a few minutes they tangle and untangle their limbs as Whitley directs them by hand. Then he sits down with a pad and begins to sketch them in pencil.

"I couldn't find the house," Lauren tells Giselle.

"You didn't tell us to expect you," Giselle says.

"But why couldn't I see it?"

Giselle raises her eyebrows at her husband, who responds, "Our house is hidden. We don't like attention that we didn't invite."

"Hidden," Lauren repeats.

"Concealed, if you prefer," he says, precisely erasing part of his sketch. "Obnubilated."

Lauren waits for one of them to expound. Neither does. She asks, "You mean you know how to pick a nondescript house."

Giselle stifles a laugh.

"No," Whitley explains, grinning at Lauren. "We choose a house we want to live in. Then we 'non-describe' it."

Rather than ask how, Lauren lets it go. Giselle rests one hand on Lauren's leg and slides her fingernails along Lauren's thigh. Lauren bites her own lower lip.

Soon Giselle kisses her. Lauren sucks her tongue for a long moment but stops, her breath heaving, to ask, "What happened to my cab driver? Why was he unconscious?"

Puzzled, Giselle says, "What's that, dear?"

"Nothing happened to him," Whitley says. "He fell asleep in the cab, waiting for his dispatcher to send him somewhere."

"Oh, Whit," Giselle says in dismay.

"He's right on Broad," Whitley argues. "I turned off his ignition. There's enough traffic there that no one'll mess with him." He continues drawing, and adds, "He's probably woke up and on his way as we speak."

"I didn't pay him," Lauren says, "I'm pretty sure."

Both her host and hostess turn to stare at her.

"I shouldn't worry too much on that account," Giselle chuckles. "That's fairly minor, as moral lapses go."

Whitley lays his pad and pencil on the floor at his feet so he can gesture freely with both hands. "This is how it is," he begins, and clears his throat. "Right now, you're like a sponge—you just soak it up in large quantities. You're helpless to avoid doing so."

"I soak *what* up?" Lauren asks.

Giselle's breasts rise and sink as she sighs. Then she says, "This is all brand-new to you, isn't it, dear?"

A week after Richie died, the day Lauren moved to her own, smaller apartment, she found two of his dirty T-shirts under the bed she had shared with him. The shirts gave her a reassuring whiff of Richie; she has kept them all this time, without ever washing them. For a while she slept in them. No one knows, because Lauren hasn't made any friends in New Orleans to whom she could confess such a strange act. Her friends in Chicago seem so distant to her these days that she has never discussed Richie's death on the phone with them.

Yet lying on a canopied bed in the warm afterwash of sex she discloses this fact almost blithely to Giselle, who accepts it as normal.

"You had the ability, just in a less developed form. See, what happened to you this morning? With that accident uptown?" Giselle says as she massages Lauren's nape. "That gave you a big taste, and it probably woke up your appetite."

"So you're saying I consumed Richie, too?" Lauren asks.

Lost in a search for the right way to answer, Giselle exhales and runs a hand through her hair. "Look, dear," she says, "it's not always wise to learn more than you want to know. Go a little slower, it will upset you less."

"How do you and Whitley know all this stuff?"

"We just *do*," Giselle says, lighting a cigarette. "And you should, too, by now. I'm not criticizing you, mind, I'm saying it's peculiar that you haven't grasped what's happened to you. It seems as though part of you has, but not the part that looks out of your eyes and speaks through your mouth."

Lauren takes a cigarette from Giselle's pack and lights it.

"It's the same as how I knew you were lying about having a roommate," Giselle says. "At the time it made perfect sense for you to tell me that, so it didn't make me view you as a liar."

"And it's just by chance that I encountered you two today, of all days," Lauren says.

"No, it's not a coincidence," Giselle says. "If not us, you would have encountered someone else. You were just aglow this afternoon. And you followed the sign."

"What?"

Giselle points in the direction of the tiny park where Bayou Road cleaves from Esplanade. "The sign that led you here, about the sale. That's enough of this, don't you think, dear?" Giselle says, and douses the candle on her nightstand with a tiny brass snuffer. "Why don't we sleep a little?"

They try. Giselle dozes off, Lauren cannot.

As they lie together Lauren notices that the bedroom walls shine with a peculiar light; it has a kinetic quality, as though flickering too fast for her to detect.

The door opens, and the weird light disappears. Whitley enters. He has left a candle burning on a pricket in the hall. Whatever it is he wants from Giselle's walk-in closet, he knows how to find it in the dark.

Lauren closes her eyes, and the flickering light returns. She opens them, and it stops.

Now she shuts her eyes again, but picks her head up as if scanning the room. And she *sees*. At the time she noticed the light, she had her eyes closed and didn't realize.

"Lord," Lauren says.

"I'm sorry, did I wake you?" Whitley whispers.

"No," she tells him. "I'm seeing things."

Whitley waves his hand for her to follow him out into the hall. Lauren rises from Giselle's bed, dons her robe and leaves the room. The object Whitley came to fetch from the closet is a brooch.

"I'm sorry to drag you out here. I just hate to wake Giselle," Whitley tells her.

"No, that's cool. I can't sleep."

"You're seeing our shields," Whitley says. "This is a skill you have that's been dormant until now, a talent you developed real, real well at some point you no longer remember. You're right, it's nothing scary."

Outside, not very far away, a rooster crows.

"It's morning already," Lauren groans.

Whitley grins. "Nope. My neighbors keep roosters but don't know enough that the things scream every time any light hits them during the night. You can't really hear it from our bedroom, and I always work all night with music playing."

"May I see your paintings?"

"Now? Surely. Come." Whitley guides her to the staircase, and they climb to the third floor of the house.

His studio has black walls and a skylight, down through which a column of moonbeam shines upon an easel, a stool, and a small table, all three made of the same blond wood, all three spattered with countless drops of paint.

"You know, I just recalled, I put water on the stove for tea," Whitley says. "Will you join me, since you're not sleeping?"

She accepts, and Whit goes downstairs to the kitchen. Lauren approaches his easel. Resting upon the easel's crossbeam is a metal triptych, an antique picture frame that folds open to reveal three separate pictures. In the leftmost panel Giselle stands in the rain on a dirt street, staring upward, and after studying the scene for a moment Lauren realizes Giselle is seeing a bolt of lightning directly overhead.

A coat of flat white covers the middle and right panels. On the center one, which is twice the width of the other two, Whitley has begun Giselle and Lauren from their modeling session a few hours ago. Rather than a painting it more resembles an ink sketch.

Seeing how recent the white paint seems upon the third panel, Lauren realizes that Whitley has painted over other art originally housed in this triptych.

Whitley makes a polite amount of noise mounting the stairs, so his arrival does not startle her. Along with the tea tray that he sets upon the table he has brought a folding chair.

"I really like this," she says, pointing at the image of Giselle in the storm.

"Thank you," Whitley says, and pours her a cup of tea.

While she stirs in a spoonful of sugar, she says, "Your paintings have a strange quality. They almost look black-and-white."

"They *are* black-and-white," he informs her, "only the black part isn't always black. They're all chiaroscuro."

Lauren opens her eyes wider to show she doesn't know this word.

"Painted with one color on a white background," he explains. "I only see two colors, so everything's black-and-white to me. I just choose a color based on how well it handles in the light range I wish to work in. They all have their little quirks and surprises."

"Did Giselle pose for that one?" Lauren asks, pointing at the rain scene again.

Whit shakes his head. "I did that from memory."

"Because I thought you might have done it when they poured the dirt onto the streets in the Quarter for that movie," Lauren said.

Whit shakes his head again.

They sit awhile. Slowly the angle of the moon through the skylight becomes sharper, cutting the moonray smaller.

"You better watch out, painting over someone else's work, " Lauren advises him. "It's bad luck."

Whitley smiles. "There is no 'luck.' Nor 'coincidence,' for that matter." He sips his tea and then adds, "In any case, the most recent paintings on there were all mine. I destroy all my own work every so often."

"Really? How often?"

"Every twenty-five years, say. The only two pieces I hang on to are both of Giselle. I'll show you sometime."

An hour before sunrise Whitley carries outside the mahogany mirror that Lauren admired in the yard earlier today. Lauren kisses Giselle good-bye and follows him out to find that he has dropped the roof on his convertible so he can wedge the mirror upright across the back seat.

"You can just have that mirror," Giselle tells her from the doorway. "That's a gift."

"You don't have to do that," Lauren says.

"Don't be silly," Whitley admonishes her. "You admire this piece; we want you to have it."

"I don't have a place for it, dear," Giselle says as she yawns. "I want you to put it up in your house. Then we can come visit it."

"Well, thank you," Lauren says, and climbs into the passenger seat.

Whitley gets behind the wheel and pulls out. The night is crisp, if a little damp. As they take Broad across town Lauren watches the sidewalk, sees a few men stagger between shadows or stir in doorways. A few more curse traffic from the corners.

No one returns her gaze.

"They can't see us," she remarks to Whitley. "Can they?"

He shakes his head. "We don't need people looking at us when we've got the top down and this thing in the back."

Broad turns into Napoleon. No one walks the street for blocks and blocks. Finally Whitley turns down Magazine. The decrepit buildings flying past on either side shine at Lauren with the unnatural glow of a photograph printed in negative.

"Things seem unearthly to me," she says.

"If we're on earth, what you see must be earthly."

When they reach Lauren's building he hoists the mirror against his diaphragm and marches it up the stairs behind her. It must weigh a ton, she figures, yet carrying it does not tax Whitley's strength enough to keep him from greeting her neighbor's cat.

She leads him into her bedroom. It takes him only a few taps of his fingertips to locate a beam inside her wall. From his pocket he pulls a mallet and a tiny hasp, which he mounts against the beam. Within a minute he has hung the mirror so Lauren can watch herself from her bed.

"I'm sorry the place is such a wreck," Lauren tells him.

"I haven't noticed," Whitley says.

"I want to have you guys over," she says, "some night real soon."

"I look forward to it. I know Giselle does, too," Whitley says. "But I really must go."

She kisses him good night, then watches out her window as he speeds away in his convertible. The sun's almost up. Lauren wants to sleep. First she needs to brush her teeth.

The bathroom stinks. She flicks on the light, half-expecting to see the toilet backed up. Nothing's out of place, so she opens the window and airs the room. The odor dissipates. Lauren brushes her teeth and goes to bed.

She cannot sleep.

The phone rings at two-thirty that afternoon. It's Giselle.

"Found out what your problem is, dear," she says.

"What do you mean?" Lauren asks. Staying awake so long has given her the jitters.

"Do you take the news?"

"Take the news how?" Lauren asks.

"The paper. We say 'take the news' down here," Giselle clarifies. "Do you have the paper delivered?"

"No."

"Maybe you need to go get yourself one," Giselle tells her. "Your accident's on the front page."

"You mean the taxi driver from last night," Lauren ventures.

"No, the accident at the coffeehouse," Giselle says. "It was on Magazine Street, wasn't it? Near where you live."

"Yeah," Lauren says. "Wow, I can't believe that was yesterday. It feels like weeks ago."

"That car sure creamed the coffeehouse," Giselle says. "They've got a picture of all this cake and whatnot on the walls. You're lucky you didn't get hurt."

As she listens, Lauren pictures the blue sedan plowing through the pastry case, can smell the faint bouquet of the varnished oak as it snaps and splinters. Most of all she recalls the rush.

"And here they've got another photograph, of the fellow who was driving," Giselle goes on. "His name's Jethro, can you believe it? Jethro Liams. They said they didn't expect poor Jethro to live the night."

"He's *alive*?"

"Uh-huh. And he's still alive now," Giselle says. "I just heard it on the radio a little while ago, over breakfast."

"I haven't slept."

"No, I guess you haven't," Giselle says. "They talked to this doctor at Charity, and he says it's a miracle. This fellow should have died before he reached the emergency room. His family made them disconnect the life support and everything. He won't die."

"That's, uhm," Lauren begins, and then wonders what she wants to say. Giselle waits patiently, and does not speak again until after Lauren has heaved a frustrated sigh.

"You watch television, dear?" Giselle asks.

"Not really," Lauren answers.

"You must have seen some of those nature programs, though," Giselle says. "One of those shows where they've got, let's say, an elk and something's happened to it, so it's wandering along dying and looking all sad. I just hate to see that. You know, I've always wondered about people who could just document a creature's suffering that way."

"I," Lauren sputters, "I, I don't see—"

"It's very simple, dear," Giselle says. "And I *like* elk, mind. They're such beautiful animals, they don't deserve the indignity of dying from mange. It takes forever, and they're so unhappy the whole time."

Lauren clears her throat.

"See," Giselle explains, "that's why there are wolves."

Giselle exhales audibly. Lauren realizes that Giselle must have lit a cigarette. She pictures Giselle smoking, dressed in a dark violet slip, holding the phone elegantly.

"Giselle," she says, "are you wearing...the things I see you wearing?"

"I'm not wearing anything," Giselle replies, "just a slip."

"Is it purple?"

"Yes," Giselle says.

"Why do I know that?"

Now Giselle speaks slowly, as though warily. What she says she clearly considers obvious. "Because," she says, "you can see me."

It occurs to Lauren that not even frank and direct answers to her questions will satisfy them. For a very long thirty seconds she and Giselle stay silent. At last Lauren breaks the spell and says, "The news says they've put him in Charity?"

"Yes, dear," Giselle says. "In whatever part of the hospital they put you in when ICU gives up on you. His name's Jethro Liams. I'd offer to have Whit give you a ride, but it's not something we can help you with."

"I understand," Lauren says.

"I'll tell you this, though: You want to stay focused. Every step you take, remember what you're doing. That'll make things a lot easier."

"Thanks," Lauren says.

"Call me. Let us know you're all right, dear."

Lauren promises she will, and hangs up. As she searches her bedroom for a change of clothes, she spies her own reflection in her new mirror and stops to stare at the mirror itself. A tiny strip of sunlight that slips beneath her drawn shade reflects across the mahogany with a reddish glint.

Finally Lauren puts on jeans and a plain green shirt. On her way down her front steps to the sidewalk she pauses to run her tongue along her teeth. They feel filthy, covered in plaque. She turns around and goes back inside.

When she enters her bathroom, the odor engulfs her much the way a roomful of smoke would. Her eyelids flutter involuntarily. The very air sways, as if with humidity, but the pressure here has nothing to do with moisture or heat.

On the ceiling above her head is the climate-control vent. To unscrew the grate she needs one of her kitchen chairs to stand on, and then she has to reach into the duct to discover what died there.

Lauren reminds herself that Giselle advised her to stay focused, so she takes her toothbrush into the kitchen and brushes her teeth there, leaving the bathroom door closed.

A lady at the information desk whose nametag reads POLLY tells Lauren that Jethro Liams cannot receive visitors other than immediate family. This lady rereads the computer screen through her pearl-rim glasses to make certain.

"I'm just a close friend," Lauren says.

"I'm sorry," Polly says.

"Can I send flowers or something to him?" Lauren asks. "Just something so that his family can see I cared? I don't want to call them right away, you know, this is very hard for them. And I don't want to wait for the funeral."

"Yes, honey," Polly says. "His family's been in to see him. You could send flowers. They don't expect he'll wake up, though."

"So what room do I send them to?"

Polly tells her a room number on the sixth floor. Lauren thanks Polly and walks around the corner to the elevators. No one stops her to ask for a visitor's pass.

The elevator is enormous and crowded, its walls all bright steel, and it travels very slowly. Among the passengers, two stand out: a lizardly man and a stern, owlish woman. The rest are fodder. The lizard smiles at her. None of the three women with him notices.

At the sixth floor, Lauren steps off and follows the signs. Although she has never encountered one in a hospital before, for some reason Lauren expects a guard posted at the door to Jethro Liams's room, or at least a lock. When she arrives, she instead finds the door propped open by a wastebasket.

Two comatose men share the room. A curtain on a rolling frame separates them. Lauren immediately knows which patient drove the sedan, only because the other is a black man in his sixties.

Bandages cover the driver's face, including his right eye. A catheter tube runs inside his gown to his groin.

On the nightstand beside him lies the true-crime book Richie gave Lauren the Christmas before he died. She picks it up. Dark brown spots speckle the volume's topside.

On the bed, Jethro Liams dies.

His final breaths make Lauren convulse with pleasure. It pours through her, pounds at her temples.

A nurse squawks in the doorway, her voice too frantic for Lauren to understand a word of it. Book in hand, Lauren saunters out of the room as the nurse charges in.

Outside in the hall, odd scenes and noises amuse Lauren on either side as she walks: A frail patient stares at his hungry beneficiaries, an elderly man cries out for a lover dead forty years. When she waits for the elevator, Lauren closes her eyes and sees the paperback book in her hands, sees it on the table in the coffeehouse where she left it yesterday, sees a cop pick it up while collecting the boy's belongings and an admissions clerk hand it to the boy's father, who then leaves it at his son's bedside.

The elevator comes. This time it's empty but for a married couple in their middle twenties. They have a baby.

Lauren leans into the back corner. As the elevator creeps down toward the ground, she pictures herself throwing the emergency switch to lock the elevator between floors, sees herself strangling the husband quickly and then sinking her teeth through the soft upper part of the baby's skull to rip out its brain, saving the horrified mother for last. Lauren sees a maintenance worker finally open the emergency trap door in the ceiling to find the elevator a gleaming abattoir with Lauren reclined on its floor in hysterics, blood blackening her teeth and making her flesh gray-white by contrast.

Her teeth feel dirty again. Lauren opens her eyes.

She finds the married couple studying her coldly. They look away. Lauren snickers out loud at them, and exits the elevator behind them, enjoying their nervous briskness.

Outside Charity, Lauren catches a cab that has just dropped someone off. The driver nods when she tells him her address.

Ten minutes later, near Magazine Street, she turns off his ignition just as she saw Whitley do last night, though she doubts this driver will wake up. She locks him in his cab and walks half a block to her apartment.

As soon as she walks in the door she dials her phone. "Hello?" Giselle answers.

"It's me," Lauren says. "Everything's cool."

"Really?" Giselle says. "I'm pleased."

"I understand, now."

"I'll bet you do," Giselle says, and laughs.

"I need to sleep," Lauren says.

"Yes, you go to sleep, dear," Giselle tells her. "Call us when you wake up, we'll talk to you then."

They hang up. Lauren walks toward her bed but notices once again the grit coating her teeth. She wants them clean.

The bathroom reeks. The air pulsates in waves. Either her sense of smell has become much, much more acute or the stench has grown so dense as to actually alter the atmosphere in this confined space.

It's not coming from the vent.

Lauren opens the lid to her hamper and yanks out the clothes she threw there when she arrived home after the accident, her jeans and thermal shirt and denim jacket, all wet with Jethro Liams's blood.

She kneels and holds the jacket to her face, keeps it there a long time, waiting for the odor to overpower her.

It doesn't.

EXODUS

THEY ARRIVED IN NEW ORLEANS A FULL DAY BEFORE the first news reports about the bodies police had discovered inside the Kenmore, Arkansas, home of Doctor and Missus Chad P. Fuller, apparently murdered by school friends of their sixteen-year-old daughter, Jerrianne—the only one, of five Fuller children and both parents, now believed alive.

So when Doctor Fuller's sensible Dodge Prospector entered Orleans Parish, no policeman had any reason to stop it. Its driver stayed well within the law. If anything, he annoyed fellow motorists by obeying posted speed limits.

Aside from the driver, Joel, the van carried six other oddly serene teenagers. In the passenger seat sat Isaiah; the first of two parallel benches seated Jonah, Micah, and Zephariah; the second, Ruth and Esther, whose name had been Jerrianne until Isaiah christened her. Of those present, only Joel still bore the name given him by his parents.

New Orleans traffic baffled Joel. Isaiah had mistakenly delivered them unto the wrong exit. As Joel drove south on Carrollton Avenue past restaurants and supermarkets, Isaiah traced a path to the French Quarter on the street map he had taken from a rest stop.

"Have we passed a Tulane Avenue?" Isaiah asked, adjusting his glasses. "Or an Edinburgh?"

"Yea, Edinburgh," Joel said, "near where we first got on this."

"All right, then we're heading towards the river," Isaiah said, checking a street sign as they passed it. "We're crossing Claiborne."

A great clang sounded several times, causing Joel to flinch. Alongside the opposite lane of Carrollton, across the wide traffic island, a streetcar rang its bell to chase a station wagon off the tracks.

"Is that a train?" Micah asked.

"No," Isaiah said, "a trolley car."

The sight so fascinated them that Joel failed to see where the street narrowed to a single lane, and had to brake hard to avoid rear-ending a taxi that merged ahead of him.

"Watch the road," Isaiah said.

"I *know*," Joel snapped, then, to cover his temper, said, "Tell me how to get to the French Quarter."

"No," Isaiah said. "We need to hang back first, someplace not too far from this trolley line. The trolley goes to the French Quarter."

"Let's just drive there," Jonah said from behind them. "Just drive through it and see it if it's like we think."

Isaiah shook his head.

"Why not?" Jonah asked.

"We don't want anyone noticing this van," Isaiah said. "For any reason. The less it's on the road, the better. The fact that the license plates say Arkansas will make it stand out in people's mind."

"But...we just drove across state lines in it."

"Yea, but soon cops will start looking for us," Isaiah predicted. "Every Prospector this color, they're going to check the plates on. In every town for, like, ten states around. We want this thing painted a different color by then."

"Spray paint will make us look like hippies," Jonah said. "Phishheads spray-paint their vans. We'll get pulled over."

"I think you're right," Joel said.

From the back seat, Ruth asked, "Isaiah, can we drive through Wendy's? I'm really hungry."

Isaiah swiveled in his seat to address her. "All right," he said, and moved his gaze onto Esther, who did not react. Esther stared at the floor of the van and picked her scalp.

"She should eat, too," Ruth said. "We have to eat regular. I mean, it's important now."

As if to agree, Isaiah turned in his seat to face front.

Before they reached a Wendy's, South Carrollton Avenue ended. "I guess I should just turn onto Saint Charles," Joel said, reading the name from a street sign as he slowed the van.

"No," Isaiah said quietly.

Joel glanced over at him, and then straight ahead, to see what Isaiah was staring at: a green hill.

"Go there," Isaiah told him.

They had to make a sharp left onto a street so tight that Joel at first didn't think it was two-way, then cross over railroad tracks onto a parallel dirt road that began at this junction and ran to their right, separating the incline from the tracks, for at least as far as Joel or Isaiah could see. The hill itself more resembled a massive earthen wall.

All of the half-dozen cars and trucks parked on the dirt road were here, near the crossing. Joel parked in the first gap long enough that it didn't require him to back in.

All seven piled out. While everyone else stretched beside the van, Isaiah and Jonah jumped across the drainage ditch and climbed to the hill's summit, where they met a woman walking three dogs.

"What is this hill called?" Isaiah asked the woman.

"This is the levee," she said. "That's the Mississippi River."

On the hill's other side, poured concrete reinforced the slope. Between the levee and the river lay a strip of woods. Behind the trees loomed old steel barges; from atop the levee neither Jonah nor Isaiah could make out any pier through the thicket, but they could see a wooden building with a parking lot connected to the dirt road.

"Is that a shipyard?" Isaiah asked the woman.

"I don't know, I suppose so," she said. "I don't know if it's in business anymore."

"I'm just wondering if they own all that property," Isaiah explained, pointing at the trees. "I don't want to walk down there if I'm trespassing."

"Oh no, I walk my dogs all over those woods in the winter, when the weather's drier," the woman said. "No one says anything. There's nothing down there but some garbage from the river."

"Must be full of ticks now, I'd think," Jonah said.

"Not especially," the woman said. "It's just hard to move in when it's more grown like this. And I'm very susceptible to poison oak."

The lady left with her dogs, each of whom gave Jonah and especially Isaiah a cold, loveless stare.

They two sat upon the peak of the levee. Soon the others except Esther climbed the hill to join them.

"We didn't get any food," Ruth reminded Isaiah.

Isaiah said, "Joel can take you now. You and Esther both."

"Let me just stretch my legs, all right?" Joel said to her. "Just give it a couple minutes. I'll take you wherever you want."

Isaiah opened his wallet and counted out fourteen dollars. As he handed it to Ruth he said, "Spend my share on yourself. If you want a shake instead of a coke, or whatever. I'll fast tonight."

"Thank you," she said.

"I know we passed a Wendy's back near the highway," Isaiah said, nodding up Carrollton the way they had come. "Joel, why don't you take them both now, and bring the rest of the food back?"

"I really need to rest for a few minutes," Joel said.

Isaiah had already shifted his attention to the driveway that ran up and over the levee, connecting the shipyard's fenced parking lot to the dirt road. Absently he told Joel, "Ruth will lie with you tonight."

"Come on," Joel said to Ruth and started downhill.

"Be careful," Isaiah warned him.

At the foot of the levee Joel and Ruth coaxed Esther into the van with them. The van pulled out and drove away from the crossing for nearly a quarter-mile, to where the road widened enough that Joel could manage a three-point turn.

Back at the summit, the others paid no attention to them, for Isaiah had begun outlining their strategy.

And night came, and cold rain, and a wind that caused trees great in age to sway and creak. And they seven sat in the van, its windows fogged from their breath. And this night dismayed Joel, for it gave him no privacy to know Ruth.

Alongside the van, runoff from the road and the hill filled the drainage ditch. More cars came to park on the dirt road. Right across the railroad tracks stood a Thai restaurant and several bars.

Each hour, on the hour, they listened to the news station on the radio, and heard no mention of Kenmore, Arkansas. When each update ended, Isaiah switched the radio off. The cassette player did not work.

After the ten o'clock news Ruth asked, "Why are we just sitting here?"

"We're waiting for a train," Isaiah said.

"But why?" she said. "You don't even know if a train's coming. I'm uncomfortable in here."

"None of us is comfortable," Isaiah said. "If—"

"This makes no fucking sense at all," Ruth interrupted him.

"Listen to me," Isaiah huffed.

She did. But before he could utter a word, he caught sight out the rear windows of a train's headlight in the distance. "Here it comes," he announced. "Micah, you watch the road."

The train halted a quarter-mile from them. It stayed there several minutes, but no one questioned Isaiah now. At last the engine resumed moving, moderately, and passed them. It pulled a very long freight train.

"Start it," Isaiah said to Joel, who turned the ignition.

With his headlights off Joel mounted the levee and at its peak plowed down the tiny chain guide that bordered the driveway; for a moment the van's bumper got stuck on one of the two-foot metal poles that had supported the chain. The rear wheels screeched as they dug ruts.

"Can't we *try* to get a motel room?" Ruth asked. "Just one of us go in and try. Then the others can sneak in after, if it works."

"No," Isaiah answered calmly. To Joel he said, "Back up a little."

"I *know* back up a little," Joel snapped.

"Police," Micah said.

Everyone paused to stare downhill. On the other side of the train, a white squadcar passed without slowing.

"They don't see us," Micah said.

Joel got the van off the drive onto the grass and drove for several dozen yards before he braked. "They can see us real easy up here," he said.

"Yea, get down on that cement part," said Isaiah.

"No way," Joel said, studying the slope outside his window. "It's too steep."

"No, it's not."

"The truck'll flip." Joel flashed his lights on the levee ahead of them. "See? There are wheel ruts up here. You have to drive on top of the levee, if you're up here at all."

"Joel, it's not even a forty-degree angle," Isaiah said. "We won't flip."

In the back Ruth said, "You've got to be kidding. We'll die." A moment later she said, "Is that water down there?"

"The river is on the other side of those woods," Isaiah told her.

"No, I mean at the bottom of this hill, here," she said. "Look. Isn't that, like, a pond up ahead?"

It was.

"If we don't crash going down, we'll get stuck," she said. "For this, we had to wait for that train?"

"*Yes*, we had to wait for that train," Isaiah said in a louder voice. "If cops see us up here, that freight train's a natural barrier between them and us." He pointed down the hill. "See? The train's even stopped again. If those cops before had seen us up here, we would've just backed down onto the dirt road and booked. They'd still be waiting."

"They'd be waiting at whatever's the next place that road crosses the tracks," Ruth said. "They live here, you're not going to fool them."

"This would give us a chance to take off," Jonah said to her. "Any precaution to keep us away from the cops, I say we do."

"We can't take a motel room, Ruth," Isaiah said. "I'm sorry. We just can't. Going anywhere near a motel will get us locked up."

Joel resumed driving. The levee took them past a tall electrical tower. Three pairs of white beacons flashed up the tower's side every two seconds or so, the lowest lamps first and then the middle and then the top ones. An identical tower stood not very far down the levee, and though the storm muted its safety lights at this distance, still they could see that the two structures flashed in rhythm.

Behind the tower, the woods had given way to a beach littered with flotsam. The river threw waves against the sand.

A little farther up the levee they reached a pier connected to a set of buildings, which Zephariah insisted was a power plant; he offered opinions rarely, so the rest tended to take his word whenever he did. Back in Kenmore, Isaiah had declared that Zephariah possessed the gift of divination.

"I'm going to back up and drive onto that beach," Joel said.

"You can still drive farther," Isaiah said. "You just cross over the front of that dock."

"Yea, but let's check this out." Joel reversed smoothly and drove down onto the sand, saying, "This way we can go near those woods you wanted to hide in."

And they did. The trees and brush grew right to the edge of the sand, too dense to admit the truck. Again Joel flashed his headlights, the high beams this time. The light did not penetrate far into the thicket.

"Come on," Isaiah said to the trio on the bench seat behind him, and opened his door. He hopped out onto the sand.

"It's raining," Jonah protested.

Isaiah pulled up the button on the side door, then slid it open for them. Drops speckled the lenses of his glasses as he spoke. "Yes, it's raining. We need to *use* that. Rain keeps people indoors, away from places like this. When the rain stops, police are more likely to get out of their cars and investigate. We have to be hidden by the time the rain stops. Come on out and get wet."

Neither Micah nor Zephariah ever questioned Isaiah. Zephariah, in fact, spoke so seldom that Isaiah himself sometimes slipped and called him Robert.

They three clambered out, leaving Joel and the women inside the van. The tufts of wisteria that hung from the trees came away easily by the fistload, though the dirt caked upon the vines smudged their hands. They cleared a lane between the trees wide enough for the van to enter. Then Isaiah had them haul washed-up boards off the beach to act as pavement. Zephariah found a cache of warped plywood further inside the forest, with which they covered almost the entire route.

"Bring it in," Isaiah called to Joel, waving the truck inside this makeshift garage.

As he drove down a slight decline, Joel admitted out loud that the wooden path helped, especially since it meant he could definitely back out when the time came.

Zephariah and Micah gathered more vines from the trees along with dead branches and some dumped trash, and they piled all of it as camouflage across the entrance to the passage they had just forged. Then out on the beach they followed the treadmarks left by the van's tires, and with their boots carefully filled the fresh ruts with sand every inch of the way back to where Joel had driven off the levee onto the beach. Before they finished the rain had already beaten the sand smooth where they'd begun.

Meanwhile Isaiah, Joel, and Jonah searched the woods nearby.

When they returned they brought a wrecked beach umbrella, a plastic rain cover for a chaise lounge, some garbage bags, and two more slabs of plywood in even worse shape than what Zephariah had found. Balanced against tree limbs and the umbrella pole, this junk formed an awning over the van's side door.

Then they searched for dry wood. The girls waited in quiet, Ruth nervously clearing the ground for a fire and Esther catatonic, until the party returned carrying a large wooden porch chair.

"Did that come from someone's yard?" Ruth asked.

"No," Joel said. "It's broken in the back. Some guy must have set it up out here so he could fish comfortably."

"You can't even see the river from there, though," Micah said. "It was behind those barges. You can't see anything. Plus, he had it up too high to fish."

"The boats make it so there's less wind here," Joel said. Though no one else had noticed it, he was right: Together, the barges and the levee protected this grove by making it a valley. Very little breeze affected their infant fire.

Isaiah had Micah and Zephariah flip the chair onto its back so that the bottom faced them under their new awning. Joel siphoned a cup of gas from the Prospector, and they splashed it onto the dry wood of the chair's underside.

They had collected also some almost dry boards and sticks, and once the fire had fully ignited Isaiah pushed the chair upright and had them heap this other fuel upon the seat, so that as the flames consumed the chair the heat primed the other wood.

By the time it grew hot enough, none of the men felt like hanging his clothes over the flames to dry. At first the work of building the fire, and later the satisfying crackle as it ate each new block they fed it, kept their minds off the soggy fabric upon their flesh. They all seven felt the fire's warmth, even Esther inside the van, so that they did not notice when the rain stopped. And by sunrise they all had fallen asleep in the van, except Isaiah, who stayed awake to tend the fire and to pray.

Morning came, and they slept until eight sharp, when Isaiah woke them by tuning in the news on the radio. Joel saw that Isaiah had removed the Arkansas license plate from the van and now held it under his arm.

"If we drive without any plate at all," Joel said, "they pull us over, no doubt about it."

Isaiah nodded to placate Joel, but his attention never wavered from the newscast. When the update concluded, it had not mentioned Kenmore, Arkansas, and all seven of the Remnant had fully awakened. Even Esther stretched and yawned, the first subtle signs of returning to her former playfulness.

"We can't drive without the plate, Isaiah," Joel said. "I won't."

"You won't have to," Isaiah promised him. "Driving a Dodge van with Arkansas plates is just as likely to get you pulled over today, Joel, especially with teenagers in it. Any hour now the bulletin goes out. The whole country's going to hear it."

"So how are we going to get food?" Joel asked. "It was a hike to Wendy's, I ain't walking it."

"Don't get Wendy's," Ruth said. "We had Wendy's yesterday."

"You can get food right where we came up the levee," Isaiah assured him while climbing back outside to sit under the awning. "Right across the tracks."

For some time they all sat there together, staring out the windows and the open door at their surroundings.

"We need to keep the truck off the road awhile," Isaiah said. "We should paint it while it's hidden here, just so if some cop does find it, they don't know it's us."

Jonah got out and stretched. "It's warm," he said, and turned his back to relieve himself onto a patch of brambles as he spoke. "Listen, I thought about this. What we need to do is switch license plates on a bunch of cars, and put one of them on the van. If we do enough of them, the cops'll already know this is a local thing that's going on here, and if they pull us over, they'll believe this is just Joel's old man's van, because they'll have heard this is going on. They'll be like, 'What's your father's license plate supposed to be?' and he'll go, 'How should I know?' They might let him go."

"Okay," Isaiah said, with the calm he displayed whenever he stayed awake and fasted to build his power. "Where can we switch all these plates without having anyone see us?"

"The train tracks," Joel said.

"Yea, where we parked yesterday," Jonah said. He zipped up and sat in the van's open side doorway.

"We just wait till the freight train comes," Joel said.

Jonah said, "I can't believe it's so warm without being sunny." He leaned forward to peer outside the awning at the haze overhead.

"Don't piss so close to camp," Isaiah said to Jonah.

They all rose and left the van. The dense plantlife made the glen muggy, much more humid than the air that greeted them outside on the beach. They found the open shore empty. Still, they each used the flora to hide behind while draining their bladders. Someone had painted a huge vampire face in black and white on the cement slope of the levee.

As soon as she had pissed, Esther returned to the van. The rest climbed the levee by the electrical tower. The tower and its twin connected via cable to an identical pair across the river, which the storm had rendered less visible last night.

After a short while they decided to visit the French Quarter. Isaiah told Zephariah to stay with Esther. "Don't let her out of your sight," Isaiah warned, very gently because Zephariah never disobeyed him.

Without a word Zephariah reentered the woods. The rest walked the levee toward Carrollton Avenue. When they reached the shipyard's driveway, they tried in vain to fix the chain guide Joel had driven over last night.

"Here's the thing," Isaiah said, causing them all to look at him. "Whoever's coming to the French Quarter has to give up a meal. My map says the streetcar costs a dollar each way."

"How about if I just cut my next two meals in half?" Jonah said.

"Cool," Isaiah said.

"I can't not eat," Ruth said.

"You're coming, anyway," Isaiah told her. "You don't count."

Joel asked, "Why doesn't she count?"

"She has to eat, *and* she has to see if she can get a job," Isaiah explained. "I'm not eating."

"I'll stay," Micah said.

"All right," Isaiah said. "If you're going to stay here, you have to stay inside the woods. Don't let anyone see you, especially from the shipyard. No one should notice us suddenly hanging out on the levee."

"Then where do we go?" Joel said. "I'm not sitting in that truck all day."

"Of course not. You just have to stay inside the woods," Isaiah said. "Or go walk somewhere else. There's a park on Saint Charles."

"Where is that?" Micah said.

"Come with us, we'll get the streetcar and you can walk to the park," Isaiah said. "Come on."

They five walked down to the street. As they passed the Thai restaurant, the smell of food awoke their stomachs. "Give us the two dollars we're not spending," Joel said.

Never one to surrender money, Isaiah led them to a cafe at the corner of Saint Charles and Carrollton. Inside, the pastries smelled so good that Isaiah nearly broke his fast and bought one for himself along with the others. He resisted.

With their food in a paper sack, Joel and Micah left Jonah, Ruth, and Isaiah at the trolley stop. A streetcar came around the turn from Carrollton. The driver held his hand up to Jonah and Ruth, and said, "No food."

"Even if they don't eat it on the streetcar?" Isaiah asked.

"No food," the driver repeated, and closed the doors. As the streetcar pulled away, Jonah and Ruth sat on the concrete to eat.

Presently there came another trolley, which they boarded.

❋ ❋ ❋

The French Quarter did not fulfill whatever expectations the Remnant had formed in Kenmore, Arkansas. Visible residents bore no relation to characters they had seen in movies. Instead, tourist families milled along every sidewalk and alley.

At Jackson Square Jonah and Ruth spoke to some street kids, while Isaiah quietly observed. Forgoing sleep and food always made Isaiah reticent to speak around anyone he didn't know.

"The easiest place is the Pink Flower," a dirty girl in a Butthole Surfers shirt told them. As she gave Ruth directions, a drop of blood formed upon the silver hoop the girl wore in her nostril.

"Your nose is bleeding," Jonah told the girl.

"I *know*," she said, annoyed.

They went where the girl had directed them. Isaiah and Jonah waited down the block while Ruth entered the club and asked for work. An oily man who called himself Paulie said he couldn't hire her without legal proof of age, and shortly after that slipped her a pager number for someone who could sell her a forged driver's license.

Jonah and Ruth quickly decided the trip hadn't been worth the expenditure. Pensively, Isaiah followed them back to the streetcar stop. While they waited for a trolley, Ruth spotted a Dunkin' Donuts down the block, but she and Jonah both knew better than to press Isaiah for money.

During the ride back uptown, they all three began to itch.

Half entranced, Isaiah scratched himself the least. Ruth just rubbed her forearm through the sleeve of her denim jacket. Jonah found himself clawing at his own nape.

"What's wrong with my neck?" Jonah finally asked Ruth, and leaned forward to show her the back of his head.

"It's red, from you scratching it," she said.

They rode a while more before Jonah leaned forward again and said, "There's really nothing there? It feels like there's little bumps or a scab."

This time she touched his neck and said, "Yea, there are little bumps. And it's kind of pink, but I think that's from scratching it."

"How about my forehead?" Isaiah asked calmly, brushing back his bangs.

Ruth and Jonah both looked.

"Oh, shit," Jonah swore. "Poison fucking ivy."

At that, Ruth rolled up her sleeve and found an irritated pink ridge parallel to the bend of her elbow. "We got to get calamine lotion," she said. "Is there a store up near where we parked?"

"That's where we got poison ivy," Jonah said, disgusted, "walking around in the woods last night. Probably we all got it, except Esther."

In response, Isaiah shrugged and let his eyelids droop. Physical discomfort meant little to him now, when each minute he spent awake and unfed deepened the reservoir within him.

Having Isaiah virtually unconscious freed Jonah to show anger, though experience had taught him not to complain out loud; they could never know for sure that Isaiah was not listening.

"That was a drug store," Ruth said to Jonah. "Back there, with the purple sign."

"Wait till we get closer," Jonah said. "There has to be another drug store."

They waited. Within ten stops another one with the purple sign turned up on a corner. Ruth and Jonah stood, and shook Isaiah to get his attention. "Come on, we have to get calamine lotion," Ruth told him.

They got off and the streetcar pulled away. Traffic had picked up, so they had to wait for the light to change. Jonah pulled from his pocket a Swiss Army knife, and opened the smaller of the main blades. "Use that one," he told Ruth as he handed her the knife. "Keep it open in your pocket." She slipped it into her jacket.

Isaiah followed them, silent. To see Ruth and Jonah lead him across the street and the parking lot toward the store, a casual witness would assess Isaiah as either sullen or simple.

Inside the drug store they entered the First Aid aisle single file, Jonah walking first and Isaiah last, so that neither the cashier's station up front nor the pharmacy at the rear had a clear view of Ruth, should anyone at either desk watch them.

"Wait," Ruth whispered. They halted, and each man examined the items nearest him while Ruth used the knife to scrape the magnetic price tags off two pink plastic bottles. Once she had stuffed both bottles down her jeans and put the knife away, she whispered, "All right," and they resumed walking.

When they reached the back aisle the woman running the pharmacy did not even acknowledge them. They followed the store's perimeter until it brought them back to the front doors, through which they exited.

Outside they crossed the street again to follow the trolley tracks. They walked on the grass between the uptown and downtown lines. After half a block, Jonah said to Ruth, "Give me some of that stuff."

She glanced to either side, then with a smirk reached inside her waistband to pull out a pink bottle. "Here," she said, twisting the cap off, "let me put it on you."

Jonah faced away from her and hunched down to give her access to his neck. Having neglected to steal cotton swabs, she daubed the lotion onto his skin with her fingers.

"This has gotten worse already," Ruth said. "Since we left the streetcar." With her index finger she tugged his collar away from his skin to expose the very top of his back. "God! This looks bad," she said.

"It's down my back?" Jonah asked. He turned around to look at her.

"Oh, Jonah, it's on your *face*," Ruth gasped, and threw her hand over her mouth.

"Fuck, man!" Jonah cursed, and stamped the grass.

Isaiah said, "Come," and led them onward.

"I'm covered in this shit!" Jonah shouted at him. "It's getting worse!"

"I've got it, too," Isaiah pointed out. "What does it last? A couple days, maybe. It's just discomfort. We'll live."

"'We'll live,'" Jonah repeated, in a sneer.

"It's on my flesh, as well, Jonah," Isaiah said. "I can feel it under my shirt. I am sorry for our misfortune, but the real issue is whether we're in prison. And we're not."

Jonah made no reply. A streetcar heading downtown passed them. "Come on," Isaiah said. "The sooner we get back to the truck, the sooner you can strip and have her put that stuff everywhere you need it."

Isaiah did not see Ruth flash the briefest smile at Jonah before she said, "Yea, we have to get back. Some of the others probably need lotion, too."

They continued walking. As they went, Jonah rubbed some calamine onto his own cheek where the rash had spread.

"We got off too far downtown," Isaiah said, without anger, after they had traveled eight or nine blocks.

"We had no way of knowing," Jonah said. "We only been down this thing once."

A half-dozen blocks later, they passed yet another of those drug stores with the purple signs. Either from tact or due to his withdrawal inward, Isaiah refrained from comment. Then they reached Audubon Park. From the sidewalk they couldn't see Micah or Joel among the dozens of pedestrians, but they did not enter to search for them.

Finally Saint Charles ended. They three climbed the levee, weary from their hike. Midway up the slope, Isaiah suggested, "Let's collect plenty of wood now, in daylight, when we can see the poison ivy and avoid it."

"I don't even know why we're going back into these woods," Jonah said.

"No choice," Isaiah said.

"Do you know what poison ivy looks like, if you see it?" Ruth asked.

"Yea," both men answered.

"Then let's find where it is, and get rid of it," she said.

"Good idea," Isaiah told her.

They spoke no more as they rounded the top of the levee and continued down the other side to the bottom. The beach looked different from how they'd last seen it, as though the river had changed tides.

At the edge of the thicket Jonah and Isaiah inspected every element of the foliage. None had white berries or leaf triplets. The bunches of vines Zephariah and Micah had used to help camouflage their entrance might hide anything within them, so they three stepped around those clusters the best they could.

Neither did they find the culprit growing anywhere alongside the wooden path they had laid during the night. Immediately as they entered their secret passage the air grew hot and moist around them. This time it smelled of exhaust.

The windows of the van had fogged slightly. Isaiah led the way beneath the makeshift awning and yanked the handle on the side door. It did not open.

Zephariah appeared at the window and tugged up the button. Isaiah opened the door and felt the cool air inside.

"You ran the engine to put on the air conditioner," Isaiah said.

Zephariah nodded. An arc of enflamed pink ran up his throat from below his collar. "For her," he muttered, nodding toward Esther.

"It gets like an oven, sitting here," Esther said.

Pleased to hear her speak a full sentence, Isaiah conceded the point and climbed in. Ruth and Jonah followed.

❋ ❋ ❋

And Jonah removed his garments, and so did Zephariah, and Ruth. And she applied salve unto them both, on their backs and their chests and their legs and arms, and unto herself on her arm, where the rash had now stretched to her shoulder. And Isaiah refused his share of lotion, saying, "Wait and make sure you have enough for Joel and Micah." And Esther watched with her arms folded.

While Ruth rubbed Zephariah, Micah appeared at the side door. Isaiah opened it for him.

"Where's Joel?" Isaiah asked.

"Went to get spray," Micah said, and glanced for a second at the trio in the back, Jonah and Zephariah in their underwear, Ruth topless.

"Spray?" Isaiah said.

"Yea, he got all red and itchy."

"It's poison ivy," Jonah said. "We've all got it."

"I don't," Micah said. "I never get it."

"Why didn't you go with Joel?" Isaiah asked him.

"He didn't have money. He wanted to go alone." Micah looked again at Ruth as he spoke. She began to put her shirt back on. "He doesn't like anyone to be around him when he shoplifts."

The guys began to dress, too. Micah climbed in and sat in the driver's seat. Because he had held the door open so long, they ran the air conditioner again. After five minutes Isaiah had Micah kill the engine and switch the ignition so they could listen to the news update on the radio. The clock on the dashboard said three past noon, so they had already missed the headlines at the beginning.

The newscaster told them about political trouble in two South American countries, and then went to a commercial. After the break, the newscaster described the arrest of a rock star's son for prostitution in Los Angeles.

Then the newscaster said: "State police in Arkansas are searching for the members of a cult who police say murdered the parents and four siblings of one cult member. Police say the group, known as the House of Jacob, was ordered by its charismatic fifteen-year-old leader to kill Doctor Chad P. Fuller and the rest of the family. Suspects' names have not been released because of their age."

Another voice came on, edited from a press conference: "It appears that Doctor Fuller and his wife objected to their daughter's having gotten pregnant, which she seems to have done on the say-so of this particular individual who headed the House of Jacob. The reason nobody knew about the cult is that they didn't do anything illegal until this. We're talking to about fifty individuals in the area who were members, most of them minors, none of whom are suspects in any crime."

The newscaster came back to identify the police spokesman by name and give what few details anyone knew about the murderers' whereabouts, which was that they had fled Kenmore in the Fuller family van. Nobody save Isaiah paid attention to this later portion of the report, because Esther had begun bawling in the rear seat.

Ruth hugged her and said, "Come on, honey." As a commercial came on, she said to everyone else, rather crisply, "Can we not listen to the news anymore, please?"

Isaiah said, "We have to—"

"You expect her to listen to that," Ruth said, her cheeks flushed with sarcasm. "There's no reason to think she might freak when she hears strangers talking about this on the radio."

"*You killed them!*" Esther suddenly screamed at Isaiah.

"Esther," Isaiah said.

"You killed my sisters! My sisters didn't do *any*thing!" she screamed.

"Honey, come on," Ruth said. "Stop yelling."

Esther broke away from Ruth's embrace and told Isaiah, with more venom yet less volume, almost calmly, "I hate you. I wish you would fucking die."

No one made any reply.

"You might as well kill me," Esther said. "I don't want to live."

"Esther," Isaiah said.

"What?" she asked, crying again. "What? What are you going to fucking say that's going to make this all right? You fucking killed my family."

"First of all," Isaiah said, "*we're* your family. And this family counts, and everyone here knows that. Now, I'm sorry about your parents and your brothers and sisters. I know you were fond of them, and if there had been any other way, that's how we would've done it. But they were *going* to interfere, your father said so. Your brother would've fractured my skull."

Esther buried her face in Ruth's arms and wept.

Isaiah said, "We took a vow, all of us: If we don't fufill the Scripture, we fail. I wish that didn't mean we ever had to hurt anyone, but if someone's going to come between us and that goal, we can't let them. We have to enact the Will of God. *Have* to."

After a moment or so, during which what he said sank in visibly upon everyone except Esther, Isaiah added, "I know you agree with me in your heart, or you would not have come with us. Right now you're suffering, but you have felt His Will just as the rest of us have. Please don't think I cannot appreciate your sacrifice."

Isaiah reclined his seat and closed his eyes. Everyone sat in reflection as though after a sermon.

"You might as well all go out and walk around," Isaiah said after a few minutes. "Leave the calamine lotion here in case Joel comes back with the wrong kind of spray."

Jonah reached for the door and said, "Good idea."

"Don't hang out on the levee, all right?" Isaiah said. "Don't attract any attention around here."

Jonah opened the door and got out. Zephariah followed him.

"You want me to stay with you?" Ruth asked Esther very quietly. With her head resting on Ruth's shoulder, Esther shrugged.

"I'll take that as 'yes,' then," Ruth said.

Esther shrugged again.

"I'll go," Micah said. He climbed out and shut the door behind him.

Isaiah opened his door and called after them, "Hey?" They turned, and he said, "If you think of it, bring firewood with you when you come back. For tonight."

Micah and Zephariah and Jonah all nodded and then vanished into the foliage. Isaiah relaxed again. Soon Esther became calm.

"You let the cold out," Ruth said.

Isaiah did not open his eyes or move as he said, "What?"

"Having the door open. It let all the cold air out," Ruth said. "It's like an armpit in here."

Isaiah sighed.

"Just run the AC again," Ruth said. "What's the big deal?"

"There's no big deal," he assured her, and moved stiffly into the driver's seat. First he turned the key the wrong way, then he turned the engine over. Not quite cool air wafted out of the vents.

Ruth said, "Could we have something on the radio besides news?"

"No," Isaiah said.

"How about if it's classical music?" Ruth said. "That stuff doesn't have anything to do with Scripture. There's no words."

"Why do you want to hear classical music?" Isaiah wondered out loud.

"Just something," she said, and when he glanced at her, she gestured with one hand toward Esther, whose features had taken on a puffy, sore quality from crying.

Isaiah relented, and they passed the afternoon listening to Beethoven and some other composers they had never heard of. Every half-hour or forty-five minutes, Ruth made him run the air conditioner. As the day grew later, the van itself absorbed less sunlight and thus retained the cool temperature longer.

Night came, and Joel did not return.

The others brought some grill sausages they had filched from a supermarket, and plenty of firewood. Jonah had even thought to steal rolls.

They stood around the fire, holding the meat on sticks in the flames. The package said the sausages were already cooked, so the men needed only to heat them.

It turned out that Zephariah and Isaiah had the worst rashes, though this fact comforted neither Jonah nor Ruth.

Isaiah, who had used none of the calamine and did not eat any food, meditated upon Joel. Zephariah had found a broken wooden boat lying on top of a bush, and Micah had helped him haul it to camp for the fire, but instead the hull had become a bench hearthside. Isaiah sat there now to close his eyes and absorb each wave of warmth the fire emitted.

Many minutes passed. Sometime after they finished the sausages, Isaiah heard Jonah say, "Shit, it's raining."

As he opened his eyes, Isaiah said, "Throw the firewood under the truck now, before it gets wet."

They did. Isaiah himself proved too lightheaded to help with more than a couple of logs, but the Remnant soon had a dry store of fuel. Yet the storm broke heavily over the Mississippi, so that despite the wooded valley's barriers against both the river and the city, rain fell through the branches from all angles, and doused their fire.

Their awning could not protect them against this storm, so everyone climbed inside the truck and Zephariah closed the side door.

At Isaiah's insistence they listened to classical music on the radio. First they heard an orchestral suite, which added dramatic intensity to what little they could see of the storm pelting the forest around them. Then the DJ announced that the news update would follow. Isaiah turned off the radio.

"That was cool," Jonah said. "I didn't mind that."

"Yea," Ruth said from in the back, where she sat next to Esther. She did not point out to the others that she had persuaded Isaiah to try this station, for fear of cooling their leader's enthusiasm.

The storm itself carried the faintest echoes of the music they had just heard. As they sat in the dark, sheets of rain slapped the roof over their heads. It proved so hypnotic that they all sat mesmerized until Isaiah saw on the clock that nearly half an hour had passed. The news had ended long ago. He switched the radio on again.

It was organ music this time, in a minor key. Isaiah turned it loud to drown out the storm. Bass pipes shook the van. No one moved, except when Micah turned in the driver's seat for a moment to look at Isaiah's profile.

The piece ended abruptly.

"Man, I thought we were underneath the ocean," Jonah said.

Zephariah nodded.

Isaiah mumbled something without turning around.

"What?" Jonah asked him.

Wearily, Isaiah lowered the volume on the stereo and said, directly to Jonah, "I had a vision."

"Tell us about it," Jonah said.

"Joel is in prison," Isaiah told him. "They were playing the radio on the address system in the drug store, and the news came on while he was stealing hydrocortisone cream. It freaked him out, and he got caught."

The van had fallen silent. Then Ruth asked, "Are they looking for us here?"

"No, that's why he's in prison," Isaiah said. "He listened when I told everyone not to carry identification. They don't know who he is. But they must have thought he was older, because he's in prison overnight. With adults."

"Can we get him out?" Jonah said.

Isaiah scratched absently at the poison ivy on his forehead, now spread halfway across his scalp. "I have no idea how we do that," he said. "I don't think they'll let him out without identifying himself, at least as *some*body."

"Then they're probably going to start looking for us in New Orleans," Jonah said.

"They're looking for us everywhere, now," Isaiah said. "We can't pull out and drive somewhere else. We have to stay off the highways for a few months. Down here we can drive around once our story gets off the news and we have a Louisiana plate on this truck."

Micah said, "We can change the plates now."

Everyone looked at him.

"It's stopped raining," Micah said.

It had, almost as suddenly as it had started. Water still dripped steadily from the trees.

"Very well," Isaiah said, in a tone that suggested he hardly considered this an issue worth thinking through. "Let's go switch all the plates down by the railroad tracks."

Micah took the screwdriver from the glove compartment. They all climbed out the side door, except for Ruth and Esther. Moisture from vegetation overhead and alongside them soaked each man the instant he set foot outside the van. But the rain had ceased.

Micah led the way back out to the levee, and they marched to Carrollton. As they traveled, Jonah noticed behind them a freight train standing idle down the tracks. "We should hang until the train moves," he said to the others, "especially since we're fucking with people's cars."

Five empty vehicles awaited them at the crossing. Waiting for the train to come shield them, Jonah explained his plan again: He would use his Swiss Army knife, Micah the screwdriver, and Zephariah a quarter. Since it would take him longer, Zephariah would unscrew the plate from just one car. Micah and Jonah would remove two each, and screw four of the plates onto the wrong cars. The fifth plate they would keep for their van.

"And Isaiah watches us from up here," Jonah concluded. "In case we get any trouble."

Isaiah nodded, and dropped onto the grass with his legs folded. By now he had amassed within him enough might that external reality would not engage his full attention again until dire need arose.

The train moved. Jonah, Zephariah, and Micah headed downhill. They reached the bottom just as the engine sealed the crossing, and they set right to work.

Inside half a minute the rain started again.

If it didn't come back at full pitch, it regained its earlier fury quickly. From where he sat Isaiah could see Jonah and Micah accelerate the pace of their work, while Zephariah remained in a patient crouch, struggling against a rusted screw with his quarter.

From the other side of the shipyard, a black dog charged down the levee toward the cars.

Isaiah drew his head up and froze.

No one else saw the dog coming. By the time it leaped onto Zephariah, Isaiah's attention had instead shifted to the dog's owners, a man and woman racing downhill behind it. Probably these two had begun running merely to escape the rain, but the man had now sprinted ahead of the woman. He reached the dirt road seconds after his dog.

Zephariah fought the dog away and grabbed the car's back bumper, trying to haul himself to his feet.

The man did not slow as he reached Zephariah. Instead he jumped onto the bumper with one foot. It gained him the leverage to kick Zephariah brutally in the face.

Micah came at the man then, and the man flung his arm outward once in a horizontal half-circle. His fist did not connect, yet Micah dropped instantly, and the man began moving on Jonah, who tore away from the cars. The man and the dog chased him.

The woman meanwhile stood at the edge of the road, one hand covering her mouth.

The man caught Jonah and dragged him back to the cars. He used a peculiar hold on Jonah's neck. After watching the two travel a few feet, Isaiah realized the man had a chainlink dog leash: He had whipped Micah unconscious with it, and now had it twisted round Jonah's throat.

Isaiah breathed a sigh of solemn resign.

Then he closed his eyes. "Father," he said, "let Thy Will be done. Make me an instrument of Your Will."

Everything staying awake and fasting had built within him—which the Remnant needed, for protection; police had actually commenced a hunt for them—flowed into action.

Whenever Isaiah devoted this energy to His Will, he perceived the world from the perspective of every one of his disciples at once, as well as from his own. So now as he saw from his own viewpoint the man and his dog beating Jonah on the hood of the nearest car, he also saw the beating up close through Jonah's eyes, and saw the blank swirl of nothingness that engulfed Micah and Zephariah, and saw what Joel saw as one cellmate held him to the floor and another sodomized him, and could even hear the proscribed rock music Ruth had put on the radio once Isaiah had left the van.

Down at the cars, the man halted with his fist drawn back. To Isaiah it seemed that the change in Jonah's features gave the man pause.

The man did not notice as Zephariah and Micah rose stiffly to their feet. Neither appeared sober. Both made a clumsy turn toward their opponent, and then bolted at him.

The woman screamed, which made the man glance up at the last second. Still he had no chance.

Micah seized the man by the shoulders. Zephariah snapped the man's head all the way backwards.

The man's neck broke. It sent a pleasing jolt up the bones of Zephariah's arms. Isaiah only enjoyed it for the briefest moment, because the dog locked its jaws on Micah's left hand. Very rapidly Zephariah killed the dog as well, though of course its neck offered a less satisfying snap.

Isaiah left Zephariah and Micah kicking the dog's corpse, and concentrated instead on making Jonah yank the leash loose from his own neck. Finally Jonah rose jerkily to join the other two. They stopped kicking the dog, and all three turned to regard the woman.

She had already taken flight in the other direction.

"Shit," Isaiah hissed.

Making them run invited all kinds of problems, especially during rain: They fell, they had trouble stopping, they could get hit by cars. Worst of all, running ate Isaiah's power rapidly. Yet there was no other way.

All three marched through the drainage ditch onto the grass slope of the levee. All three aligned themselves facing one direction, toward the fleeing woman. With no flourish whatsoever all three broke into a straight-legged dash after her.

The woman did not check behind her as she ran.

Micah proved the fastest of the three. As they pursued her, Zephariah twisted his ankle in a small hole hidden in the grass, and fell.

Isaiah focused on Micah and Jonah, who outpaced the woman. She had nowhere to go, for the train still cut the levee off from the rest of the city. Lightning flashed.

Dead ahead she came to a silver storm fence, fifteen feet high. Razor wire curled along the top. The rain drummed against a sign that said NO TRES-PASSING.

The woman threw herself onto the fence and began to scale it.

Micah arrived and tackled her to the ground. The long run had weakened Isaiah already, so the woman's desperate clawing had some effect on Micah.

Her fingernails dug chunks from the gash her companion had opened across Micah's face with the metal leash.

Then Jonah got there. Micah braced the woman's head against the sod with both his hands, and Jonah kicked her skull in. Five times he smashed his boot into her face.

The sixth time Jonah missed and instead kicked Micah's arms out from under him. Micah collapsed on top of the woman, who did not move. Jonah lost balance and fell on his back beside them.

Isaiah relaxed, adjusted his glasses, and found he had forgotten to breath. Now he pulled oxygen into his lungs and glanced down along the railroad tracks. Freight car after freight car rumbled past, with no caboose in sight. The rain worsened. Isaiah beckoned Zephariah back onto his feet.

The rain did not relent. They all slept a long time. Isaiah had exhausted himself to the point that he suspected neural damage.

He awoke to gray daylight on the trees and no sound whatsoever, other than the river's flow. His seat, like the driver's seat to his left where Micah snored through a ruptured septum, reclined almost horizontally.

Though none but Isaiah suspected why, he always managed his followers more easily for a day or two after expending energy the way he had. Even Ruth ceased complaining.

Now, as he wished them to, they came awake, gently, and listened to him.

"Joel is dead," he said, and put on his glasses. "I saw it in my sleep."

Everyone nodded sadly, mournfully. Together.

The welt on Micah's face from the dog chain had turned purple, except around his eyes—the blow to his nose had blackened them—and the festering pocks where the woman's nails had punctured his skin.

"And we need to, uhm," Isaiah tried to continue. Their calm bothered him, and he stared at their faces.

As one, his audience slowly blinked.

"We need a drug store, is what we need," he managed.

Everyone else nodded.

"An ankle bandage, a bunch of peroxide," Isaiah listed, "and, Jonah, I think they have, like, a kit that you use to fix broken teeth."

Jonah responded with a faint nod. The left side of his face resembled a clump of dried bait on a pier. Getting pummeled on the car hood had cost him an eyetooth.

"Micah, we have to get you somewhere with a sink," Isaiah said. "The problem is, we're vulnerable now because I had to burn all that power last night. I have to rest for at least a day before I can begin another fast."

Once again, they all blinked in time. Their eyelids smoothly closed and reopened at some unseen command.

Isaiah spun around to face forward. "All right," he said. "Let's just listen to the radio a little while, then we'll go. Let's hear what they say on the news."

He switched on the radio.

Nothing happened.

"The keys," Isaiah said. Reclined in the driver's seat, Micah did not stir. The keychain dangled from the ignition. Isaiah leaned across and turned the key to Accessory.

The radio did not come on.

Isaiah turned the knob again, to make certain, and then told Micah, "Turn the engine over."

As Micah carried out this order with the sluggish air of an invalid, Isaiah added, "We need some AC, anyway."

Micah twisted the ignition and held it. The only sound came from his foot pumping the gas pedal to the floor.

No one swore.

"What do you think?" Isaiah asked Micah. "Is the battery dead?"

Micah studied the dashboard as though absorbing data from the gauges and speedometer. "Yea," he said. "Maybe. I don't know."

"All right, then, when it's dark we steal a new battery," Isaiah said. "We can find out for sure that way."

Something bumped against the rear of the van.

For some reason it pleased Isaiah to see everyone else snap awake at the noise, even if they did so mutely. He glanced out his window.

The bright green ground was swirling, several feet higher than he'd last seen it.

"Am I dreaming?" Isaiah asked, adjusting his glasses.

He was not. The river had risen to swallow the woods, and their van. Isaiah moaned as, below his seat, he spied seepage in the bottom of his doorwell.

Outside, tiny lily pads covered the water. Currents swept them around any vegetation that broke the surface.

A small log floated past. "That's what made the noise," Isaiah said.

"What?" Ruth asked from the back.

After inhaling deeply and exhaling, Isaiah replied, "When we picked this place to hide in, that lady with the dogs said it was cool here when the weather was dry."

"So this place is bad now," Ruth ventured.

"Look out the window," Isaiah told her. "It's underwater."

Everyone did, except for Zephariah, who grunted as he massaged his twisted ankle; for him to express discomfort implied severe pain.

"God," Ruth said.

"Look out the back, would you?" Isaiah asked her.

Ruth and Esther both turned around, and together they gave a small cry. "Shit, it's flooded all the way to the levee," Ruth said. "I can't even tell how deep it is."

"Where's the, the number?" Isaiah asked Micah. "The number they trace cars by. Car thieves file it down. Do you know what I'm talking about?"

Reclined in his seat with his eyes closed, Micah shrugged. Zephariah shook his head. Jonah showed no sign of hearing through the throb of split nerves that wracked his jaw and skull.

"Then let's not take chances," Isaiah said. "We have to burn it."

Ruth said, "Burn what?"

Isaiah nodded and said, "The van."

"Then...where do we sleep?" she said.

Isaiah pushed his glasses up the bridge of his nose. "Well," he intoned, and gave everyone a wry grin, "we'll work on that when we get out of here."

"Wait, they could be waiting out there," Ruth said. Isaiah actually welcomed the dissent. "If we come wading in out of the woods and there are cops down where it happened, they'll grab us."

"What else can we do?" Isaiah pointed out. "Sit here?"

No one said anything, and suddenly they all noticed the gentle rush of the water along the sides of the van; the sound had begun while they slept, so that they all awoke with their ears accustomed to it. None had heard it until now.

CADIZ & CADIZN'T

IT'S DAYTIME. IN THIS DREAM I still live in New Orleans but I'm with Lee. I don't know what that means since Lee has never even visited New Orleans. But we walk off Cadiz Street down the alley full of those annoying Japanese plants to the entrance to my old apartment. The lock on my door sticks the way it always does. Lee and I walk into my living room. A pile of mail sits heaped upon one of my stereo speakers. Without asking me Lee starts sifting through my letters. *LEE* I say *MY MAIL IS NONE OF YOUR BUSINESS.* That doesn't faze him. He holds up a magazine that I've never actually subscribed to and tells me *THIS ISSUE HAS THE ANNUAL CARPET BUYER'S GUIDE IN IT. MY COPY GOT STOLEN OUT OF MY MAILBOX AND I DON'T WANT TO HAVE TO BREAK INTO THE STORE IN THE MIDDLE OF THE NIGHT TO GET ANOTHER ONE.* Which is almost something Lee would say. Despite my never having heard of this magazine in real life I want to trick Lee out of adopting my copy. I offer to make him coffee with chicory. NO THANKS he says. So I turn on the stereo and start dancing with him and that works. He puts the mail back on top of the speaker and puts his hands around my waist. The stereo plays a strange whine that contains hints of guitar and voice. It's the same sound as when a radio has two different stations halfway tuned in. We dance. Soon Lee slips his hands into my underwear.

I've forgotten how weird my bedroom in that apartment looks. While Lee fucks me I stare at the walls. Whoever rented the apartment before me tried to marbelize the walls but gave up. After painting the room peach they let the veins of red and blue dry without sponging them. Instead of marble the walls resemble the inside of a scrotum. Then we sleep. Barely have I turned the light off before I hear the lock turn in my front door. Someone casually enters my vestibule and walks down the hall toward the bedroom. Lee snores, loud. A man in a rich olive suit with an oxblood tie comes in. Suddenly I remember I don't live here anymore. This man lives here now. I feign sleep. The man finally notices us and says HELLO? I don't move. HELLO? he says again. This time Lee and I stir at the same time. Lee says WHO ARE YOU? The man says MY NAME'S AARON. WHY ARE YOU IN MY APARTMENT? I rub my eyes and say I USED TO LIVE HERE. I FORGOT I MOVED. Aaron takes this news easily. I'M SORRY I say WE'LL GO. Aaron says politely IT'S ALL RIGHT. I GET SOME OF YOUR MAIL. Behind him I begin to see signs that he's painted over certain veins and outlined others with metallic paint. I SAY I SEE YOU'VE CHANGED THE WALLS. Aaron nods. IT ONLY HAPPENS VERY SLOWLY he says. Lee stares at us with the sheet wrapped around him. I NEED TO TALK TO YOU Aaron tells me. He means without Lee. So I climb out of bed and follow him naked into his living room. We sit down together on my green knit couch. Aaron says YOUR FATHER IS VERY ILL AND UNHAPPY. I shake my head and say MY FATHER DIED TWO YEARS AGO. Aaron looks at me. I think he's realizing he won't get to fuck me. Now he's ready for me and Lee to leave. Fine. I don't need a recap of my life since I lived in that apartment.

Outside it's daytime. Lots of kids I grew up with accompany us along with Aaron. The kids are still the age I remember last seeing them but they're as tall as I am. Their increased size makes them doll-like. They run and hop sideways to keep up with us. We walk around the corner to the trolley stop. It's the back of the Winn-Dixie I used to shop in on Carrollton. We're standing on the loading dock by a streetcar stop sign. A briny green canal flows past us. The loading dock is an actual pier now. LOOK Aaron says YOU REALLY DON'T KNOW WHO I AM? Lee glares at him. Aaron says I STARRED IN BOTH EVIL DEAD MOVIES. I study his face. NO I say THAT WASN'T YOU. This news deflates him. I WAS IN A ROCKY MOVIE THOUGH he huffs. Lee says I SEEN THAT ONE. IT WAS ALL RIGHT. Then the streetcar comes. It cuts the water. I look down and through the murk I can see the brass wheels turning along the track. The brakes gurgle rather than hiss.

Except for Aaron we all depart aboard the streetcar. I'm still naked. As we pull away from the loading dock Aaron watches us and kicks a pebble into the water. The streetcar turns down Bienville Street. *BIENVILLE STREET ISN'T AROUND THE CORNER FROM MY HOUSE* I say. Lee goes *YES IT IS.* He points at a street sign and says *LOOK* as though I hadn't seen them already. *THIS IS A SECRET PASSAGE* he says. We pass houses nicer than you would really see along that part of Bienville. Then the streetcar ferries us down a sidestreet behind that restaurant. Around the turn we pull up to Johnson's Pier where I used to go on the ferry to see Aunt Glenda. She lived on a beach where there were no streets. New Orleans always reminded me of her and I miss them both. Which I suspect is the whole point of this dream.

LOVELADIES

As soon as I steered Olga into traffic, I glanced upward and saw the sky darken. I pulled the carriage over at a bar up Decatur and told my passenger and his family I would just need a minute. They did not object. I went inside to the payphone and called Olyphant, Pennsylvania, collect.

Nana Mitchell had died.

When I came back to the carriage, the passenger's wife asked me, "Is everything all right?"

"I am afraid not, ma'am," I said. "Bad news, of a family nature."

I mounted my seat, took my reins and directed Olga toward the heart of the Quarter. You learn to read a mark down here; this passenger wanted the more war-oriented historical tour, which I usually give down the other end by the Marigny. The hell with it, I could take them down Bourbon and improvise. Any rebel who lets his woman ask another man rude questions puts up with too much, anyway.

The passenger's sons could not care less about history, but I made sure they caught a glimpse of stripper ass through the door at Big Daddy's. By the time we reached Bourbon and St. Philip, where I identified an anonymous blue house as the Pirate Lafitte's private seraglio, my suppressed sobbing began to affect my speech.

"You sure you want to go on with this?" the nosey wife said to me.

"Certainly."

"Because you could just take us back, you know," she said in a tone meant to soothe me. "That would be fine. I mean, if you've gotten some bad news."

O, would this woman's prying never cease?!

To please her, I piloted the carriage back toward the river, where I had picked them up. "My grandmother has passed away," I told the woman, hoping by my curt delivery to stave off further interrogation. "She raised me."

"Oh, yeah? Where you from?" the passenger said, as though this question were somehow germane.

"California," I told him.

"My brother lives in California," he replied. "What part you from?"

Now I became incensed, as much by the challenge of expanding upon this casual lie I had told them to protect my privacy as by my curiosity to see how gauche this passenger might get. I picked: "San Francisco."

"Oh, my brother's in LA," he said.

"I lived in LA until last year," I said. "What part of Los Angeles?"

"Uh," the passenger said. "Shit... I forget. It's not West Hollywood, it's some other name with 'west' in it."

"Well, I lived in Westminster," I said.

He bit. "That's it! Westminster! My brother lives there."

"What's his name?"

"Scott Schreiner."

I halted Olga at the stop sign on Chartres and turned to face the passenger. "Scott?" I asked, suitably overwhelmed by the coincidence. "Looks like you, a little younger—?"

"He's older, actually," he said. "But everyone says he looks younger than me. He always did."

"Guy was married, right?"

"Not anymore." He shook his head.

"I *know* not anymore," I told him. "He stayed at my apartment when she brought home that—well, there's children present."

"How do you like that? You know Scott."

For a moment I let him dangle in the still evening, his head nodding with pride. Then I said, "Your brother owes me fourteen grand, chum."

When I dropped them by Jackson Square, the passenger slipped me an extra sawbuck and said, in a low voice so his wife wouldn't hear, "Look, I'm sorry about Scott. My whole life, I'm making good for him. He don't fucking learn. Someone'll shoot him some day."

"It won't be me, I assure you," I told him.

From the sidewalk his wife waved and said, "Sorry about your bad news."

I left Olga there in front of the park and ran across the street. I smoked a joint on top of that staircase that leads to the Riverwalk. From the platform I could see the river, and I could keep an eye on Olga below. For the first time since taking this job, I did not feel like working.

I used to whistle two pitches at once. It takes hours of practice, I haven't done it in years. But Nana Mitchell taught me how to do that.

By watching closely and asking the right questions the right way, I learn a secret about each person I meet. Nana Mitchell taught me that, too.

My brother in Olyphant told me she had died seven months ago the day I called. I had not spoken to him in several years, and we did not waste much time on small talk. He wanted to know where I've been, whether I was calling from a police precinct, that sort of thing.

I much prefer my brother the way he appears and behaves in my dreams. In person he has grown into an irritating and self-righteous man, quick to find fault. My subconscious tends to recall his better side.

This one dream I must have had three or four times now, where my brother and I are watching television in Loveladies, a resort town on the Jersey shore. Our parents once owned a summer cottage there. My brother and I sit watching the Friday night television shows with all those smartmouth kids on them, and we're drinking glasses of purple water.

The reason that last detail intrigues me is that one summer night when I was ten or eleven our parents went to a party and left us in the bungalow alone. We invited over a neighbor girl, Luanne, and she showed us how to flavor water with stuff from Pixie Sticks. You just had to add sugar. My water turned purple. Later that night I talked her into showing us her pussy. It was my first time ever seeing a girl's pubic hair, and certainly my brother's, too. (He has never thanked me, needless to add.)

Yet I recall clearly what we watched on television that night—House on Haunted Hill, on Creature Feature, which means it had to be Saturday. Why should my dream recreate history so painstakingly and make such glaring mistakes? Surely the purple water refers to that Luanne incident, and Nanny and the Professor deliberately conflicts.

But my brother's young in this dream, and a perfect gentleman. When I wake from this dream I miss him, though of course I do not phone him. My brother as he exists today back in Pennsylvania, I don't know that I would even care to drink with him.

❀ ❀ ❀

After I had turned Olga in at the stables for the night, I returned to Mariella's apartment and showered. We made love for an hour, and afterward I cried on her breast.

"What did your brother say she died from?" Mariella asked. She meant to be helpful, prompting me.

"I didn't ask him," I said, which was untrue. I had asked; my brother had not answered me.

"That's fucked up," she opined, before embarking on a pot-inspired feel-good rant. Her point, if she had one, involved communication and spiritual feedback. Mariella couldn't help these outbursts; she grew up in California.

Evening gave way to night, and her blather lulled me. A slumber too flimsy for dreams overtook me for several hours. I awoke shortly before midnight. Mariella had drifted off soundly beside me. I dressed without stirring her and left in her Toyota.

In my wallet I had a bank card with seven dollars in the account. Any day now the bank would deduct the checking fee, which would leave a negative balance. The only place I could withdraw less than ten dollars was at a super-market on Carrollton, and they closed at midnight. For the past week I had reminded myself daily to stop at that cash machine, and each day I forgot until past midnight.

I arrived with ten minutes to spare. No one paid me any attention. I forgot to avert my face from the camera, although I had heard they only retain the videotape from an ATM for forty-eight hours. My transaction would not at-tract police attention for weeks, if ever.

Crisp fiver in hand, I marched to the one checkout lane still open and stood in line behind a girl in a paisley frock, the sort of dress vegan-types wear in Seattle or Berkley. Idly I studied her hair clips. She had two barrettes that said sue in Fisher-Price lettering. I waited for a glimpse of her face.

When she paid she turned sideways to dig through her purse, unaware of anyone's watching her. Thank God, she looked young enough to get away with the highchair hairwear; cutesy older women nauseate me.

As she waited for her change, I noticed that she had etched a list of things to do on her hand in ballpoint: PICK UP OKRA. CALL ALISON. RETURN MOVIES.

She hoisted her bag and left. I bought cigarettes. By the time I reached the parking lot, Sue had already disappeared.

❀ ❀ ❀

I don't know whether anyone from the Lupovic family ever visited Loveladies or ever will, but they show up there every so often in my dreams.

The Lupovics lived on Laburnum Avenue in Olyphant. I dated Jan Lupovic throughout my last year of high school. We were lovers, and despite being easily the dumbest girl I ever touched, she won my heart.

In these dreams we creep from house to house, down alleys of dull gray sand. Sometimes she wears a bathing suit, sometimes jeans cut into shorts. Once she had her communion dress on.

These are happy dreams. During one I asked her to marry me and she agreed, which of course she had done in real life. But in the dream we were leaning against a cinderblock wall with a pink sunset painting the sky overhead. Jan tugged off the top of her bikini and said, "I will love and cherish you for the rest of your life. I will be the most devoted wife you ever have."

Then a screen door wheezed open, and Mr. Lupovic trotted out from the shabby white house beside us, followed by his wife and son, Jerome, and Mrs. Lupovic's redhead sister, Charlene. Although they hadn't overheard, they all knew already about our nuptial plans.

"Good work, son," Mr. Lupovic—I always called him Mr. L—said, beaming and shaking my hand. "I know you'll make us proud."

"I'm going to make you an Indian blanket," Mrs. Lupovic told me warmly. Pueblo blankets had been her great joy; she hung them on her living room walls and bought her kids ponchos every time she visited the Southwest.

In my dream she handed me a photo of herself alongside a gigantic half-completed blanket, with a pattern that included Jan's and my silhouettes in red. "I can't finish it until she grows more red for me to weave," Mrs. Lupovic confided, pointing toward her sister.

Charlene nodded sleepily at me, and I saw from her short shaggy hair that she was clipping the stuff off so Mrs. L could knit with it.

"I'm so happy, I can't wait until you two are married," Charlene said, her hair looking worse than when she used to cut it herself.

Jerome too congratulated us, and we all watched the pink clouds above us form two hearts with an arrow through them.

Had Jan's family reacted to our wedding plans so enthusiastically in real life, I might never have left Olyphant. They wouldn't all despise me now, because Jan would still be alive.

❋ ❋ ❋

On Wednesday afternoon I walked out of Kaldi's with a cup of coffee, and this thankless Korean stray I recently put up for several weeks nearly recognized me. My temper flared at the sight of her.

Her name's Jin-Yi or Jin-Yo or somesuch. She sat begging on the curb, and in the quarter-second before our eyes actually locked a tourist couple stepped in the way.

"Can you help me out with some change?" she asked them, rising to her feet. "Expectant mother, I'm really hungry. Please?"

Even with her gut thrust forward, her stomach barely stuck out enough for them to notice if she hadn't announced her condition. The tourists winced at her without slowing their pace.

It took some effort to walk toward the park without looking back. I mounted the carriage and steered Olga into traffic, wondering whether that oversized pimple I had just seen was my baby.

My first customer came from Tennessee, here with his wife for their second honeymoon. He wanted the military tour, she wanted the ribald version. I compromised. On each block I singled out a historic bordello and traced its origin to a specific military period. The Blacksmith Shop on Bourbon I dated to the Crimean War.

"That was in Europe," said the customer, obviously a historian of some note in West Bumblefuck, Tennessee.

"Right, and when they lost it, they were exiled to New Orleans," I said. "At that time, Louisiana was under the rule of the Spanish Governor O'Reilly."

"Yes, we saw a plaque about him," the customer's wife put in. "He killed all the Frenchmen."

I wished my carriage had a catapult seat so I could eject them both into the Mississippi. "That's exactly right, he had two hundred Frenchmen shot to death at the place we call Frenchmen Street," I said. "Over by the old mint. They were the first Americans killed for refusing to bow to a foreign power."

Intuition made me forgo my usual punch line: *They shot two hundred Frenchmen—sorry to report, they ran out of bullets.* I dropped the customer and his wife off. He tipped me three dollars and they waddled away across Jackson Square. A week from now, they would discuss New Orleans history with their friends at a tractor pull.

Next I picked up four inebriated women who wanted to photograph every-thing, even me.

"No, ma'am," I said.

"Oh, why not?" the photographer said, aiming the camera at me.

I thrust my hand in front of her lens. "I am a Mennonite, ma'am," I said. "It's against my religion to allow my picture to be taken. I don't even have one on my license."

This revelation amazed them. "But doesn't that mean you can't drink?" another girl asked me.

"Just because I am religious, ma'am," I said, "doesn't mean I am a fanatic."

They laughed and I drove on. Down Decatur Street beyond the Brewhouse I pulled over to let a car pass. Before moving again, I glanced into a daiquiri shop beside us.

The girl tending bar—I knew her. From...from the supermarket on Carrollton. Her name was Sue.

Sue did not appear to enjoy her work. She frowned and rolled her eyes as she hauled a huge tub of ice forward to a sink I could not see. This job humil-iated her.

"Isn't Van Morrison from New Orleans?" one of the four girls asked.

"Sure, I can show you his house," I said, pulling away.

Often my dreams use grim imagery to make an innocuous point. For some reason, the grimness doesn't register until I awaken. It jars me sometimes.

The hardest ones to shake take place in Luanne's house after the fire. I poke around in the ashes, finding dolls with their hair melted into clumps.

Of course, real-life dolls would have burned to cinders, but I never actually crept around in Luanne's house after the fire, so my unconscious has to guess. These dolls look the way I imagined hers did when the firemen finally sprayed down the flames and entered Luanne's room, where the fire had started.

Soot stains their naked flesh. There are lots of them, all over the house, nestled among the charcoal embers. Here's something odd: Their eyes stay open until I pick them up.

❁ ❁ ❁

For years I have avoided waking up during daylight unless I must. On Monday I made a rare exception and hit that daiquiri stand on Decatur Street around three-thirty. I entered from the sidewalk and studied the beer list without glancing at the bartender. She ignored me.

Then I dropped my hands to my sides. "Oh, it's you," I said to her. Her eyebrows rose as she looked at me.

"Sue, isn't it?" I asked.

She nodded. "Have we met?"

"Sure, I'm James," I told her.

"When did we meet?"

I exhaled and studied the ceiling. "Jesus, I don't remember," I confessed with a laugh. Then I bit my lip in concentration, pretending to strain my memory. I already knew what I would recall next. "I know who introduced us, though—Alison."

She bought it. "Oh, right. How is Alison, have you seen her?"

I shook my head. "Not in weeks," I said. "Didn't know you worked here."

"Yeah, well," she said, rolling her eyes, "wish I didn't."

We chatted awhile. With little prompting she told me where she lived off Carrollton, how long ago she had come to New Orleans, where she had lived prior to coming here, and how much rent she paid for each of her last five apartments.

All the while I kept her talking, because I had just realized the source of my attraction to her: Her eyes, cheekbones and brow resembled Nana Mitchell's. Uncannily.

"What do you do?" she asked me.

"Spend my trust fund," I quipped. "My father invented punk rock and lawn darts. I get a huge check every week." That covered me.

Luckily I caught myself and left then, on an up note. Too often with a clever woman (or one clever enough not to trust me right away—Sue would have cold-shouldered me had I not had Alison's name to drop) I waste a good opening impression by sticking around. Not this time. As soon as I made her laugh I hit the road.

I had things to do, anyway.

❊ ❊ ❊

Nana Mitchell only appears in my dreams in one of two ways. Either I am pedaling her around Olyphant on the cycle carriage I received for Christmas at age five, or we're at her house and she's in her rocking chair.

One odd aspect of the rocking-chair scenario is that usually the dream begins with me standing next to her, and I'm tall enough that I look down on her scalp from above. Then she takes me in her hands and sits me on her lap, and I fit in there perfectly. (These story conflicts only trouble me after I awaken.)

We read books, just as we did in life, and again my subconscious overlooks no detail to play it real. Every time I spend a dream in the rocking chair with her, I wake recalling with precision some book I haven't seen since before the Beatles disbanded.

One time Nana and I sat paging through an enormous pictorial guide to common garden creatures, illustrated with paintings of vicious insects and other brutal fauna. In one series of scenes, helpless ants plunged into a pit dug by some hairy monster that ate them. The monster lay hidden in the sand at the bottom, her mandibles sharp and hungry.

When I woke from that dream, I felt the exact sickening fear that had plagued me after seeing that book for the first time at age four.

Through great determination, I avoided letting Sue see me on the carriage. The temptation to steal a peek—and risk eye contact, the only way anyone will notice me while I work—proved great but surmountable. The reason I accepted this job so enthusiastically, aside from the pay and a perfect excuse to waste time wandering the Quarter daily, was that no one can recognize me at the reins so long as I do not make myself obvious. Every day I pass someone I prefer to ignore, and as yet none has spotted me.

I could only visit Sue on my days off, since my work clothes (not to mention Olga's aroma, which only a thorough shower can erase) would give me away. That worked in my favor, though. Had I dropped in there several days in a row rather than on consecutive Mondays, she would have raised her guard, thinking I had a crush on her. Instead she came to regard my visit as a tiny respite amid her otherwise bleak work week.

After the third time I came by, I doubled back around the block and took a vantage point across the street, from which I watched patiently, and learned that Sue's shift ended at eight o'clock.

Two days after that, on Wednesday, I answered Mariella's phone. "May I speak to Mariella Guccialo?" a policeman asked me.

"She's not here now," I said, truthfully.

He told me his name, and asked, "Who am I speaking to?"

"I am her brother Jack," I told him. "Is anything wrong?"

"Well, yeah," he said, hesitating just slightly. "Found her Toyota torched down in the Ninth Ward."

"Oh, Jesus," I exclaimed, and my alarm was sincere.

"How come it wasn't reported stolen?"

"I didn't know it *was* stolen. She's out of town," I said, thinking rapidly, "and she lent the car to one of her friends."

"What's the friend's name?"

"Brenda something. I'm sorry, I haven't met her," I said. "Does it look like the car was stolen, or could this have been an accident?"

"Sir, this was no accident," the cop told me with a snicker. "Someone burnt your sister's car up, and they didn't want no one to find it, neither. They put it way down the levee, on the other side of the industrial canal."

"How did you identify it?" I asked, and immediately wished I hadn't phrased the question that way.

The cop didn't catch it. "Triple A had the serial number on file," he said. "Can I call your sister?"

"Actually, no. I have no number for her," I said. "She's driving around in the Southwest with her boyfriend in his camper. She'll be calling me tomorrow or the next day, though, and you can bet I'll have her call you then."

The cop thanked me and hung up.

For several minutes I stood by the phone, furious and yet relieved. Had the cop come to the front door, I would have had serious trouble by now. This way he would not show here for two or three days, at the earliest. I calmed myself: So what if I had to abandon this apartment sooner than I had planned? Events might easily have taken far crueler turns.

Besides which, no one would identify Mariella anytime soon, even if someone did find her.

⊛ ⊛ ⊛

Supermarket dreams drive me up a wall. I spent the summer I was fourteen working illegally in a supermarket. I forged my work papers; you have to be sixteen to get a job in Pennsylvania, unless you want to deliver newspapers. I got my brother his first job there too, another favor he has yet to repay.

These dreams irritate me because I feel as though I am working without pay. Yet strangely, in the most frustrating one I ever had, I did not work in the store. Instead I was a customer.

The store had two or three stories, though in all my travels I have never seen a supermarket with more than one floor. But the supermarket this time was huge and intricate, with elevator banks and different departments.

I paid for my purchases before realizing I had forgotten something. The clerk made me leave my bags at the checkout. As I went upstairs the PA announced that the store would close shortly. Various departments closed before others, and navigating the store became a task in itself.

Soon I forgot what I had wanted upstairs. Then I returned to the elevators, to find them turned off. I had to wander a labyrinth of stairways to get back down to the checkout, and when I arrived the counter had closed. My groceries had disappeared.

I found a stock clerk cruising the aisles, replacing all my items on the shelves. He refused to believe they belonged to me.

Sue's name turned out to be Suzanne, rather than the more prosaic Susan. I found that out the first night we made love.

Those barrettes I had seen her wear that first night foreshadowed a trait of hers: Her taste tended toward gaudiness—not nouveau riche vulgarity like Mariella's gold fingernails, but a child's graceless love of showy things.

Watching her get ready in the morning, I could tell she had taught herself how to dress. Without fail, she would choose one item that pressed her appearance too far—a headband, say, or suspenders, or leggings under a skirt. My attempt to educate her resulted in a tiff a few days after I had moved into her apartment.

"You just don't *like* these earrings," she said.

It never occurred to me to disagree. The earrings she meant were miniature pizzas.

Once my lack of reply sank in, her face went cold. "So you're a fashion critic too, now?" she asked.

"Well, they're too cute," I pointed out helpfully.

By the time she left for work twenty minutes later, Suzanne had requested I pack and leave before she returned that evening.

At that point I was not leaving the apartment much, though she had no way of knowing. I'd had to tell Mr. LeCerce at the stable that my family needed me back in Chicago, that I'd call him the day I got back. No way could I have kept the job secret from Suzanne while coming home reeking of mules every night. Olga would miss me, but they all do.

My sixth sense had advised me to keep out of sight awhile. I trusted it. Plus, I could afford to stay home all the time, because I had six thousand dollars.

Most of the surprises Mariella gave me happened after she was gone. When I entered her bank code for the first time (she had scrupulously avoided using it within even my peripheral eyesight, as though I were some sneak thief, and only a king-hell dose of X pried the digits loose from her), I discovered she had nine grand in the bank. Probably she avoided on principle letting any man know she had enough money to cover the bills. Women are like that.

She had a five-hundred-dollar daily limit, which meant I had to visit the cash machine sixteen days in a row to amass eight thousand. But I smoked a joint on the seventeenth day, and it made me paranoid, so I avoided the bank. That night the cop called me about her car.

I had already spent two grand of my earnings, and staying home helped me hang on to the other six. For starters, I paid Suzanne's rent and had this fag Lou deliver pot. Thus she couldn't really tell me to leave.

That afternoon when she told me to hit the bricks, in fact, I doubt I still remembered our argument ten minutes after she left for work. Over a joint and a pot of tea I watched television. I hadn't spent any time in front of the tube in years. I'd supposed I knew how depraved trailer-park pinheads could get, but these new talk shows were a revelation. And "reality TV," shows where they stick strangers in a condo for six months and videotape them everywhere except the bathroom—nothing on television even vaguely resembled this stuff, last time I'd checked.

There were new cop shows, too, where actors would reenact crimes and at the end the screen showed photos of the real culprit. These programs came on later, though, in the evening, by which time I had smoked enough pot that I could not stand to listen to any more stilted dialogue. After dinner I just turned the stereo up and let the screen catch my eye from time to time.

Finally a face came on that I recognized. At first I thought it must belong to an actress, until it didn't move. Still photographs on these shows were of dead people or murderers only.

Sandra. It was Sandra.

A moment later the screen filled with a slow-motion video image: a man standing close to the camera, looking intently at something below and in front of him. Behind him was an almost-empty supermarket.

The man moved for a few seconds. He was operating an automatic teller machine, and this tape had come from the security camera.

Then the tape froze and blew up one clear angle on the man's face as he walked away.

The face was mine.

I sat up and grabbed the remote. By the time I had the music turned down, they had cut ahead to another section of tape that showed me in the background, getting on line behind Suzanne at the checkout.

"New Orleans police say they do not know this man's identity," the announcer said as both freeze frames of my face filled the screen, side by side. "The fact that he knew Sandra Barnett's PIN code indicates that he may have been a close friend. If you recognize this man..."

Any dream in which I discover a pit instantly attains a mood of violation, a mood so powerful that often I cannot clear it from my head after waking until I leave the house. Usually such a dream will echo at me once or twice later in the day.

The worst pit dream I have suffered while living in New Orleans involved a horse trail in New Jersey. At least once every summer my parents would take my brother and me to a dude ranch two hours across the Pine Barrens from Loveladies. On one visit I feigned nausea so they would leave me at the bunkhouse. Then I went exploring on foot, alone, foraging my way through grass taller than I was. And I found a pit, a huge sinkhole with a wrecked car shoved into it.

In that car I spotted a magazine with a girl's tits, so I overcame my fear and climbed down to retrieve the smut. It took me some time to understand that it

was a film catalogue. The photographs showed sex, but they also showed blood
and knives. Text accompanied the stills, describing the films. In one, a woman
fucked and then stabbed her lover, then her husband, and hid both corpses in her
closet. In another, girls in Communion dresses—the text led me to believe they
were children, but these models were not underage—lay around an altar being
raped by a motorcycle gang.

Never had I felt anything comparable to the anger this filth aroused in me.
I spent hours below ground, kneeling on the hood of that abandoned wreck,
poring over that catalogue.

When this pit appeared in my dream twenty years later, that anger sprang
fresh upon me, even though the porn pamphlet did not await me in the hole beside the horse trail. When I cleared the flora well enough to step through, I found
the pit full of steel poles. Too late. I could not avoid slipping in among them.

But when I landed upon the metal poles I saw that this gaping rent would not
swallow me. Dozens of these poles, each slightly smaller in diameter than a street
signpost, obscured wherever the pit led below.

Down each of these poles from above slid a girl. I looked closely and saw that
the poles vanished up the girls' cunts. And I knew all the girls, though now they
lay in a fetal curl with peaceful grins I had never seen them wear in life. The poles
did not pierce out of the top of them, though somehow I knew the shafts all to
be the same length, and different girls had swallowed different amounts of steel
inside their vaginas.

It occurred to me later after much thought that each girl's cunt looked to me
the way I had known cunts to look at a specific stage of my life—Luanne's was
a vague slit, Carrianne's had a sparse coat of fur but did not spread open wide,
and so forth.

Perhaps I spent too much time analyzing this dream. O, but how it evoked that
day at the dude ranch. After I had already shaken the dream off and gone about
my day's business, I suffered a fit of anxiety on Royal Street. I had to get a cup
of coffee to calm down. From nowhere had come a vivid memory of my father
beating me that night alongside the highway during our drive back to Loveladies.

My brother had noticed the sun-bleached film catalogue inside my nylon jacket,
and squealed. Typical.

✸ ✸ ✸

My fear, of course, was not that anyone would recognize me, but that some-one might recognize Suzanne and bring the show to her attention. That never happened.

It gave me an agonizing week, though. I kept waiting for the shots of me draining Mariella's account to surface. They never did.

Suzanne was just too suspicious of me from the start, sad to say. Pity people who cannot trust others; such misers deny themselves more than anyone could steal from them. Suzanne gave up her PIN code easily enough, but balked as soon as she noticed anything missing.

"Did you take money from my account?" she asked me.

"What?" I said, glancing up from the paper.

"Did you have to take money out of my account, for some reason?" she rephrased the question. "There's two-fifty missing."

"Maybe you wrote a check you forgot," I suggested.

She shook her head but then, looking at my face, said, "Well, maybe. I'll find my checkbook." With that, she disappeared into the bedroom. All night she hid behind pretense. The next day she went to work with a suitcase and never returned. They cut the phone and the cable TV off that afternoon and I cleared out.

In the part of Olyphant where I grew up, virtually every street ran up and down hills. The few exceptions became well known to me when I rode my bike, because only on these straightaways could I coast on accrued momentum.

The Lupovics live at the peak of Laburnum Avenue. To come home from the Lupovics' house I have to pedal like mad downhill, then cut extreme left when I reach the five-way intersection at the bottom. You cannot see it from up Laburnum, but Murray Street runs flat all the way to Marcus, where my parents live.

Sometimes when I dream of Nana Mitchell, she's riding with me in the cycle carriage I got for Christmas when I was five. Somehow it's big enough to fit not only Nana but Jan as well, both of them in the back while I pedal and steer up front.

Jan's always very young. "Where are we going?" she'll ask Nana Mitchell as we race down Laburnum toward the intersection.

"I couldn't say," Nana Mitchell will answer, and we go faster and faster, the houses fly past us so quickly they seem to revolve, faster we go down and faster,

I control the wheels by force of will and the street's clean but full of acorns and oak leaves, there's a fire waiting for us at my house.

"How will he pedal us up that next hill?" Jan asks Nana Mitchell.

Nana can't say. Only I can. Only I know we can coast the whole way home from here.

STAY OUT OF
NEW ORLEANS

Enoch and Diane strolled around the French Quarter for most of their first afternoon in town. Much of what they saw disappointed him: pagan statuary, T-shirt shops full of lewd trinkets, and clubs where men and women danced naked. Dirty teenagers loitered on every corner. Enoch gave a quarter each to the first and second kids who begged him for change, only to have them rudely dismiss him for his kindness.

Late in the day, after the police placed metal poles into the asphalt to barricade Bourbon Street against drivers, a bearded man with an eight-foot wooden cross took his place in the center of the blacktop. The man's cross had the words HE DIED FOR YOU! painted vertically down the long beam. Revellers waded around him, oblivious.

"Hi, there," Enoch said.

"Hello," the man replied. He smiled at Enoch and Diane both.

"Good to see you spreading the Word," Enoch said. "This place sure needs it."

"Oh, I agree," the man said. "I agree."

Diane wanted to go. Now. "See you again," Enoch told him.

When they got out of the man's earshot, Enoch asked, "Did that make you uncomfortable? That I talked to that fellow?"

Diane shook her head, just barely.

"No?" Enoch asked. "Because it seemed like it did."

"It's just," she began, and didn't finish.

After waiting for an answer, he prompted her, "It's just what?"

"I'm not comfortable, is all," Diane said, keeping her eyes on the sidewalk. "That's not me. I'm a more private person."

"I don't see how it affects your privacy to have a conversation with some-body who may seem a little simple—"

"He's on the street with a *crucifix*, Enoch," she pointed out. "In the middle of this tourist trap. I don't feel comfortable having strangers stare at me while you talk to him. It has nothing to do with what I believe, I just don't like strangers staring at me. And I think that man's peculiar. I'm sorry, but that's just not the way to reach out to people. In the middle of all these drunks, with mobs of—"

"That's how Jesus did it."

She had no answer.

Two men walked a harnessed black pig in some kind of costume down Bourbon Street toward the homosexual clubs. The crowd around the pig kept Enoch from seeing what vesture they had placed on the animal.

An older man passed in front of Enoch and Diane at Conti Street wearing a top hat and a long black jacket, the first seeds of fray nibbling the back edge of his collar. They walked a little while longer, and passed a couple a few years their senior who had three kids with them. Enoch smiled at the parents.

"I have to say," he told Diane once the family had marched away, "it bothers me to see people bring their kids out here. There's just stuff here children do not need to see."

"Well, it *is* a very historical place," she said.

"Granted," Enoch said. "But if you peek in the doorways of these bars you can see naked women from the street. I don't think it's right. Children are too naive to make informed moral choices, and parents ought to protect them."

They passed a strip club where a pair of mechanical legs in black stockings kicked out through an upper window every few seconds. Glancing in the door-way, Enoch saw a woman lying naked upon the bar, or more accurately saw her reflection in the mirror hanging at an obtuse angle from the ceiling above her.

"Like that!" Enoch said. "For instance."

Diane gave a small nod of surrender.

They walked back to their hotel. Enoch found both the building and their room rather old, and not in the best sense. He didn't say as much, however.

As she gathered her clothes for the gym, Diane invited Enoch to join her, mostly to be polite, since he never set foot in a health club. She changed in the bathroom, with the door shut. They had been married three days, hardly enough time to become comfortable dressing in front of each other.

"So, what time do you want to go for dinner?" she asked through the closed door.

"Let me see," Enoch replied, and consulted his wristwatch. "I should be back here around seven, seven-thirty. Let's eat at eight."

When she came out from the bathroom in her workout clothes, she asked, "Where are you going?"

"I'll try to visit the—well, at least establish contact with," he corrected himself, "the Collection."

Diane kept looking at him, expecting more.

"Oh," she said.

"It's better for when I write this trip off if the expense record starts the day I landed," he explained.

"The houses here don't have dashed addresses," a very polite although somewhat effeminate man told Enoch on Royal Street. "Whoever wrote that must have made a mistake."

"I copied it from their printed literature," Enoch said. "Do the addresses at least follow a grid?"

"The Quarter goes up to thirteen starting from Canal Street and up to... ten, I think, from the river."

When the man turned his head, Enoch saw two earrings in his right ear.

"Which way is Barracks Street?" Enoch asked.

The man directed him toward the eastern end of the Quarter. Enoch thanked him and set off down Royal.

Across the street, the late day's sun shone amber upon the bricks and woodwork of the buildings' third and fourth stories. At the corner Enoch stepped into the syrupy gold light, a haze so heavy that he walked directly into the path of a moving car and forced it to brake.

"Sorry," he said to the driver, who waved him across, no doubt believing Enoch drunk.

When he reached the shade again, Enoch did feel intoxicated, or at least impaired. The cold clarity inside the shadows cast a blue filter over his sight. A woman half a block ahead of him wore a white shirt that stood out as though the hour had already reached dusk; somewhere farther from the equator, Enoch guessed, it probably would have. He glanced up at the still-bright sky, at the darker tendrils seeping across from the east. Here celestial bodies obeyed laws different from the ones he knew.

As he traveled Royal, each alley and doorway murkier than the last, Enoch wondered how a newcomer could tell a dangerous neighborhood from any other in this city. He crossed through the sunshine again, two blocks after the first time, and already the light had grown visibly weaker, the ensuing shade deeper.

The woman in the white shirt ahead of Enoch paused for several seconds while a stranger accosted her, until with a curt shake of her head she resumed walking. Frantically the stranger glanced in both directions along the cross street, then turned toward Enoch.

It was a girl, beautiful and quite young. Her gaze locked upon Enoch's as he came closer.

"Sir?" she said, wearily. "Can you help me? I've just had my purse stolen."

"Did you see who took it?" Enoch asked her.

She nodded.

"Let's get a policeman," Enoch said.

"No," she said. "I tried, and they said they couldn't do anything because I'm from out of state."

"Really?" he said. "How long ago did you get robbed?"

She thought about it. "Maybe an hour ago," she said.

Rubbing his chin, Enoch said. "Would you know where to find these people who robbed you?"

"No," she said. "They're drug addicts. By now all my money's gone and they're high on crack."

Enoch nodded.

Lips quivering, she said, "All I want is to go home. A bus ticket costs thirty-two dollars."

"Where do you live?"

"I'm from Missouri," she said. "I don't want to have to sell myself to get home."

"You don't have to do that," Enoch said. "Don't even think that way."

The girl nodded.

"What's your name?" he asked.

"Stephanie," she said.

"Stephanie, you need to call your family," Enoch said.

"I don't *have* any family," she told him, sobbing.

Six or seven white-haired vacationers approached. As though drawn by their scent Stephanie spun to greet them. Her perfume wafted past Enoch, very faint but too sweet. Sweat tainted it, feminine perspiration. Enoch had only become familiar with such odors scant days earlier, so perhaps many women he'd met had smelled this way without his detecting their aroma.

"Can you help me?" Stephanie begged the aged group.

"What's the matter, young lady?" a man in a stiff new shirt asked. Enoch guessed the man's age at sixty-eight.

"My purse has been stolen," Stephanie told him. "They took my purse and all my money. I can't get home."

By the time she had mentioned the ticket price, which had escalated to thirty-eight dollars, the man already had his wallet out. He reeked of liquor. Many strangers here did, and Enoch supposed that the drunks would grow in number with the onset of night.

"Come with us for a drink," the older man said to Stephanie.

"Yes," said a lady behind him. "Come to Pat O'Brien's with us. Our treat. You'll feel better."

Holding her hand out for money, Stephanie said, "I can't come with you. I'm sorry. Thank you, though."

Their voices faded from Enoch's ears as he continued down Royal. Soon he reached Barracks Street.

The first and second block he saw of Barracks called to Enoch's mind a tidy summer community: small wooden houses, parking stickers on rear windshields. But no porches. Most of the houses had either wooden or cement stoops; on five or six of them, someone with a stencil had spraypainted the words PLEASE DO NOT SIT ON THESE STEPS in white. Enoch glanced up and saw jagged spikes rising from the top of a fence. Nails, they looked like.

The street was empty, except for a man walking two black dogs, a cocker spaniel and some kind of terrier. The man's expression seemed irate. He exchanged nods with Enoch as they passed.

The address Enoch needed didn't exist. A park surrounded by an iron fence occupied the entire block. Just enough light remained for him to see a few men on the grass inside throwing tennis balls for their dogs to fetch.

Across the street all the buildings connected in a single row, except for one alley in the middle of the block. The fifteen-foot stretch of sidewalk without a curb showed that this passage had once been a driveway. A bright steel storm fence ran across it now. Nothing here seemed a likely home for the Collection.

A terrible scream gave Enoch a start.

It came from the pig he and Diane had seen on Bourbon Street. The two men had recruited a third, thinner fellow clad entirely in black, and all three were now pulling the pig along the sidewalk. It didn't want to come.

The fellow in black opened the front door of the building next to the alley and the men dragged the pig inside. The door slammed shut behind them, which muted the pig's squeal until they dragged him out a side door into the alley. The pig wailed all the way down the alley and around the back of the house.

"They're not slaughtering that pig, are they?" said a man from just inside the park. During the commotion Enoch had not noticed the man's arrival at the fence beside him.

"No, you can't kill an animal in city limits," Enoch said. "Can you?"

"People do it every year, during Mardi Gras," the dog owner said. "I find it disgusting, myself."

Enoch went back to the hotel. As he walked, he noted sharp obstacles atop every gate he saw. On brick or stone walls, the builders had embedded glass shards in the uppermost layer of mortar. It surprised Enoch that he and Diane had missed this detail earlier, in plain daylight.

When he arrived in their room, Diane nodded at him without speaking.

"What's the matter?" Enoch asked.

Diane shook her head, staring out the window.

"I went to the address, and the building didn't exist," Enoch told her. "I'll have to call information and find the correct address."

For a brief instant Diane shot him a grimace, as though it pained her that he should speak.

"Maybe I'll just phone Mister LeCerce," Enoch said. "I'm sure I wrote his number down."

"This man," Diane said.

Enoch listened, patiently.

"This man made advances at me," Diane said. "In the gym."

From nowhere the thought of a drink of water crossed Enoch's mind. "Advances?" he urged her on, as gently as he could.

"Yes."

He drew a breath in, released it. "Advances like what? Did he touch you, or—?"

"No." Her gaze had returned to the window. "He had shorts on that showed his—his penis, and so forth."

"He showed his penis to you."

"No, no." With her left hand Diane erased an invisible blackboard in front of her. "No. He just—wore these shorts. Right in front of me. You could see it."

"Through his clothes," Enoch clarified.

"The outline of it. All of it."

Anger rose in Enoch's stomach. He resisted it, and spoke calmly. "Do you want me to call the hotel and complain?"

Diane shook her head.

"Think that over," he said. "There'll still be time later if you change your mind."

"I just want somewhere else to work out," Diane said.

When Enoch outlined (in the vaguest terms) his dissatisfaction with the gym at his hotel, Mr. LeCerce immediately recommended his own health club. Enoch wrote the club's address next to the one Mister LeCerce gave him for the Collection. After they hung up, Enoch tore the sheet of paper in two and handed one half to Diane.

"Mister LeCerce assures me you'll love it. Your name's at the reception desk, and you'll be his guest," Enoch told her. "Ask for A.D. LeCerce."

She took the slip and nodded.

"He says it's one of the oldest clubs in the country," he went on. "Women have only been allowed to join in the last five years. Blacks, too. He makes it sound very elegant."

Diane smiled. "Thanks," she said. "How late are they open?"

"I don't know," Enoch replied, taking from the side pocket of his suitcase *The Christian Traveler's Guide to New Orleans*. Under the Health And Fitness category he found the club by its address and gave Diane the phone number. She dialed and spoke to them.

"They're open until ten," she said to Enoch. "I'll just go get a cab."

"I didn't think you were going there tonight," Enoch said.

"Well, I didn't get to work out this afternoon, with this stranger swinging his, his—"

"Diane, I'm not objecting," Enoch said quickly. "I'm just confused. I thought we were going for dinner."

"Oh," Diane said. "I guess we could just eat after I get back. Or I could meet you."

"No, that's all right," he said. "I can just get room service. You could eat in the restaurant downstairs when you get back. It's open late."

Still wearing her jumpsuit from her earlier visit, Diane put on a gray T-shirt with a white CRUSADE FOR CHRIST logo ironed onto the front. She packed Enoch's *Christian Traveler's Guide* and the slip of paper with the club's address into her gym bag and left.

Not long after she'd gone, Enoch phoned room service for dinner. He considered ordering a movie, too, but none of the choices sounded worthwhile. His steak arrived promptly.

After he ate, he stared out the window, trying to think of something else to do until Diane returned. Each possibility that rose to his mind—the Aquarium, the Riverwalk, the revolving bar atop the World Trade Center—was something he'd rather wait to do with her.

So he turned the television off and tuned the radio to a gospel station. Friends had insisted Enoch listen to jazz while in New Orleans, but the disc jockeys' puerile jokes kept him from enjoying the station everyone recommended. The gospel station, by contrast, displayed barely any hint of on-air personality between the recordings.

While he listened, Enoch decided to unpack his bags into the bureau. Earlier Diane had claimed the closet for her clothes, and told him to use the battered dresser.

None of the drawers opened or closed properly. It reminded Enoch of furniture left ownerless at the end of a charity drive. The narrow drawers at the top felt flimsy as he loaded his socks and underwear into them. Two of the three wider drawers below slipped off their metal runners when he pulled them halfway out.

A tiny dead roach lay in the dust on the bottom of the middle drawer. This sight stopped Enoch cold, three folded polo shirts stacked in his left hand. Then he moved his clothes, everything he'd put away so far, back into his suitcase. Diane would not appreciate having his luggage in plain sight for their entire stay, but—

The lowermost drawer refused to shut at all. Enoch lifted it up and down, jiggling it upon its treadle. The drawer seemed to work fine. He pushed it again, and again felt it stop, and he guessed that some object—something firmer than clothing; perhaps a Gideon Bible—had fallen from one of the other drawers to block the bottom one's path.

So he slid the drawer out all the way. Behind it inside the bureau lay a gray cardboard box. When he brought it into the light he found dust collected along one narrow edge of the box, the edge that must have faced upward while the box stood hidden inside the dresser. Enoch's jostling the dresser with its drawers open had allowed the box to fall flat.

The lid slid easily off the box. Inside lay a manuscript of photocopied pages from a thick comic book.

Enoch had little experience with secular comics, but the manuscript's length seemed to him excessive: three hundred pages, at least. He flipped through it. The entire sheaf was a comic book.

A small figure stood at the top of the first page, a man dressed in a top hat and ragged tails. The tiny fellow gestured with his hand as though introducing the story, yet he said nothing. In fact, the first page contained no dialogue whatsoever. Neither did the second, nor the third.

The story began with a man wearing a rumpled hat, walking in the rain. In the first few frames demonic creatures darted their heads out from behind buildings to smirk at the man after he passed. The man turned to check behind him, and of course found nothing there. At the bottom of the page he entered a seedy building. The second page began with the man seated on a bed. A woman knelt before him, gratifying him sexually with her mouth.

Normally Enoch would have stopped reading right there, yet the lack of words made him curious. Perhaps this artist had some point to make. This imagery seemed extreme, even for a secular comic. Without text it gave no obvious call to leer. It certainly didn't seem intended for children.

The rest of the second page depicted various sex acts, half of them in close-up. So did the third page, and the fourth. As he examined them, Enoch marveled at his own lack of disgust. His new familiarity with the subject matter had supplanted the revulsion he'd taught himself as a teenager.

The sex stopped on page six. The man left the building and went home to bed. A panel of him asleep in the dark showed an X-ray map of the man's blood vessels in white. An arrow linked one of the arteries in the X-ray to a circle containing a blowup of the cellular flow within. The blowup showed corkscrew-shaped creatures invading the man's bloodstream. These creatures had the same triangular eyes as the demons from page one.

Throughout page seven, the man's disease ravaged him. The first image showed him urinating, his face tortured. Others had him curled on his bed in pain. From panel to panel he developed more lesions. By the page's bottom his air of misery had progressed to one of madness. Chancres ate the flesh from his cheeks.

At the top of page eight the man sat on an exam table in a doctor's office. The doctor frowned, his arms extended in a helpless shrug. Then the man exchanged money with a black teenager for a handgun, went on a shooting spree on a crowded street that resembled the French Quarter, and died when police shot him down. At the climax that little figure in the top hat reappeared, grinning again.

This silent host reminded Enoch of a man he and Diane had seen walking Conti Street earlier, a man dressed the same way. Perhaps that was an archaic style down here, among older men who prided themselves on their eccentricity.

Enoch placed the manuscript back in its box. For some reason he wanted to put it in the same position he'd found it, behind the drawer. He doubted now that the box had gotten there by accident. It belonged to someone who had stashed it inside the bureau; tugging his clothes out of the drawers, Enoch had made it fall horizontal.

Instead he placed the box in the bottom drawer and closed it.

When Diane returned, she entered carefully, so as not to wake Enoch. He heard her anyway as she took her nightgown from the closet. For a few moments he observed his wife unawares as she placed her right hand against her hip and glared at his suitcase.

"I started putting my clothes into the drawers," Enoch said, lifting his head. "There's a roach in one of them."

Diane faced him, a little embarrassed at having reacted angrily while he spied on her. "Why didn't you just kill it?" she asked.

"It's dead. But that means they live in there. I didn't want bugs on my clothes," he said.

"No, of course," Diane agreed.

Enoch sat up and checked the clock. "It's after eleven," he told her.

"Yeah." Diane walked into the bathroom to change.

"Did you eat?" he asked.

"No," she said, and closed the door.

Louder, he said, "All right, then let's go eat downstairs."

"No, that's okay," she replied through the closed door. "I'm pretty tired. I had a good workout."

"I would expect so," Enoch said, not loud enough for her to hear clearly.

A few minutes passed. Diane emerged from the bathroom and crawled into bed beside him. Enoch kissed her on the neck, which he knew she liked. It didn't arouse her this time, however. Swiftly he slid his hand inside her nightgown, down her stomach onto her pudendum. With a shift of her hips she pulled away.

"I'm really tired, Enoch," she said. "All right?"

He removed his hand and examined it. "My hand's damp," he said.

"What?"

"My fingers are wet where I touched you," he said. "Are you sweating?"

Diane pulled the front of her nightgown closed. "I guess I forgot to take a shower when I left the gym."

"I read where you can get infections from doing that," Enoch said.

"That's not for you to worry about," Diane said. "That's *my* business."

"No, your health is my business, too, now. I'm your husband."

Very audibly she exhaled. A vibration rippled across the mattress as she impatiently rapped her fingers upon it.

"Diane..."

"*What*?" she snapped, with as much venom as Enoch had ever heard from her.

He switched on the bedside lamp and said, "Diane, what's the matter?"

"*Nothing* is the matter, I just need to sleep."

"Something doesn't sound right about your voice. And your eyes don't look right," Enoch said. "Did you have anything to drink that someone could have dropped something into?"

Diane smirked at him and rolled over. "Go to sleep," she said.

But she herself didn't. Several times as Enoch drifted back off she jolted him awake by rolling over or fidgeting. Finally she got up.

"Enoch?" she slurred. "Do you mind if I put on the television, real low?"

He yawned his permission and slept.

White noise woke him. The sun had all but risen, and Diane had fallen asleep in her chair with the television on. The station had gone off the air.

Enoch climbed from the bed long enough to shut off the TV and shake Diane. "Hey, why aren't you in bed?" he asked her.

Her stiff neck made her wince.

"Come to bed," Enoch said.

She did. He held her close and massaged her neck and shoulder with one hand. Diane fell back asleep.

Enoch didn't. The room's window faced away from the sunrise, but what clouds he could see turned bright magenta as the sky lightened to the blue of a robin's egg.

An hour crawled past. The city seemed impossibly clamorous outside. Finally Enoch got up and stretched. No point forcing himself to rest, morning had arrived. He prayed and took a shower, then donned some casual clothes.

Dressed, he bent gently over the bed. "Diane?" he asked, poking her. "Diane?"

All at once she bolted awake. "What is it?" she demanded.

"I—I'm just going outside," he answered, reeling back. "I didn't want you to wake up and wonder where I'd gone."

"Fine," Diane said, and rolled over.

Her crankiness annoyed him, but his annoyance passed by the time he reached the elevator. The halls were empty. Enoch pressed the DOWN button. As he waited, the smell of mildew—of something (the carpet?) made wet and never allowed to dry—evoked a memory of a camp in upstate New York where he'd taken a retreat the summer he was fifteen. His Christian Youth Module had booked the weekend based only upon the camp's brochure, perhaps based most of all upon one illustration that depicted the site's days as a renowned spa in the late 1800s. The dour people who now ran the camp had not redecorated the buildings during Enoch's lifetime, and every room reeked of wet rot. Vividly Enoch recalled how unclean he felt returning to his lodging after necking with a girl named Rita in the woods just after dark.

The elevator came.

Downstairs a man behind the concierge's desk politely acknowledged Enoch's exit. Out on the sidewalk two black men in hotel uniforms stood chatting and smoking cigarettes.

"Excuse me," Enoch said.

The doorman regarded Enoch curiously, almost reluctantly. The other, a porter, ignored him.

"Where can I get a cup of coffee and a paper?"

The doorman thought a moment, then said, "Cafe du Monde, sir."

After a silence, Enoch asked, "Where would I find that?"

The doorman gave directions as though Enoch had committed a faux-pas by needing them, and the porter weighed in with a put-upon glance.

The cafe took Enoch a quarter-hour to reach, but he did not mind the walk. Early daylight made the French Quarter pretty and innocuous. Passing through Pirate's Alley in the shade of the cathedral felt almost brisk, and the light when he emerged into sunny Jackson Square did not stupefy him the way it had the previous evening.

Stripped of crowds, the square radiated far more charm. Despite wanting something to eat, Enoch paused to watch a middle-aged woman who had just applied the first paint to a canvas. She smiled at him.

But hunger drove him into the cafe, actually an outdoor cafeteria of wobbly iron tables under a massive tent. A Vietnamese waitress, eager for her shift to end, smiled at him and said, "Sit wherever." The cafe served only coffee with chicory, hot chocolate, and small square fried doughnuts called beignets. He nearly rose from his table to leave, but he was too hungry to hunt down a restaurant.

The coffee was good. The beignets came smothered in confectioner's sugar. As he ate, Enoch noticed pedestrian traffic growing denser on Decatur Street. Families strolled together past the mule carriages lined up outside De Gaulle Park. By the time Enoch finished and rose from his table, the sidewalks had reached a steady pulse.

The crowd carried him up Decatur Street until North Peters split away to follow the same route as the Riverfront streetcar. Soon he reached an outdoor market and wandered among its stalls. None of the merchandise interested him. The mounting humidity made him too sluggish to browse.

On the other side of the market Enoch walked onto a street and saw that it was Barracks, the one he had searched yesterday for the Collection. A block to his right this street ended—began, rather—in the sheer cement wall that separated North Peters from the trolley tracks. That dog park where he'd wound up yesterday must lie to his left, and the Collection lay across the street from the park. He checked his pocket, found the torn slip upon which he'd written the correct address Mr. LeCerce had given him, and set off there.

Sunlight and exercise put Enoch in better spirits that even the drunkards he saw sleeping in doorways did not lessen. He walked all the way to Bourbon before it dawned on him how early the hour was; nobody would be at the Collection yet.

He continued anyway, figuring he might as well locate the building. It wouldn't mean going much out of his way back to the hotel, and far fewer tourists roamed the streets at this end of the Quarter. In a small way it now bothered him to think a mob had swept him in its own direction when he'd left the cafe.

Only two owners had brought their dogs to the park. Enoch noticed piles of rags heaped against the park's far wall, and came to realize that each pile contained a sleeping person.

Across the street, the row of attached buildings lacked posted addresses. Enoch tried to estimate by counting, but the gap between the two numbered buildings at either corner was twenty-five, so he could only guess.

The steel fence that enclosed the only alley on the block stood at least fifteen feet high. As Enoch stood before it, the waist-high black pig approached him down the driveway, either warily or lazily but without sound.

"Hey," Enoch greeted the pig. "Hey, how you doing?"

The pig stopped four feet from the fence and watched Enoch, its only reaction an occasional lilt in its nasal panting. It still wore its costume, or at least part of it: a pair of red horns on its head. The red leather harness around the animal's torso had runes hammered onto its straps.

The dog owner's comment about ritual sacrifice chimed in Enoch's head. Even so ugly a creature...

"All right, fella," he said, and left.

He returned to the hotel to find his room empty. A piece of hotel stationery lay on the table; on it in pencil Diane had written:

> *ENOCH,*
>
> *I WENT TO WORK OUT AT THE GYM. I'LL BE BACK LATER*
> *LIKE LUNCHTIME.*
> *LOVE YOU,*
>
> > *DIANE.*

With a sigh he sat down. The digital clock on the nightstand said eighteen minutes after ten. "I had no idea it was so late already," Enoch said aloud.

Nothing on the television interested him, and he had already had breakfast, satisfying or not. He put the gospel station on the radio again. After a quarter-hour he remembered that comic book in the the bureau and opened the bottom drawer to look for it.

The bottom drawer was empty.

Instead he found the box in the middle drawer, and told himself, "I know I did not put this here." When he opened it the pages themselves showed no fingerprints or creases.

Enoch switched off the radio and sat at the small round table to read. For some reason, he did not want Diane's note to share the tabletop with this comic, so he folded the sheet of stationery and slid it into the left rear pocket of his jeans. He flipped through the story of the man driven mad by venereal disease.

Drawn in a similar though more realistic style, the second story actually used dialogue balloons, but no dialogue. Instead the balloons contained drawings. The weird host introduced the story without comment, just a malevolent grin and his hands folded over his heart.

In the first panel a girl stood alone on a street corner, staring toward her right. In the second, she checked toward her left, as if nervous. Then an elderly couple came, and the girl began speaking through tears; her balloon showed two black kids dashing away with her purse. The elderly man gave the girl forty dollars.

"It's Stephanie," Enoch said, and held the page closer to his eyes. After a few seconds he decided, "Yes, definitely." This artist had used as his model the girl Enoch had met on Royal Street yesterday. So close a likeness could not result from chance. Even the almost-shabby clothes matched. The artist either knew her or had spied upon her confidence routine.

On the second page Stephanie pled her case to a variety of strangers, mostly older tourists. On the next page she counted the huge wad of bills she had amassed, and traveled to a ramshackle house. Inside this house she sat leaning against a wall, smoking a tiny glass pipe. Her irises became strange circles within her eyes.

An unsavory man—he didn't look black, exactly, perhaps South American—spoke to her; his speech consisted of a white object on a plate. Enoch looked closer. The object was in fact a pile of powder.

Stephanie left with the man, and smoked her glass pipe in his car as he drove. Then she sucked little rows of the powder up her nose; the man had brought her to a very seedy hotel room. Another similar man had joined them.

Suddenly all three were having sex. Stephanie squatted on her hands and knees, upside-down, with one of the men entering her from behind while she took the other's penis in her mouth.

Enoch had of course heard of such acts—more accurately, had been warned against them—but of course he had never seen them. He couldn't tell whether the man in the back was performing intercourse or sodomy.

The two men indulged both those urges simultaneously in closeup through-out the next page. Stephanie took a break to sniff more powder. Enoch recognized the odd box on the three-legged stand in the background as a camcorder. People's need to capture such depravity on tape baffled him.

The artwork achieved an all but photographic realism, especially when documenting the girl's face as she used her mouth on the men's genitals. The very nature of this act struck Enoch as demeaning and immoral, yet he had to grant that Stephanie managed to make it appealing, at least visually.

At the top of the next page, the men's heads had changed, unnoticed by Stephanie. Now they were gleeful demons, similar to the ones that taunted the VD victim in the previous story but more clearly visible.

They began to stab her with knives.

For several panels she fought back, her body now a mess of blood, her face contorted in terror. Both attackers remained sexually aroused throughout her murder, even as they withdrew the videocassette from the camera and fled the scene.

In the final panel, a group of teenaged boys knelt in front of a television with a VCR on top. The boys smiled sadistically. On the screen Stephanie's body lay on the floor, riddled with stab wounds. If the older man in the funny clothes had not appeared leaning against this panel, Enoch would not have known the story had ended.

He placed the manuscript back in its box with extreme care. All at once he declared, "This thing is warped," and chucked the box into the bottom drawer again.

Now Enoch's head ached. He had longer than an hour to wait until Diane returned, so he lay on the bed and massaged his eyelids.

When Enoch woke up it was nighttime. Diane had just opened the door and come in, her gym bag slung over one shoulder.

"Where have you been?" he asked.

"I went to the gym," she answered. "Didn't you get my note?"

"You said you'd be back for lunch," Enoch reminded her, glancing at the clock. "It's almost nine o'clock! You've been at the gym all this time?"

Diane studied him for a moment, eager to placate him but impaired some-how, sluggish. Then she said, "Where else would I go, dressed like this?" She gestured clumsily with her hands at her clothes.

Enoch rubbed his face and said, "We have to go eat. I haven't eaten."

"Where do you want to go?" Diane asked him.

"I don't know, somewhere close by," he said, and picked up the phone. He dialed the front desk, and instructed the concierge to find them the quickest reservations possible.

Diane sat at the table. As Enoch rose from the bed he said, "Listen for the phone, will you? I need a shower."

She nodded, her eyes dull.

When he had dried off and dressed, Diane showed Enoch the message she had taken from the concierge: They now had reservations very shortly at a family-owned restaurant on Royal Street not too far from Canal. Diane's handwriting listed heavily to the right, a trait it normally didn't exhibit.

They took a cab to the restaurant, where a hostess seated them at a table near the front windows. This area of the dining room had softer, dimmer lighting and a constant trickle of nightlife outside. Every so often a mule-drawn carriage would pass. Diane ordered filet mignon, and Enoch had smothered duck. The food surpassed their expectations, though so would the check.

Midway through dinner Enoch recognized a pedestrian through the window, an older man he couldn't quite place until he noticed the top hat. It was the host from the comic book. His features had struck Enoch's memory on first sight because the cartoon version of this man in no way caricatured him. The pronounced nobility of his nose and chin translated perfectly into pen and ink.

Enoch caught himself staring after the man had passed.

"What?" Diane asked.

"Nothing," Enoch said. "I didn't say anything." He warded off further conversation by waving his hand.

They ate rapidly, and very soon felt full. They couldn't finish their entrees. When they rose from their table to go, Enoch carried two styrofoam containers filled with their leftovers.

Outside the restaurant, the air felt thick, still. Enoch came to a stop. Diane halted beside him, yet didn't look at him; instead she faced oncoming tourists. A dull, filmy gleam shone in the whites of her eyes.

"Look at *that*," she said. "That is dis*gust*ing."

A stranger approaching them had facial scars of some kind. Enoch didn't gaze at them directly because Diane's voice seemed louder than usual, certainly loud enough for this passerby to have just heard.

"His face is—*ucch*!" Diane gagged before she could complete her opinion. The man reached them, furious. Enoch paled, but then realized this man's anger had nothing to do with them. Rage had prevented the man from listening to Diane.

Enoch watched the man pass, and then went rigid. Enoch's jaw hung open.

"What's wrong with him?" Diane asked.

"He has syphilis, I think," Enoch told her, and then heard himself adding, to no one, "It can't be."

"I can see right into his cheeks," Diane said. "Syphilis does that to your face?"

"Only if you don't treat it in time," Enoch said, not believing the sound of his own voice. "That man..."

Diane's eyebrows rose. "Do you *know* him?"

"No," Enoch said, shaking his head. "He's dangerous."

"If you don't know him," she reasoned, "how do you know he's d—"

Several shots fired, down the street where the man had gone. Enoch pushed his wife into the doorway of the restaurant and held himself against her as a shield. Down near the gunfire a woman screamed, and then several shouts brought more shooting. Ancient brick facades muted each shot's report, softened the sharpest edges of the sound, made it somehow less menacing.

"It's the police," Enoch told Diane. "They're killing him."

"How do you know?" She wet her lips.

The gunfight ceased.

"How could you tell that the police had gotten him?" she asked again as they relaxed and stepped out of the doorway. Up and down Royal Street, people thrust their heads out of doorways and windows, out of bars and apartments, amazed by what they'd just heard.

"I just know," he told her, shivering. "I have to find Stephanie."

"Stephanie?" Diane said.

"You don't know her," Enoch assured her.

"I know a Stephanie," Diane insisted.

"Not this one," Enoch said. "Come with me." He led her up Royal Street, away from the shooting, toward the corner where he'd met Stephanie yesterday.

They traveled briskly, and just as that particular corner became more or less distinct ahead of them, Enoch grasped the futility of coming here now, expecting to find the girl at work. Obviously she couldn't pull this sort of stunt in the same location, day after day.

Yet the impulse to come here had, if nothing else, brought him and his wife away from the gunfire, so Enoch continued. When they reached the corner where he'd encountered Stephanie, he kept his hands in his pockets and checked the cross street in either direction.

"How do you know this girl?" Diane asked.

"She pretends she's gotten robbed," Enoch explained. "I don't really know her. I met her here yesterday, and she told me someone had stolen her pocketbook. She tries to get money from people for a bus ticket, then she spends the money on drugs."

Diane digested this information, and then said, "So you need to find her now to give her money."

"No! Of course not," Enoch said. "We have to tell her she's in danger."

"From that man who got shot."

"No." Enoch tried to swallow, couldn't. "From drug people she knows."

Diane scanned passersby to make certain no one else had heard him.

"Diane, I'm sorry," Enoch said. "The gunshots and everything panicked me a little, and I guess I'm not making much sense."

She nodded.

"Let's just go back to the hotel," Enoch suggested, and hailed a taxi.

Enoch slept much more soundly than he expected, considering he'd just spent an entire day asleep.

When he awoke, Diane had already risen and dressed. She sat at the table, writing a letter.

"Morning," he said.

"Oh," she said, and put down her felt pen. "Good morning."

Enoch cleared his throat. "Want to order breakfast in?" he asked.

"I thought I'd just grab something at the gym," Diane said.

"The gym?" To clear his vision, he blinked several times, and saw her gym bag packed and waiting beside the door.

"Yes, they have a restaurant," she said. "It's more of a health club, actually, than just a gym."

"You were at the gym all day yesterday," Enoch said.

Diane nodded. She took her letter off the table and ripped it into halves, quarters, then eighths.

"How often do you suppose we'll get to travel someplace like this?" Enoch said. "We ought to spend some time together here. You should see something besides the gymnasium."

"I was just going because I didn't want to wake you," Diane said, still shredding. "I figured I would be back before you woke up."

Enoch sat upright. "Let's go to the zoo," he said. "How do you feel about that? We can take the streetcar up to Audubon Zoo."

"That sounds great," she said, and dumped the particles of stationery into the wastebasket.

"Let's just eat downstairs and then go ride the streetcar." Enoch stood and scratched himself. "I need a shower, did you already take one?"

"Yes," Diane said. "Go ahead."

"All right, then," Enoch said, and pointed at the table. "Were you writing a letter home?"

"Oh, no," she said. "I was leaving you a note, in case you woke up." She nodded toward the wastebasket. "So you'd know where I was."

Yawning, Enoch stretched thoroughly. He entered the bathroom and turned on the shower. The room filled with steam. One aspect of this hotel he could endorse wholeheartedly was its water pressure. The hot cascade warmed his skin, honed his appetite.

It also made him feel more flexible. Afterward, while drying himself with a towel, he had the idea to make love to Diane right now, in the full light of morning. So he opened the bathroom door, as if to let fresh air inside, and peeked toward the table.

"Diane?" he called, and then, louder, "Diane, where are you?"

Gone.

Awkwardly, since the idea of seduction had aroused him, Enoch padded out of the bathroom nude and searched the room as though Diane might be hiding somewhere in it. She had left no note, so he assumed her gone only momentarily, to get ice or a newspaper, perhaps.

Waiting for her, he shaved and put his clothes on. He dressed casual again, since the brochure he'd read said the zoo occupied just part of a large park that he and Diane would probably explore. For a moment he debated whether to bring a sweatshirt or his windbreaker, then he resolved to ask Diane when she came back, figuring she'd stepped outside the hotel or seen people who had.

Enoch stared across the room.

Diane's gym bag had disappeared.

"She went. To." Words failed him.

With the fingertips of both hands he rubbed his temples to slow the burning blood within. The pressure inside his skull decreased, and Enoch did a slow sweep of the room, searching for any detail that might suggest a conclusion other than that his wife had defied him. He found none.

Diane had taken Enoch's *Christian Traveler's Guide* from him the day before yesterday and had not returned it to his suitcase. Instead he looked up Health Clubs in the Yellow Pages. None of their names or addresses struck him as familiar.

With the phone already in his hand Enoch decided not to call Mr. LeCerce and ask for the club's address a second time; it could scarcely make a good impression. Diane would come back, and Enoch would put his foot down. No point getting frantic in the meantime.

Very deliberately he relaxed, listened to the radio. A municipal affairs program came on, and he turned it off. In a detached way he knew he should feel hungry, yet something told him not to eat until he settled matters with Diane. Calm or roiling, his stomach might still tie itself in knots.

After half an hour's staring out the window, Enoch retrieved the manuscript box from the bureau's bottom drawer. He flipped the pages quickly, so as not to let the first two stories retrigger their unpleasantness.

When he reached the third story he held its first page close to his eyes, combing the images for some clue whether they were drawn or photographed. Kids Enoch saw riding the bus during high school had worn jackets with rock album covers painted on the back by airbrush, but none with such clarity. Yet each panel contained a vital charge too perfect to shine from a photograph, unless the copier or laser printer that created these pages had distorted them subtly. A lecturer Enoch saw in Memphis claimed that pornographers routinely used the airbrush to remove models' blemishes, and that such finessing violated Scripture.

The third story had no dialogue. It also seemed not to have any narrative. It began with two women smiling at each other; each had her right index finger inserted completely inside the other's vagina. One sported upper arms large enough that, confused by her crewcut, Enoch mistook her upon first glimpse for a man.

The rest of the panels on the page imitated a movie camera, pulling back to show the two women's location: a locker room. Other women changed their clothes merrily, grinning at the two exhibitionists, admiring one another's breasts and buttocks. Aside from this slow revelation, nothing happened on the entire first page.

At the top of the second page, Diane entered the locker room. Enoch scoured the page to make sure the resemblance was coincidental. It *had* to be. It wasn't.

The sunlight from the window behind Enoch had assumed the color of marmalade.

On the page, Diane marched down the aisle between rows of lockers; the other women eyed her appreciatively. One in particular, a redhead with short hair who still looked feminine, made eye contact with her. Diane chose a locker and undressed. Everyone watched.

Naked, Diane strolled into the steam room. The redhead followed. Inside, they at first sat across from one another, bodies dripping perspiration, legs open wide. Then the redhead crossed the steam room. Diane awaited her anxiously.

The next page contained only one panel, as real as a photograph from *Time* or *Newsweek*. The full-page picture showed Diane reclining against the wall, her head thrown back against the tiles in ecstasy. The redhead had two fingers inside Diane's vagina while she licked the sensitive top part, where the lips folded together.

Enoch dropped the entire manuscript onto the bed. The pages fanned slightly, as would a deck of cards. Then he stood up, pulled the shade to quell the thick sunlight, and ran a hand through his hair. The instant the manuscript left his direct vision, Enoch's mind struggled to pretend he had not seen what it had shown him. After half a minute he picked the pages back up, and saw to his horror that the story did not end where he'd stopped reading.

On the next page, Diane and this woman worked out together. In one panel Diane leg-pressed while her partner did ankle lifts; next she did French curls and the redhead worked the horizontal bench. It pursued that pattern until the last frame, wherein the two women left the workout area, arms around each other, headed back to the ladies' lockers.

Seething, Enoch nonetheless wondered aloud, "What happened to the old man who introduced the other two stories?"

Enoch dumped his own suitcase onto the carpet, searching for his jacket. It did not turn up anywhere in the heap of clothes. He opened the closet.

The closet was empty. All Diane's clothes, and her suitcase, had vanished.

Enoch found his jacket and his sweatshirt draped over the chair, where he'd left them earlier when choosing which to wear. He put on his jacket and left.

In the elevator as he rode down, a drunk couple necked beside him. When the doors opened on the ground floor, Enoch walked to the desk. Not until the concierge hung up his red phone and asked, "Can I help you, sir?" did Enoch realize he didn't know what he expected the concierge to tell him.

"Sir?" the man asked again.

"Yes, I hope you can," Enoch said, and gave the concierge his room number. "I realize this is probably an unusual request, but I'm just wondering if you saw a woman in a sweatsuit carry some luggage out of here about an hour ago."

"Oh, sir, I couldn't tell you," the concierge said. "Would she have had us hail her a cab?"

"Probably," Enoch said, though he hadn't thought of it.

"Then you could ask the doorman," the concierge suggested.

As Enoch stalked outside, he pulled a graduation photograph of Diane from his wallet. "Excuse me," he said to the doorman. It was the same one who had grudgingly directed him to Cafe du Monde yesterday morning.

"Yes, sir?" the doorman said.

"Have you seen this woman?" Enoch asked, holding out the photo. "She would've left about an hour ago, I guess."

The doorman nodded. "Helped her with her luggage. Boyfriend didn't tip me."

"What boyfriend?"

"The guy who drove her," the doorman said. "It was a..." He closed his eyes, trying to recall. "It was, like, a Hyundai. Not a Hyundai, but one them Japanese cars. In real bad shape. Hood was a different color from the rest of the car, and like that."

Enoch's stomach felt punched. "What did this fellow look like?"

"I don't know, young guy with a stupid haircut," the doorman said, and stepped forward to hold the door for the besotted couple who had ridden the elevator with Enoch.

Enoch stepped after the doorman, and said, "Hold on. Did she know this guy, for sure?"

"How would I know?" the doorman said.

The doorman said something else, but Enoch didn't catch it. Instead he stared across the street at a passing pedestrian: the host from the comic book.

"Thanks," Enoch said to the doorman, and scooted down the front steps after the oddly attired man.

❈ ❈ ❈

For someone past middle age, the host maintained a surprisingly swift pace. Enoch trailed him through the Quarter from a block behind, and several times had to jog to keep up.

From Royal Street the man turned toward Bourbon, and Enoch lost sight of him across the crowd there until crossing through it himself. The man had gained almost a block; he made a left on Dauphine, and Enoch had to run again.

Just as Enoch reached the corner, the man disappeared to the right around the next one. Enoch charged after him, noticing that his own jacket felt too heavy, though whether due to exertion or to overall discomfort he couldn't say.

The man made another left onto Rampart Street. Enoch lagged just a little, just enough to catch his breath.

When he reached Rampart, he saw no sign of his quarry. "Damn it!" Enoch cursed, stamping on the concrete. Two men working at a tire shop stared at him.

He walked Rampart to the next corner. The man had vanished.

Enoch headed back the way he had come. Halfway down that one block of Rampart Street, he paused to study a building he had passed moments ago, an ornate gray building, taller than most in the French Quarter—taller, at least, than any structure that exuded a similar sense of age.

Across the doorway's stone arch the builders had sculpted words, letters barely legible in a forgotten style: HEALTH & RECREATION LEAGUE OF NEW ORLEANS. The iron-and-glass doors of the health club reminded Enoch of a Catholic church in Pittsburgh where he had attended an ecumenical meeting.

For a moment Enoch stood very still. Sweat tickled his cheek, and he swiped a hand across his forehead. The amount of moisture gathered there surprised him. His face as reflected in the door's panes of glass revealed far more anxious confusion than he intended.

He tidied his hair as he pushed through the doors into a vestibule of polished stone. A brief staircase and a set of swinging wooden doors brought him to the front desk, where a young woman greeted him, "Hi, can I help you?"

"Yes," Enoch said. "My wife works out here. Can I just go in and talk to her?"

"I can page her for you," the receptionist said. "What's her name?"

"Diane Mellon," Enoch said. "I mean, Diane Schrader."

"Schrader?"

"Yes, we just got married," Enoch said. "I'm not used to it, yet."

The woman laughed and pressed several numbers on a house phone. Then she spoke, and her voice boomed across the building. Each time she paused, Enoch could hear her last syllable echo in the club's farthest recesses.

"Diane Schrader," the receptionist said. "Diane Schrader, please come to the front desk. Diane Schrader, please see the front desk."

They waited. No one came in or out, but three different people called. After some time had passed, the receptionist said, "You know, if she doesn't respond, we could try again in about fifteen minutes. In case she's in the sauna or the showers, where they can't hear the PA."

Enoch nodded.

A middle-aged man came in from outside and said to the receptionist, "I'm here to see Laura Schell."

"Hi, I'm Laura," the receptionist said. "You must be Mister Scanlon."

"That's right," Mr. Scanlon said.

"Has anyone shown you the club yet?" Laura asked him, nodding over her shoulder.

"No, I haven't seen it," Mr. Scanlon said.

"Just a sec," Laura said. She picked up the phone and pressed a button. "Ginny, I have to give a tour for a client. Would you come up front to the desk?"

Laura rose from her seat and said, "This way, Mr. Scanlon." As she led him into the hall, a girl with straight black hair appeared and took her seat.

"Are you being helped?" Ginny asked Enoch.

"I'm just waiting for my wife," Enoch said. "Say, can I ask you something?"

Ginny nodded.

"What's that man's name who came in here just a few minutes ago? The last man to come in before Laura's appointment," Enoch said. "He's an older man, and he dresses in a peculiar manner. Almost antique clothing."

She thought about it a moment, and said, "I haven't worked here that long. You could be describing a number of the regulars."

"Oh. Well, I just thought I'd ask," Enoch said. Suddenly he felt suspect. "I met him here, and I've forgotten his name, so I couldn't say hello just now."

"Have you just joined?" Ginny asked.

"Just joined?"

"The club," Ginny said. "Are you a new member?"

Enoch nodded, a little too rapidly. "Yes. My wife and I both joined last week. Very happy that we did."

"Good," Ginny said. The phone rang, and she answered it. Someone made an appointment with her. Then she hung up.

"Do me a favor," Enoch said to her. "I'm going to go see if my wife waited for me inside. If she comes here to the desk, tell her to wait for me?"

"Sure," Ginny said. "What's her name?"

"Diane Schrader," Enoch said. "Thanks." He set off into the club, amazed at how well simple lies could work.

The first room he crossed had a weight-machine section on the right and a line of treadmills on the left, all of it empty but for two men using the weights. Beyond that, Enoch passed a large bar and small offices for personal trainers.

Then he climbed a staircase. One flight up it brought him to a swimming pool, another flight to a track, and then to a long gym full of boxing gear and tennis tables. As he entered, another weight room became visible on his left, one that seemed familiar.

It was the one he had seen Diane use in the comic.

Alongside this weight room ran a hallway, and at its far end lay the doorway to the women's locker room where Diane and her redhead companion were headed at the story's end.

A bead of sweat escaped Enoch's hairline and descended his neck until his collar absorbed it.

As he peered through a cloud of anger to discern the sanest among his options, Enoch saw the women's locker entrance move closer, advancing on him. Just before it swallowed him, he realized that he had in fact dashed forward to it at full speed.

Inside, the locker room did not resemble the one from the comic, not at all. The sinks were pink instead of white, and the basic layout did not match. Here where he had entered he stood in a foyer, a small anteroom with three sinks and a wall-length mirror. To his right the lockers lined the wall around a turn. He could hear water splashing somewhere back there.

Enoch did not recognize himself in the mirror over the sinks. His cheeks seemed bloated, his hair cowlicked. His flesh shone red and slick.

A woman screamed.

To his right Enoch saw her, startled on her way to her locker from the shower. With a flash of white buttocks she spun back around the turn, the way she had come.

"There's a *man* in here!" she cried.

"Ah," Enoch said.

Then he met the floor.

He looked up and saw who had put him there: the muscular crewcut woman from the comic book, the woman he had mistaken for male.

She picked up a house phone from the wall, pressed a button and said, "Send George to the womens' lockers, we've got a guy in here," and hung up.

Enoch began to crawl toward the exit.

"Stay put," the woman said testily. "We'll escort you outside."

For a brief flash it appeared to Enoch that the three security men who came to remove him could hardly conceal their glee at being summoned inside the women's locker room.

"Are you a member?" an officious man with white hair asked as they guided Enoch toward the stairway.

"No," Enoch said.

"How did you get in here?"

"I walked in off the street," Enoch said. "I'm just looking for my wife. She comes here."

"That still doesn't allow you to enter the premises," the man told him as they walked down, "especially not the ladies' shower stalls."

"I didn't go anyplace near the showers," Enoch informed him.

They didn't speak for the remainder of the trip down the steps, past the offices and the bar. A pretty blonde girl walking a treadmill stared at Enoch as the security men whisked him by.

When they reached the front desk, Laura paused from berating Ginny to glower at Enoch and say, "Mister Schrader, if I or my staff see you set foot inside the front door of this club, we will have you arrested."

"I was looking for my wife," Enoch told her. His head hurt.

Apparently the big woman upstairs had sucker-punched him.

"I don't want to hear it," Laura said, and turned back to abusing Ginny, whom Enoch could now pick easily as the younger of the two; the girl's eyes threatened tears at any moment.

"I don't care what you *thought*," Laura hissed at the girl. "If thinking was part of your job, *you* wouldn't have gotten hired, Ginny."

The security men steered Enoch toward the front doors.

"Wait! That's him!" Enoch cried.

"That's who?" Laura asked.

"That man," Enoch said, and pointed at the figure he had followed here, now clad in an old-fashioned undershirt and shorts, journeying from upstairs to the bar, paying no notice to the conflagration at the desk. "That's who I asked you about," Enoch told Ginny. Then, to Laura, he said, "I need to speak with him, *please*? I can't find my wife. I'm not normally like this."

Everyone held still while Enoch's plea sank in. "Please let me talk to him, just outside," Enoch said.

"I shall ask him if he wishes to speak with you," Laura said. "If he does, he'll come out front. You wait out there, away from the doors, and either he'll come out or one of these gentlemen will inform you that he's chosen not to, and you shall leave."

"Agreed," Enoch said. "Thank you so much."

The security men took him through the swinging doors, down the stairs, and outside.

"You can wait over there," the man with the white hair said, pointing. Enoch obeyed.

While he waited, Enoch watched a strange foreign van driving on two flats pull into the tire shop next door to the club. An abandoned building across Rampart Street had once been a department store, Enoch guessed; plywood filled every window and all but one doorway, and gates shielded the entire storefront. That one unboarded doorway hung open, dark, with no sign announcing what business lurked inside. Brand-new, this store must have resembled the ones back home where as a child Enoch had gone shopping with his mother. A much older, smaller building adjacent to the store thrived, as though via roots that burrowed through the soil to sap its younger neighbor's vitality.

The club's front doors swung open.

The host from the comic book—yes, this was no other—stepped outside in his shorts and sneakers and shirt and said, "Are you the young man who asked to speak with me?"

"Yes, sir," Enoch said.

"Please, call me Avram," the man said. His remarkable physical condition made it hard to place his age.

"All right," Enoch said. The man's comfortable voice made it easier to address him as a familiar. "Avram...I need to find my wife."

"Oh, yes?"

"Yes," Enoch said, "and I don't know why, but I think you can help me find her."

"I will certainly help you if I can," Avram assured him, "although I cannot see how."

Enoch combed his hair with his fingers, to calm his tormented appearance. "Ah," he said. "Well, you're—you come here regularly, don't you?"

"Yes," Avram said. "Often daily, for many years."

"I can see why you would," Enoch told him. "It's an elegant place."

"I am quite glad you say so," Avram said, gathering some wind. "Few things in this city have provided me with joy so consistently as this club. Positively an oasis. In fact, I can safely assert that many of my fondest memories have this building as their setting." He shook his head. "But you were asking for my help."

"Yes, I thought you might have seen my wife working out here, a few days ago," Enoch said.

"How would I know her? Have I met her?"

"She, uh." Enoch paused, stuck for a description, till he recalled her graduation photograph and pulled it from his pocket.

Avram took it from him and held it at arm's length, squinting.

"Why, yes, I do recall her," he said. "Oddly enough."

"Have you seen her today?" Enoch asked.

"No," Avram told him. "I have seen her exactly once, two days ago. In fact, she sticks in my mind only because she wore a T-shirt that said, 'Crusade For Christ.'"

"Yes," Enoch said. "Her."

"Her shirt offended certain club members who belong to what we call today the Gay Community," Avram said.

Without meaning to, Enoch grunted.

Avram quickly added, "I must say, it certainly gave no offense to me."

"That day you saw her, what...?" Enoch gestured with limp hands, unsure which if any question he wanted to ask.

Avram helpfully panned through his memory, and spoke slowly, carefully. "I saw her in the women's weight room," he said. "That day I used the punching bags by the boxing ring, and a young gentleman I sometimes encounter there pointed her out, because of the slogan on her shirt. And, as I say, it did not offend me, so I took little notice of her, though I left the club at the same time she did."

None of this information told Enoch anything.

"Come to think of it, she raised an alarm in leaving, as well," Avram said, "because her companion clearly did not belong on the premises. The staff here can be, I suppose, tetchy."

"I've noticed." Enoch had begun to feel a steady throb where the woman upstairs had socked him. "Wait, what companion are you talking about?"

"A young man who came to the desk to wait for her," Avram said, and then changed his mind and corrected himself, "Now, that may not be what in fact took place. I am merely repeating gossip I overheard after the incident, so any of it could be distorted. He may have just wandered in at the same time she left."

"Did this guy really exist, do you know for sure?"

"Oh, yes," Avram said. "As I mentioned, I saw them."

Enoch mopped his face with his sleeve and said, "Is there anything about this guy that would make it so that I could find him?"

Avram considered this question. Enoch could not tell whether interrogation had taxed the man or Enoch's own situation had begun to appear foolish.

Then Avram politely cleared his throat before speaking, and said, "I have seen other young people dressed in a similar 'style,' if that indeed is the word, on Decatur Street where it meets St. Philip. At an establishment called, I believe, Kagan's."

"Kagan's," Enoch repeated to himself. "That's at Decatur and St. Philip."

"Yes," Avram said. "How long have you been here, in New Orleans?"

"A few days," Enoch told him.

"It is," Avram said, his tone one of cautious recitation, "a beautiful city, but not an ideal home for all, and perhaps worst for those who take to it most avidly."

When he saw that Avram had paused for him to agree, Enoch said, "I haven't seen enough of it to know what you mean. I don't find it inviting. In fact, I never have."

"May I ask why you chose to visit, then?"

"I need access to a..." Enoch pursed his lips as he searched for the most generic way to describe the Collection. "There are materials here that I need for work. I am a religious scholar."

Avram raised his eyebrows. "That's an odd coincidence," he said. "I curate a private collection of manuscripts used by scholars."

Enoch's mouth fell open and out came, "Is your last name LeCerce?"

"Yes, it is," Avram said, smiling.

"I'm Enoch Schrader," Enoch said, disturbed at the adenoidal edge in his own voice.

"How do you do, Enoch?" Mr. LeCerce said. "I am so pleased that we get to meet, at last. Sorry we haven't arranged a viewing for you yet, but I see you have other matters on your mind for the moment. As soon as you have time available, I look forward to showing you the Collection. I know you will be fascinated."

"But I can't really think about that right now," Enoch groaned.

"Yes, of course, that's right," Mr. LeCerce said, ashamed at his own enthusiasm in the face of Enoch's predicament. "May I be frank, Enoch?"

"Go ahead."

Mr. LeCerce drew a breath and advanced diplomatically. "New Orleans figures in many people's best memories and in many people's worst. If someone comes here and suddenly changes—suddenly decides to live here, in a fashion he or she never before desired—that person will stay here, despite efforts by loved ones to remove him or her. It becomes a question merely of how much grief those loved ones wish to withstand."

Someone exited the club beside them.

"I think I understand," Enoch said.

"Come inside," Mr. LeCerce invited him.

"No, they won't let me."

"Nonsense," said Mr. LeCerce. "I'll talk to them."

"I really can't," Enoch said. "Mister LeCerce?"

The older man looked at him benignly.

"Do you know anything about a comic book with you in it?" Enoch asked.

Mr. LeCerce's features sharpened. "A *what*?"

"A comic book." Enoch outlined one in the air, using both his index fingers. "I found a comic book in my hotel room, and you're one of the characters in it."

"Did you?" Mr. LeCerce said. "I know nothing about it."

"Maybe the artist just saw you around the city," Enoch said, "and used you as a model."

"Quite possibly," Mr. LeCerce replied. The topic had stirred awake his overpowering reserve. "Enoch, it has been a great pleasure meeting you. I am afraid I must go, I am not dressed for outdoors."

They shook hands, and Mr. LeCerce went back inside the club.

❀ ❀ ❀

Enoch's watch said one-forty, which was much later than he'd expected but still did not explain the nocturnal quality this day had assumed by the time he crossed Chartres Street on St. Philip; nor did the dense cloudbank overhead.

That sharpness peculiar to early nightfall—when twilight heightens contrast, causing pale objects to glow—imbrued everything he saw, the stores, the sidewalk, every passing face and car.

He approached Decatur. Ahead of him, sitting in a former doorway not far from the corner, an unwashed couple groped and shared a cup of beer. As Enoch reached them, their odor made him gag, and the man smirked at him.

Enoch recognized the man, whose beard had grown unruly since they had last spoken.

"You were on Bourbon Street," Enoch said to him. "I talked with you. You were holding a cross."

"Yup," the man said, and the girl laughed. Something moved inside her sweatshirt; the man had his hand in there, touching her breasts.

Through gritted teeth, Enoch said, "You call yourself a Christian?"

"No, everybody else calls me Christian," the man said.

The girl explained, "His *name* is Christian, asshole."

"'Christian asshole,'" the bearded man mused. "I've sure met some people you can apply that name to."

A light sheen of dirt covered both their faces, probably dried sweat. From ingrained habit Enoch refused to let them engage him in a quarrel, particularly since even from a distance their breath stank of beer.

"Can you tell me where to find a bar called Kagan's?" Enoch asked.

The girl giggled. The man had lost interest in Enoch, and jabbed a finger toward the corner. "It's around there," he said.

"Enoch!" Diane gasped, before she could stop herself.

Enoch spun around.

Diane had frozen in place, walking toward him with a young girl—not the redhead from the comic book, but Stephanie, who obviously didn't recall meeting Enoch on Royal Street the other night. Stephanie glanced from him to Diane and back, confused.

Both women carried cigarettes and plastic cups of beer. From lack of experience Diane held hers awkwardly. Her mouth looked wrong, too. She had put on dark lipstick.

"What are you doing here?" Enoch asked, feeling his temperature rise.

"Enoch," Diane said. "Enoch, I'm sorry."

"You're sorry about what?" Enoch barked. "Running out while I'm in the bathroom?"

"I'm sorry we got married," she said. "It was a mistake."

"Damn it, you can't just talk about being married in the past tense! That's not good enough!" Enoch hollered at her. He regained some composure and added, "Are you saying that you intend to divorce me?"

Diane nodded, her manner consoling. A pink crosshatch of tiny blood vessels glazed the whites of her eyes. "Whatever is easy for you," she said.

Stephanie said to him, "Can you spare any change at all? My pocketbook got stolen last night."

"What, again?" Enoch said. His sarcasm made her laugh.

"Enoch, this is Stephanie," Diane said, and then waved her cigarette toward the lovers on the doorstep and said, "And that's Nilda and Christian."

Diane's three friends behaved as though she had violated some code by introducing them. As he studied his wife's face, Enoch saw that, like these others, Diane now had a barely discernible grime scumbling her skin.

A robust twenty-year-old with his hair dyed blue and black shuffled around the corner. "Diane," he said, irritably, "give me a smoke."

Enoch watched his wife lodge her beer in the crook of her arm so she could fish a pack of cigarettes from her pocket and flip its top open for this surly dolt, who withdrew two and said nothing.

"Who *is* this?" Enoch said.

"Who the fuck are you?" the punk shot back.

"Enoch, you should leave now," Diane said.

"Is this dick your husband?" the punk asked her.

Diane nodded and said, "Leave him alone, Jeffrey, please? Let him leave."

"The fuck I will," the punk said, advancing on Enoch.

Anger helped Enoch stand his ground, until the punk's fist smacked his eye with a *pop!* somewhere between the smart clack of billiard balls and the bang of a squeezed bag full of air.

Sprawled on the sidewalk, Enoch blacked out very briefly, and awoke to a kick in his stomach. Pain curled him onto his right side. Then he heard Diane speaking and sat up.

His wife stood pleading with the punk who had just assaulted him. "Come on, Jeffrey," she was saying. "I'm asking please, give it back to him and let's go?"

"*You* can go, if you want," the punk told her as he rifled through Enoch's wallet. Enoch hadn't even felt him take it.

The girl named Nilda flicked a cigarette butt. It landed on Enoch's leg. "Oh, sorry," she said, but did not move to brush it off him.

The butt rolled off Enoch as he hauled himself to his feet.

"I want a policeman," Enoch announced.

"Suck my dick," the punk spat, counting the money he had just reaped from Enoch's billfold.

Louder, Enoch said, "Police! I need a policeman! *Police!*"

Tourists among the tide on Decatur turned their heads. Nilda and Christian sniggered.

With the sudden fury of an incensed dog, the punk sprang from beside Diane to kick Enoch in the buttocks.

Enoch dropped onto the sidewalk again, and quickly scrambled to rise and run. The punk let him stagger a few paces away before following, at a commanding stride. Again his boot caught Enoch's backside.

The punk swung a third kick, which missed, and then he stood firm. "Get the fuck out of here," he shouted at Enoch.

Enoch looked in shock at his bare wrist, and said, indignantly, "That's my watch you're wearing!"

The punk stamped the concrete, and Enoch tore away. Behind him as he fled he heard laughter, mostly female.

At Chartres Street he turned around to check whether anyone had pursued him. The scene back near Decatur had not changed except that Diane had come over to light the punk's cigarette.

Even at this distance, with his right eye swelling worse each second, Enoch could not mistake the glee suffusing Stephanie's smile. What she had just witnessed had not merely amused her but fueled her in some perverse way.

As he neared Bourbon Street, Enoch heard a man say, "Hey, buddy." He had to turn his head so his left eye could see the two policeman approaching him.

"I've just been robbed," Enoch said.

"You look like you've been fighting," one cop said.

"No, sir. I was punched without warning, and the guy took my wallet while I was unconscious," Enoch said.

"Do you have any identification?" the cop asked. Behind him his partner leaned against the hood of a car, shaking his head.

"Yes," Enoch said. "Wait, no. It's in my wallet. This punk-rock imbecile that robbed me has it, right up there." With his thumb Enoch pointed over his shoulder.

"Uh-huh," the cop said. "So what did you do to this guy?"

"Nothing," Enoch said.

The cop exchanged a chuckle with his partner before turning back to Enoch to rephrase the question, "If I ask *him*, what's *he* going to tell me you did?"

"How should I know?" Enoch said. "He attacked me."

"Just for no reason."

"His reason shouldn't make any difference," Enoch argued, his voice gone ragged. "He punched me and stole my wallet."

"How'd he know you had money in your wallet?" the cop asked.

With a sigh, Enoch said, "I have no idea. Maybe my wife told him."

"Then this guy's a friend of your wife's?"

"Yes." Enoch felt beaten.

"You didn't say that before," the cop pointed out.

"I know. Frankly, I didn't think it was any of your business and I still don't," Enoch told him. "We've only been married a few days, and she's decided to become my ex-wife."

"She just told you this."

"Yes, sir," Enoch said.

"And that didn't have anything to do with the fight you got in," the cop said, which made his partner laugh. "Let me guess: This guy *isn't* her new boyfriend."

They let Enoch leave. The relief of escape elated him, and he turned the wrong way on Bourbon. It took him a block to realize his error. Yet the neighborhood became quieter in this direction, more residential. Marching back into the fray didn't appeal to Enoch with his eyelid now the size of a baseball.

At the corner he saw a store. Just before he reached its doors he read the sign: NELLY DELI. Above the words stood a man wearing a chef's hat and holding his hands on his hips, prostitute-style.

Enoch kept walking. At Barracks Street he turned left. The man with the two black dogs passed, scowling when he saw Enoch's battered face.

Finally Enoch reached the block across from the dog park, the block with no numbers to tell him which building housed the Collection. He came directly to the fenced alley, and whistled for the pig. It did not appear.

His shoes would not help, so Enoch pulled them off. With his fingers and toes he scaled the storm fence. As he climbed, the steel wire dug into his knuckle joints. The thought came to him that the owners might have placed nails or some other sharp obstacle at the top of the fence, as per local custom.

They had not. Across the apex ran a standard steel rod. Enoch swung his left leg over and used his knee to hoist the rest of his weight. As he slid himself over the top, the shaking state of his hands concerned him.

With no warning the rod gave.

Enoch met the ground with such force that he could not tell whether he'd landed on concrete or earth. Above him the broken steel rod bobbed in the air, torn free of its mooring yet still affixed to the storm fence's uppermost edge.

And then the pig set upon him. Due to his massive concussion and the endorphins deadening his nerves in response to his fractured spine, Enoch viewed this attack objectively, almost as he would had it occurred to someone he didn't know. Except for his paralysis he might have laughed at the absurdity of having a farm animal maul him in an American city.

The pig went for Enoch's throat.

THE LIVING

I FOUND IT A WEIRD COINCIDENCE THAT OLIVER CALLED ME, since I had thought about the bar during breakfast. In the past five years I hadn't set foot in the bar, so I didn't even know whether Oliver still worked there, but that morning I had woken up with it on my mind because I'd had a dream set there. In the dream my wife was still alive.

Oliver said, "How you been?"

"Not too bad," I told him.

"Good," he said.

"Good to hear your voice," I said.

"Yeah, it's been, I don't know." He thought it over. "Long time."

"So what's going on?" I asked him.

He sniffled. "Seen a ghost," he said. "In the bar."

"Who did, you?"

"Yeah," he said. "Me and Jeanine and about ten customers. Damnedest thing."

He talked about the experience for five minutes without describing the specter itself. I didn't ask questions. Evidently Oliver had called to discuss ghosts. People in the French Quarter will call you in the middle of the night and ask you to look something up in your dictionary for them. That's part of why I moved to Kenner in the first place.

"Well, all right, good to talk to you," Oliver said at last. "You're okay and everything?"

I assured him I was. We hung up.

Oliver's call came so abruptly that only afterward did I feel any anger, when I recalled wondering whether he'd been in Al's apartment when my wife took the bad shot.

⊗ ⊗ ⊗

Jeanine called later that day. "So he told you about our ghosts?" she said. "Most incredible thing, it really was."

"Oliver just told me about one of them," I said. "You have more than one?"

"Oh," she said. Her tone made me feel as if she'd let on more than she meant to.

"Where's the second ghost?"

"There's not really—well, the way Oliver's talking about it, there's only one ghost, he says," she told me. "It only counts as one."

"But you saw more than one?"

"Not really," she said.

The topic changed. She told me about some guy she'd dated for months, whom she finally allowed to move into her apartment; around Mardi Gras she came home earlier than planned one night and caught him in her bed with two men. "One of them was from *Iowa*," she said, plainly insulted by this fact.

Apparently it hadn't ruined her Carnival, for she told me a couple of stories about what she did at parades uptown. Hearing about someone else's Mardi Gras antics is like hearing about someone else's orgasm.

"Why did you decide to call me?" I asked suddenly. I may have sounded a little peeved. "You see a ghost, and you and Oliver both think to call me?"

"No," Jeanine said, but nothing else.

I apologized to her about sounding so curt, and she claimed she understood. Maybe she did.

Normally just hearing from Jeanine wouldn't irritate me that way. Oliver, perhaps, and definitely Al, but Jeanine never did anything to me. It's not her fault that she reminds me of when I lived in the Quarter.

Actually, though, my weird mood had started before hearing from them. It probably started when I dreamed about my wife. I could say it went back further than that, to when I lay in bed thinking about her the night before, but that was nothing unusual.

I had that dream again two nights later. My wife sat beside the piano in the bar. I came up behind her, and the touch of her felt real. Her breath felt warm, and her hair smelled the way it used to.

Somehow it came to me that I was dreaming, that she wasn't really there. She vanished. Knowing it was a dream didn't hurt the setting, though. The bar looked real, and I glanced around to find a group of tourists staring at me, eyes wide. Oliver had his face down in his hands on the bar, and Jeanine stood at the payphone, dialing frantically. Her hair was shorter than I'd ever seen it.

Then the phone beside my bed rang, and I woke up.

ACKNOWLEDGEMENTS

"You and I wear the comfortable looseness of doom
and find it becoming."

Edward Estlin Cummings
(1894-1962)

UNINDICTED CO-CONSPIRATORS
According to authorities, the following individuals
are currently at large outside Louisiana:
Randy B. Money
Deborah Stein
Myshkin Warbler
Brandi Morris
Wendy-Charly Lemmon
Daisy Cross

The author thanks Joe Philips & Susan Wood for publishing,
Geoff Munsterman for editing,
and Louis Maistros for being Greek.

"Enjoin while you are young."

Esther Curran Orr
(1895-1994)

CRESCENT CITY BOOKS
New Orleans, LA
www.blackwidowpress.com

The Sound of Building Coffins by Louis Maistros

Stay Out of New Orleans: Strange Stories by P. Curran

THE VALENTIN ST. CYR MYSTERIES by David Fulmer

Chasing the Devil's Tail

Jass

Rampart Street

Lost River

The Iron Angel

Eclipse Alley

The Day Ends at Dawn